Corporate Myopia

Write Decisions
http://www.nhentertainer.com/index.html
2004

Corporate Myopia

Harold L. Prevett

Acknowledgements

I am sure this book would never have been published if my daughter, Jeanne Sable, had not jumped in with her writing and editing skills. Her diligence on my behalf will not be forgotten. Charles Sable's technical advice concerning military aircraft and procedures was also of great help in lending credibility to the story. My son, Harold Jr., kept me sane by manning the computer, which I found impossible to master, and enlisted my grandson, Tom, to help with the formatting. Finally, I thank my wife, Olivia, bless her heart, for never complaining about the hours spent alone while I wrote, and for allowing one of her experiences as a teenager to be included in the story.

Chapter 1

The Twelfth Combination Lock

Roger Durand, CEO and chairman of the board of Sunrise Industries, Inc., was tired of arguing. The lengthy meeting had crammed enough discussions, projections, charts and graphs, estimates and prophecies into one Friday afternoon to last a month. If he didn't adjourn soon, he'd be facing the commute from New York to Connecticut through heavy rush hour traffic.

"All right, Hig," he relented. "You start a new company. Draw funds from Merchant's Savings. It's our bank. Use it for the holding company. You serve as president. Reimburse our bank on a timely basis, and remit funds to Sunrise Industries as profits increase, keeping ten percent for your share. I don't want to know anything at all about this new venture. Understand? Nothing! If you buy chemicals, wood products, or any other materials from Sunrise Industries, your payment terms will be the same as any other customer's." He reached his pen across the table and rapped it in front of an astonished Andrew Higgins. "Now, Hig, I'll give you another month around here. That should be enough time for you to organize this enterprise of yours."

Sylvia Durand entered the back door of the detached four-car garage at Golden Vista, the estate of Roger Durand. The chauffeur had the station wagon warmed and ready to go. "Thank you, Gilbert," said Mrs. Durand. "But I'd like to surprise Mr. Durand and drive to the railroad station myself. He sounded upset when he called. A long Friday board meeting

1

usually means trouble." Gilbert nodded politely and returned to his living quarters in the upper story of the ample structure.

Roger Durand relaxed to the rumbling of the train. It helped him reflect on the recent discussions and plans for expanding his corporation. It was mid November 1941, and war seemed a distinct possibility. No doubt Sunrise Industries could comfortably expand into other very profitable fields, when war came. He settled back in his seat, daydreaming of the possibilities.

The next time Roger gazed out the window, the familiar little newsstand next to his favorite lunch stop told him the train had already arrived in Milford. The crowded waiting room moved slowly by. Then came the concourse where he expected to see his faithful driver, Gilbert. Instead, Roger spotted his wife engaged in animated conversation with a woman and a young man—townspeople, most likely. *My social butterfly,* he thought as he stood up to grab his briefcase. *She's better known in this neck of the woods than I am.* The train ground to a halt and Roger alighted from the platform. He walked back a few cars to where Sylvia was still chatting with the two people.

Approaching her from behind, he tapped her on the shoulder and said, "Are you my driver this evening? If so, I just might lure you to some nice secluded parking spot and perhaps kindle a fire."

Sylvia turned to him, laughing, and said, "Oh Roger, are you sure you're not disappointed that Gilbert didn't come to pick you up?" She hugged her husband and turned to the two smiling friends. "This is my husband, Roger," she said. "Dear, I'd like you to meet Mrs. Emerson and her son, Carl. Carl is a friend of Kim's."

Roger nodded to the lady and shook hands with the young man. After the exchange of a few pleasant remarks, the Durands excused themselves and strolled to the lot where Sylvia's beach wagon was parked.

Driving home, Sylvia explained that she first met Mrs. Emerson and Carl a few years ago after a PTA meeting at the school their daughter, Kimberly, and the boy attended. Carl was one year ahead of Kimberly. "I remember Kim went out of her way to make sure we 'bumped into' them in the corridor. I think she was a little sweet on the boy. He graduated last year. Now he's been classified 1A in the draft. Mrs. Emerson is worried that he may be called very soon—his number is so low. I wonder if Kim knows?"

"Is there a Mr. Emerson?" Roger asked.

"Oh yes. He is a conductor on the very train you came in on. I guess they came to talk to him about something. He doesn't get through conducting until the wee hours of the morning, so they're usually asleep when he gets home. Darling, I'm glad you don't have a job like that."

"Ha!" was the rejoinder from Roger. "His job ends when he gets off the train! But my job is like a chain dangling around my neck. It has a combination lock with a dozen numbers that I'm afraid I'll forget, so I keep the chain on and bear the burden."

"For heaven's sake, what do you mean?" Sylvia questioned.

Roger replied, "I'll give you an example. At today's marathon board meeting, we acquired company number twelve! As usual, Higgins led the charge and convinced most of the board that we should form another company and take advantage of the opportunities the coming war is sure to bring. He saw that I was cool to the idea, and sort of snickered, 'What's the matter, Rog? Afraid to make money?'

3

"Well, I couldn't let that pass, so I said, 'All right, Hig'— He hates to be called Hig. Guess it sounds too much like 'Pig'—And I told him to go ahead and start a company. Told him how to finance it, and that's it. Said I didn't want to hear another word about it, ever! So, you see, dear, this is the twelfth number on the combination lock!"

"Roger, since you don't want to know anything about company number twelve, why not forget it and say the lock has only eleven numbers?" suggested Sylvia.

Roger grinned at his wife. "Yes, you're right. I'll forget all about 'Hig' and whatever business he dreams up. When it flops, maybe he won't be such a wise ass. But enough of company talk. How come you and not our hired man came to get me?"

Sylvia yawned and rubbed the back of her neck. "I just wanted to get out for a short while—get away from Kim and her noisy friends. And I just love driving this beach wagon. I think I'll keep it for a long, long time."

Roger raised an eyebrow. "My dear," he commented, "if war comes you may not have any choice but to keep it a long time. I'll wager they stop making new cars once we get into the war." He watched the buildings grow farther apart as they drew nearer their home. "Will Kim's friends be there for dinner when we get home?" he asked. Without waiting for an answer, he added, "I hope not. I feel like relaxing. Can't stand some of her friends' mindless chattering. Where does Kim get these friends?"

"Darling, don't be an old fuddy duddy. They are just young, full of life and energy! Anyway, they will be eating in the rumpus room; it will be just you and I at the table. Your brother George and Laurie declined our dinner invitation. They'll be attending a science lecture at Yale."

Roger said, "They should move to New Haven, they go to Yale so often."

Sylvia replied, "Don't forget, Laurie is interested in science. She has a chemistry degree from NYU and taught it at New Haven High School."

Roger said, "Yes, I know. My brother met her at some science lecture at Yale. I guess they attend those lectures as some kind of romantic rendezvous. I hope some of her smarts rub off on him."

Sylvia's eyes left the road for a moment to fix on Roger. "He is as smart as you. Maybe smarter," she said.

Roger was taken aback. "What do you mean by that?" he blared. Sylvia made no reply. A moment later, he dismissed the comment as a joke. "I'm just kidding you," he said calmly. "So what's the lecture about?"

"Some economics professor, giving a talk about Germany's industrial innovations to overcome their lack of natural resources in the war over there. George says food, fuel oil and chemicals are likely in short supply, and synthesizing them is a priority, no doubt."

"Good," said Roger. "Just as well they miss dinner. We can have a quiet one and enjoy each other before our guests arrive."

The couple drove in silence for the next ten minutes. Finally, Sylvia coasted to a stop at the covered main entrance to the magnificent home. Gilbert opened the driver's side door and let Sylvia out, then respectfully greeted Roger and did the same. Ever solicitous, he bade them a pleasant evening and drove off to the garage below the comfortable domicile he and his wife, Martha, occupied next to the groundskeeper's quarters. He had only to drive Kim's friends home later, and his day's work would be done.

Friday evening, as always, was a relaxing affair at the Durand household. No need to hold back on an extra cocktail or two with their friends, the Popes, during the ongoing bridge tournament. This round, they concocted a new rule: the couple who loses the most Friday evening games in a three-month period must throw a lavish party and invite at least 25 people.

"Let's talk shop for a little while. Then we can call it our quarterly IRS revenge party," John Pope proposed with a wink.

Roger brightened and replied, "That's a definite possibility."

The bridge game went on until 2:30 A.M. Then came a late night snack and a cocktail, and the overnight guests were off to their room. The house was finally quiet.

Late the next morning, which was rather pleasant for November, the Popes were partaking of brunch with their hosts on the enclosed patio overlooking the swimming pool and tennis courts, watching the teenagers frolicking about.

"Who are those brave young souls wearing swimsuits in November?" asked Mrs. Pope.

Sylvia replied, "That's our daughter, Kim—there in the blue bathing suit. She, the other two girls, and the two boys in the pool are all school friends. Those two boys playing tennis are, I guess you might say, Kim's part time boy friends. Anyway, it's a heated pool, and you know how kids are. No one wants to look like a sissy. We'll just see to it they don't lie around after they come out of the water. The dressing rooms are just inside."

Intently watching the tennis game, Roger commented, "Those two players aren't very well matched. The cocky one with the curly hair is Douglas Graf. Folks own a lot of property in town. Their home, a couple blocks away, is equipped with tennis courts, so he sure as hell must play a lot. The other boy, I just met him yesterday evening." Turning to his wife, he said, "His name is Carl, right Sylvia?"

Sylvia nodded. "His dad is a conductor on our train line here," she told the Popes.

Roger leaned back in his chair. "That's right. Guess he hasn't been exposed to tennis courts, swimming pools, and all those good things."

Kim jackknifed off the diving board one last time, cleanly piercing the water's surface with minimal splash. The two other girls followed suit, only to be cannon balled by the two male swimmers. The huge splash caught the attention of the two tennis players, who were just finishing their game. They entered the glass enclosure as three dripping girls emerged from the water and tiptoed across the opposite end of the pool area, arms folded against the chill.

"Hey, who won the match?" one of Kim's girlfriends yelled.

Carl took a giant step forward and pointed proudly to his chest. "I did, of course!" he joked.

Douglas seized the moment by shoving Carl from behind. The girls screamed and giggled as the fully clad boy balanced on the edge of the pool for several seconds, arms circling like propellers, then careened into the water with a huge splash.

When Carl surfaced, he yelled out, "You dirty b . . .", checking his expletive as he noticed the door to the patio open to where the adults were seated.

Sylvia exclaimed, "Why did Douglas do that? Now I'll have to have Martha dry and iron his clothes."

Roger, rocking with laughter, turned to Sylvia and his guests and said, "Hey, just two roosters trying to impress our young chick."

Sylvia cupped her hand beside her mouth and said, "That Douglas is a little fresh!"

As all of Kim's friends huddled outside the dressing rooms, Douglas said loudly to Carl, "Now you can change your clothes with Kim and the girls. You should thank me for pushing you into the pool!"

Kim remarked, "Doug, you're awful!" whereupon Steve and Bill said, "Hey, can we join you too?"

Martha, the Durands' maid, made a wry face and physically turned each youngster toward the appropriate dressing room. Then she handed Carl a clean bathrobe and told him his clothes would be ready in an hour or so.

Freshly showered and dressed, the group departed to the rumpus room to play pool, ping-pong, and use the exercise equipment.

George and Laurie Durand soon returned from New Haven and engaged the other adults in deep discussion about the lecture they'd heard.

"You know," said George, "German chemists have developed synthetic oil and gasoline for their war machine, synthetic food for their people, and a multitude of items they call ersatz to sustain the war effort. We damn well better get into the war and stop the madness over there, or we will see goose-stepping all over the place with a nut running the world!"

Roger listened patiently to his brother and finally said, "But you know, George, they can't produce synthetic fuels in quantities to sustain the war for very long. When we get into it, I am sure the fighting will be over in less than a year."

"Hell, Roger, it will take this country more than a year to tool up for a war! Don't forget—the Germans have slave labor making guns, ammunition, tanks, and the whole damn array of crap to keep the fight going. They don't have labor problems there. They produce or die!"

"George, I think you and that professor at Yale are over-stating the situation. When we join the fight, they'll fold quick as a lousy hand of cards."

George responded, "Roger, your over-confidence could cause the Allies to lose the war!"

War talk continued until almost noon, when lunch was served in the patio overlooking the flower gardens on the south side of the mansion. Seated at the lunch table, Mrs. Pope wondered aloud, "Aren't Kim and her friends going to join us for lunch?"

Sylvia responded, "They drive to a place to eat and dance on the road to Hartford. Probably be back sometime around midnight. It's their weekend routine. They pile into two cars and off they go for a good time."

"Not this time," George said. "I was walking around the other side of the house and saw a car near the garage. Gilbert was helping Carl replace a tire on his car. When they were done, the boy drove off by himself. Gilbert told me the rest of the kids had left in Douglas's car. Nice guy, Gilbert. He even put away the tools and the air compressor, so Carl wouldn't be late catching up with his friends. He says that boy is a whiz mechanically. Did you know he modified the car's engine? Took an 40 horse power job and made it 85!"

Sylvia said, "Oh yes, he's a very intelligent boy. Kim tells me that he finished first in his class every year in high school, and won special honors for his work in chemistry."

Roger said, "Well, I hope he has decent tires on that tin can of his; some of these young fellows drive around in such wrecks."

George remarked, "No, it's not bad at all for an old car. Gilbert couldn't understand why the tire went flat—No punctures or cuts. In fact, it was new."

Carl did not go to meet his friends. He drove home, his thoughts swirling around the flat tire. That thing was only a month old, and a good brand. Had Douglas, the only one free to roam around while the rest went to shower and dress, come upon his car and let the air out? *Well, I guess I can't prove it,* he concluded.

Carl reached home late that afternoon. When he walked into the kitchen, his mother exclaimed, "My, you're home early. Thought you would be out until after midnight."

"Well, Ma, Kim had two girlfriends and four of her boyfriends as guests at her beautiful home, using the pool and tennis courts, and eating a lunch that was more of a banquet. Anyway, afterwards we decided to go to the dance hall up toward Hartford. We were going to take my car and Doug's, but my right rear tire went flat, so everybody piled into Doug's car. I told them after I got my tire fixed I would meet them at the dance hall. Then I thought, hey, I'm the oddball. Three couples and me alone? Bad idea. So I decided to come home."

"That's too bad, son," his mother said. "Dad is getting off a couple hours early this evening. As long as you're here, how about picking him up at the station while I fix a nice snack for all of us? I'd rather not go after him now."

Carl was happy to oblige. His mother thanked him and said, "I know Douglas, but who are the other boys and girls?"

"They are Kim's classmates—Steve and Bill—a couple of clowns—always joking. The girls are Susan and Hazel. They'll be graduating in June. Doug and I are the oldies of the bunch!"

His mother stopped wiping the counter, critically eyed Carl, and said, "Say, I'm surprised your clothes are still so fresh. I guess being an oldie, as you say, is an incentive to keeping yourself neat and clean."

Carl sheepishly told his mother about the surprise dip in Kim's swimming pool, and the Durands' maid taking care of his wet clothing.

"The pool? In November?" his mother cried. "It will be a wonder if you don't catch cold. You owe one to Douglas for doing that!"

Carl shook his head. "No, Ma. I owe him two," he muttered.

His mother shrugged her shoulders and said, "I think you better leave now and pick up Dad. By the way, there's a letter for you on the coffee table."

Carl picked up the envelope and stuck it into his coat pocket.

"Love ya," he shouted as he headed out the door.

Traffic was light on the way to the train station. Carl arrived with time to spare and coasted to a stop in a good parking spot. He pulled the envelope from his pocket and opened it. As he read the salutation, his breath caught in his throat and he felt his pulse begin to race.

Greetings from the President of the United States of America. . .

WOW, he said to himself as he read the official notification. He wiped his palms on the upholstery and tucked the letter into the glove compartment. *This changes everything.*

Carl found his dad waiting in the station's ticket office, conversing with the ticket agent. He overheard the man say to his father, "Well, Tom, guess we will be seeing you more often now that new riders are coming on board."

"Yeah," his father responded. "But if more trains are put on, no doubt I'll be busier than a one-armed paper hanger. Got to go. My ride is here."

On the way home, Carl asked about his Dad's conversation with the ticket agent. He replied that the boss told him the railroad wanted more personnel available in the event of war. Troop trains, military staff, supplies, and more material would necessitate breaking in new conductors, engineers, and dispatchers. His father's talk left Carl wondering if joining the Army had been a sensible choice. He felt a few pangs of fear. He asked his father if he'd be wise to jump the gun and join the service.

"Yes and no," his father replied. "Since you are classified 1A, if you had a high number in the draft, I'd say wait before joining up. But your number is so low, I say enlist before you get drafted. Ma and I hate to see you go, but by joining up, you may get a good assignment."

Carl swallowed hard. He'd already received orders to report to Fort Devens headquarters on Monday, December 8, 1941. Travel vouchers were enclosed along with a request for a transcript of his high school scholastic records and diploma. He was waiting until his father and mother were together to tell them the news.

His father rolled down the car window and lit a cigarette. "Hey, it's Saturday. I thought you would be out catting around with your friends, or that rich girl who calls you so often. Ma told me you would be partying at her house. Did you two have a fight?"

"Nah, Dad. I was at her house and had a good time. The seven of us decided to go to Marlin's Dance Hall near Hartford. We were going in my car and Doug's, but mine had a flat, so they all went in Doug's car. I was to meet them at Marlin's after I got the tire fixed, but four guys and three girls—not much fun moonlighting alone."

"Oh, yeah. After the dance," responded his dad. "Three's a crowd and seven is worse. Say no more. But Carl, you haven't had those tires more than a couple months. They cost over twenty dollars each. My gosh, they shouldn't go flat!"

Carl said simply, "Well, one did."

After the dishes were cleared, the Emersons settled in the living room for the evening. Carl cleared his throat and said, "You know that letter that came for me today? Well, it came from the recruiting office. I have to report for duty on Monday, December 8, at Fort Devens Massachusetts."

Mrs. Emerson dropped her magazine. Her hands flew to her face. "Oh no!" she cried. "So soon? Why in less than a month you will be gone!"

"Ma, you make it sound as though it's the end of the world or something. Devens isn't far. I'll see you both a heck of a lot. Don't worry."

His dad said, "I guess you are lucky. You could have been sent to some base in the boondocks way out west!"

"Mary," he said to his wife. "Devens is about four hours from here. If he behaves himself, he could get leave every so often and come home."

His mother replied, "Well, I hope so. And maybe they will stop fighting over there soon. My land, aren't they tired of it?" Carl and his father exchanged tight grins.

After the conversation, Carl retreated to the garage and began tinkering with the motor in his car. It was 2:30 a.m., and he was still fiddling around under the hood when the kitchen phone rang. He darted inside to answer it. It was Kim, asking if he was all right, or whether he'd had some problem on the way to the dance hall.

"No, no. Nothing like that," Carl said. "Just a flat. Your chauffeur and I took about 40 minutes trying to find any trouble with the tire. You won't believe this, but it didn't have one puncture, and the valve stem didn't leak. We both were puzzled.

You know, it was practically brand new. Anyway, four guys and three girls, I would have been one too many, don't you think?"

Kim replied, "Gee, you should have come anyway. Steve and Bill are so silly. When they danced with Sue and Hazel and myself, if you could call it that, they just tossed us around like burlap sacks. It was funny at first, but we got tired of it after a while. You and Doug are good dancers. Besides that, I kind of missed you."

Carl's stomach did a little flip. "Gee, I apologize. Guess I was feeling sorry for myself."

Kim added, "You know, I like you and Doug. But sometimes Doug upsets me. He's so headstrong!"

"Yeah! Like when he shoved me into your pool. I owe him one, or maybe two. Kim. . ." He paused. "I've got something to tell you, but in person. Let me know when I can see you."

"Can't you tell me now?" she asked.

Carl said, "I would much rather tell you in person. Nothing earth shaking, but still, I want to see you when I tell you. OK?"

"All right, Carl. I'll give you a call tomorrow and let you know when I'll be home."

That ended the phone conversation and Carl went to bed. The next day Kim called and told him she would be home in the evening. When Carl arrived, Kim took him to a sitting room off the main entry hall. As they sat on an exquisitely carved velvet loveseat, Kim urged Carl to tell her whatever it was that he wouldn't say over the phone.

Carl grasped Kim's hands and looked into her eyes. "Kim, I was classified 1A in the draft and as luck would have it, my number is only 304. It could be drawn real soon. I did what seemed the best alternative to being drafted. I went to the Army recruiting office and joined." He felt a little shock wave run through her hands. "Anyway, a letter came yesterday, and they want me to report to Fort Devens on Monday, December 8. That's it. Soon Uncle Sam will call the shots for me."

"No, oh no!" Kim responded, visibly shaken. "Where is this camp Devens? Will I be able to see you once in a while? Maybe you should have waited until you were called. Gee, I wish you weren't going. Maybe you'll flunk the physical. I hope you have flat feet and they reject you!"

"Hey, hey. Slow down." Carl embraced her. "I'm not going to disappear. Devens is only three or four hours away. So I can get back here on weekends."

"Oh, I hope so," said Kim, wiping a tear from her eye. "But before you leave for the Army, promise you will see me often? I hate this thing that's going on over there. We're not involved, so you guys shouldn't have to go into the Army."

"Now Kim, relax!" He held her face between his palms and kissed her tenderly. She stared into his eyes for several moments and said, "You know, that's the first time you ever really kissed me. Those other few times were just little pecks." She threw her arms around him and kissed him again just as her mother entered the room.

"I hate to break up a serious conversation, but Kim, don't you have some serious homework?"

"Yes, I know, Mother, but Carl just told me he has to report for military duty on December the eighth."

Mrs. Durand said, "Carl, I'm sorry you have to go in, and so soon! But I sure wish you good luck. And oh, by the way, we will be having a big party here soon. When we fix the date, Kim will give you a call. I want to invite you, as I am sure Kim would like that."

Kim looked puzzled but said, "I sure would." She walked Carl to the front door. He squeezed her hand and left.

Kim later asked her mother, "Why the big party?"

Her mother waved her hand and replied, "Dad and I were the losers in this round of bridge games we play with the Popes. We agreed to have the party according to some crazy rule we dreamed up. If Dad has no commitments, we will have it a week from this coming Friday. I'll let you know, so you can tell Carl and your friends. We'll have a band and lots of goodies. Maybe we will buy a real nice gift for Carl, as a going away present!"

Kim called Carl and told him the plan for the party was on. He asked her to thank her mother and said that he looked forward to the occasion. He asked who else was coming that he might know. She replied, "Bet you're thinking the guests will be older, like my parents. But there will be at least a dozen of us teenagers. You know most of them. And we can have the rumpus room to ourselves. I haven't been able to reach Doug, so I asked Hazel to contact him."

Carl laughed. "Hey, I don't mind older people. Some day we will be older people. All right, I'll be there around four-thirty."

Hazel finally reached Doug and told him he was invited to the Durands for a real good time. She complained that she had tried calling him repeatedly but he was always out. Doug explained, "I've been practicing 'touch and goes' at the local landing strip. I joined the Army. The recruiting sergeant told me, because I have a student pilot license, there's a good chance I can go to flight training school and perhaps become a pilot, which means I would be an officer—you know, a lieutenant. That's better than a private any day! Tell Kim thanks for the invite to the party. I'll see you there."

Hazel, speechless, hung up the phone.

Chapter 2

A Parting Gift

The party was a festive occasion with lavish food, beverages, and a topnotch 12-piece band playing the latest dance music. The great room served as the dance hall for the older guests, with chairs and tables arranged around the perimeter for dining and socializing.

Kim and her friends took over the rumpus room. The victrola was turned up loud enough to be heard over the boisterous talking and laughter of the young crowd. After an hour and a half of dancing, three servants entered the room with large serving carts loaded with food, soft drinks, and eating utensils. One of the maids rang a small silver bell and announced, "Dinner is served." Seeing no response, she spoke into Kim's ear.

"Come and get it!" screeched the young hostess. The music stopped, and the hungry throng scrambled to the serving carts and helped themselves. The noise diminished as eating took precedence over conversation.

As if on cue, Mr. and Mrs. Durand appeared at the doorway and bustled to the area where the audio equipment was set up. Mr. Durand put a chokehold on the microphone and startled everyone by yelling, "Attention, you kids! Where is the young man who is going into the Army soon?"

"That's me. Here I am!" was Douglas's reply.

"Well, come up here, young man. We have something for you," Mr. Durand shouted over what sounded like a sharp cry from Kim.

As Douglas approached his hosts, Mrs. Durand's smile turned to surprise. Her husband read her expression and mirrored her confusion.

"Yes, Mr. Durand, what is it?" Doug asked.

"Well, uh, here is a present for the boy who will soon be a soldier. Good luck!" he stammered, presenting a fine wristwatch to the somewhat astonished boy. He urged the guests to "carry on," then spotting his daughter, turned away and said, "Kim, come and talk to us in the hall."

Kim hurried after them as her parents disappeared into the adjoining hall. Mrs. Durand said, "Kim, why in the name of all that is sensible, didn't you tell us that Douglas was going in the service too? We intended the gift for Carl. He must feel really slighted. You knew I invited Carl to the party and . . ."

Kim interrupted her mother. "Listen to me, Mother. I had no idea Douglas was going in the service. Hazel said she forgot to tell me. When I heard Doug respond to your question, I yelled, 'Wait Dad, no!' but I guess it was too late."

Kim's statement calmed both Sylvia and Roger. Roger mumbled, "Hazel's a featherbrain." He turned to his wife and Kim. "Does Carl know we were going to give him a present?"

"Of course not, Roger. Why do you ask?"

"Well, maybe he will think, since Douglas lives close by, that we feel a kinship toward him and his family. You know, we really do have more in common with them. Heck, I wouldn't recognize Carl's folks if I tripped over them. We have nothing in common with the Emersons. To hell with feeling bad. Come on, let's get back to our guests."

Kim was upset by the turn of events, but managed to conceal her feelings back at the party. Hazel asked why she had called out "no" to Mr. Durand when Doug was called to the microphone.

Kim said, "Oh, I was afraid he was going to make a long speech. When Dad's had a couple cocktails, he can be long-winded."

Hazel accepted Kim's excuse and laughed knowingly about Mr. Durand's long-windedness.

Carl had been seated near the two girls, listening to the conversation. He looked at her glumly and shrugged his shoulders. Kim thought, *my poor Carl. Oh how I wish this awful thing never happened.* But she maintained a jolly façade, and danced with several of the boys who asked. When Carl finally got his turn, he swept Kim around the dance floor and said, "Kim, it was nice of your folks to invite me to this great party and it sure was generous of them to give Doug a watch. I hope he appreciates it. I know I would."

Kim bit her lip and looked into Carl's eyes, but said nothing. She thought, *Carl, that was meant for you!*

The party lasted long into the next morning. When Douglas was leaving, Kim called out, "Doug! Let someone know when you leave for the Army!"

Later, as Carl was preparing to leave, Kim took his hand and led him into the sitting room. She said, "You know, Carl, this evening, things just didn't go as planned at all. Don't read anything into what happened. I, we, really care about you, and did not intend to hurt your feelings." She kissed him.

Carl said, "Kim, don't worry about it. I still like you a lot and always will." They strolled to the front door and parted.

That evening at supper, Carl's mother asked about the big party. He replied, "Oh, it was something. The Durands really know how to entertain. They even gave Douglas a going-away gift—an expensive wrist watch."

His dad remarked, "I imagine the Durands and Doug's family are close friends. You know, they belong to the same country club."

"Yeah, I guess so," Carl answered softly.

Chapter 3

The War

On Sunday morning, December 7, 1941, Carl was cleaning, polishing, and lubricating his pride and joy, a souped-up 1930 Ford Tudor five-seat sedan, preparing it for storage. He anticipated being in the service for at least a year or two. Tomorrow was reporting day at Fort Devens. He swirled the polishing cloth rapidly on the car's bumper and watched his reflection grow clearer until the uncertainty in his own eyes stared back at him.

Suddenly, the door to the kitchen opened and his mother screamed, "Carl, come here! Oh my God, how terrible!"

Carl ran into the room in time to hear the radio announcer say:

The battleship Arizona has been sunk by the bombing, as were several warships. The casualty toll is believed to be very high . . .

Carl turned to his mother. "Who bombed us?"

His mother gave him a few of the details she had heard: The Japanese. It was a sneak attack—a huge fleet of planes, completely undetected. "Of all days, on a Sunday," she added. "And tomorrow you . . . Oh Lord, why?" She put her arm around her son. He felt her tremble uncontrollably and tried to comfort her. The phone rang. It was his father, asking, "Did you hear the news? Oh, I guess you did. I can hear the radio. How's Ma taking it?"

Carl said, "She's upset. Told me I shouldn't have joined," he said quietly with his hand cupped over the receiver.

"Tell her to take it easy and not worry. I'll be home tomorrow morning before you have to leave. Watch your mother now." He ended the call.

Basic training at Devens was arduous, to say the least. None of the new recruits had much time to write letters. After thirty days, the ordeal ended and letter writing commenced. Carl wrote:

Dear Ma and Dad,
I thought that I would have to sleep a couple of months after going through basic training. They kept us going from five a.m. till dark. They scalped us, they ran us, they exercised us, and they marched us! They marched us to the mess hall, they marched us to the barracks. They marched us to the exercise field, and they marched us to the marching grounds. If the outcome of this war depended on what country did the most marching, we would win hands-down! On the day they scalped us, one guy tacked a sign on his bunk: "One comb for sale. Cost: 50 cents. Will sell for 10 cents." Well, our sergeant saw the sign and said, "What do you know. We have a comedian here!" and made the guy do 25 push-ups. The sergeant said the sign was all right. But the thumbtack in the bunk's mattress was

damage to government property. None of us dared to laugh at that. The food here is so-so. They call it mess. I kind of wonder about that. Well, Ma and Dad, take care and don't worry. I'm doing OK."

Love, Carl

Another month passed and Carl wrote two letters. To his parents, he wrote:

Dear Ma and Dad,
Our sergeant really amuses us poor grunts. But we don't dare laugh at his harangues. Yesterday we were ordered to stand at ease after he took muster. While we were at ease, another company of GI's was marching by, all bearing rifles. One GI in our group said, "Serge, why don't we have guns too?" Our serge glared at him and said, "Grunt!" (He always refers to us as grunts but when an officer is present, he calls us soldiers.) "You wouldn't know the barrel from the stock of a rifle. When the Army gives you a rifle, you're expected to kill the enemy. You have lousy aim and miss him, the enemy shoots half your ass off! And you know what, Grunt, the Army ain't got no use for a half-assed grunt!" I tell you, we had all we could do to not laugh. Serge would have had a field day giving us push-ups.

Tomorrow we will be taking some kind of an IQ test. The rumor is the test will be a screening for other military training. I'll keep you posted.

Love,
Carl

Carl relayed the same information to Kim, sweetened with appropriate nuances consistent with writing to a girlfriend. He added an inquiry about Douglas, and ended with:

I miss you, I miss you, I miss you. When I know what the Army has planned for me as a result of the IQ test, I will send you my new address.

Love,
Carl

Carl's new orders were to report to the base commander at Wright-Patterson Army Airfield in Dayton, Ohio, where he would be assigned to flight training. Before departing, he was granted a seven-day leave.

The day Carl arrived home his parents were both waiting for him. His father shook his hand. "Welcome home, son. It appears military life agrees with you."

His mother threw her arms around Carl. When she finally released him, tears rimmed her eyelids. "My little boy—All grown up. But look at you—You're all skin and bones. Doesn't the army feed you? Go talk to your father in the living room. I'm going into the kitchen to fix you something to eat."

After the biggest meal Carl could ever remember ingesting, he called Kim. The next seven days were a blur of dancing, visiting, and over-eating. But Kim stood out as the main attraction.

Flight training school required that Carl learn to fly the latest military aircraft and become proficient in enemy aircraft identification. The training covered B-17 bomber engines, fuel requirements, communications equipment, navigation, aerodynamics, safety, survival and armament. It lasted eight months, requiring hours of after-class study. The scarcity and brevity of the letters he wrote home attested to the vast amount of material he had to cover. Carl's instructors were impressed by his scholastic ability. A shortage of teachers increased the number of subjects allotted to them. Because of his high grades, they suggested to Colonel Sharp, the school commander, that Carl be certified to teach. Carl met with Col. Sharp to discuss the offer. The colonel said, "Carl, some of the boys who left here may never be seen again. Think it over."

Carl accepted the offer. His parents were overjoyed that he wasn't shipped overseas and attributed his infrequent writing to the pressure of his studies.

Kim wrote that she wished he was not so busy and would write more often. She wrote that Mr. Graf, Douglas's father, had met her dad at the country club and thanked him for giving Doug the wristwatch.

He said, "I wouldn't give him a wristwatch. Why, he's lost three good watches in the past two years!"

Dad said jokingly, "I should have given the watch to someone else." Mr. Graf also told him that Doug was ordered to report to Luke Army Airfield in Arizona, and left a

*few days after you went to Devens. So you
see, Carl, boys around here are slowly
dwindling. What are we girls to do?*

Love, Kim

Near the end of his schooling, Carl received the following
letter from his girlfriend:

*Dear Carl,
    Yesterday, Hazel and I went to the
movies and saw "Going My Way" with Bing
Crosby and Barry Fitzgerald. It was a sad
movie, I thought. Anyway, Hazel and I
were talking about you and how so many of
our boyfriends were gone. We were just
about ready to leave for home when she
said, "Oh, I forgot to tell you. Douglas
wrote me. He left Arizona about a week ago
for England. He's a fighter pilot on
something he called a P-51, whatever that
is."
    I said, "Why didn't you let me know?
Douglas, a fighter pilot! Don't you read the
papers, Hazel? That's a fast combat plane.
I hope Doug doesn't get in trouble."
    Carl, stay where you are.*

*Love,
Kim*

Carl had been an instructor for eleven months when
Colonel Sharp informed him he'd been selected to maintain,

calibrate, and retrofit Norton bombsights and electronic equipment on B-17 aircraft currently in service at a US Army base in England. He left for the classified base a week after receiving his orders.

Chapter 4

Rising to the Need

A few months after the U.S. entered the war, shortages of some raw materials began to hamper production for a number of subsidiaries of Sunrise Industries, Inc. As the war required more and more materials, goods for civilian use were curtailed. The company that manufactured cooking utensils was now producing helmets, bayonets, shell casings, and a host of smaller defense items. Another subsidiary that processed linseed oil and related products now manufactured explosives. Soon, household goods such as pots, pans and paper products, dishes, mops and brooms, manufactured by other affiliates, were consigned to Sunrise Industries' several retail stores. Stores and manufacturing plants not utilized for the war effort were phased out. Roger Durand issued the following notice from his office:

March 12, 1942

To All Affiliates of Sunrise Industries, Inc.:

Whereas numerous products, wholesale or retail, and manufacturing plants not involved in the war effort may no longer prove useful to this corporation, they will terminate operations when so ordered. Unlisted companies will be notified by their holding company, the Sunrise Merchant's Trust. Funds due to discharged personnel, disposition of pension moneys and insurance funds will be computed by the trust company. All personnel affected will be reimbursed if eligible.

(signed) Roger Durand,

Chief Executive Officer

The corporation concealed the appearance of being a monopoly, possibly evading government anti-trust action, by listing only a fraction of its affiliates. Listed affiliates bore their company name, followed by the words, "a division of Sunrise Industries," while unlisted affiliates such as Everbright Paints bore their company name only.

A bank can loan funds for business ventures, Durand reasoned. By agreement, the bank was the holding company for the business, even though the financial institution itself was owned by Sunrise Industries.

As the war fueled Sunrise Industries' profits, fulfilling Andrew Higgins's prophesy, Durand simply attributed the increased revenues to his own superior management practices.

Mandatory gasoline rationing and carpooling did not affect Roger Durand. The large quantity of gasoline allotted to his corporation was of course available to him. Yet, he often used the train to commute. The large profits bolstered Durand's spirits, and he felt patriotic riding with servicemen. He joked with them and fancied himself a true pillar of the community.

His brother, George Durand, unlike Roger, became concerned and thoughtful as the war dragged on. He purchased war bonds and contributed considerable money to the Salvation Army and Red Cross. He often asked his niece, Kim, about Carl, Douglas, and others she knew in the service of their country. He was attentive and sympathetic to her, while her father acted indifferent to her worries about her friends.

One evening when George and Laurie visited for dinner and a bridge game, Roger told George how an engineer in one of their factories had figured a way to cut the cost of fabricating an intricate aircraft part. He said, "We secured the Army contract to make the part. They estimated the cost at $2,000. They accepted our bid for $1,900 and we were contracted to make 600 of them. But thanks to one of our engineers, we knew how to make them for less than $300 apiece. We sure will make a bundle on that deal, eh?"

George responded, "Roger, I hope you get the contract revised. Hey, even $600 would have been a reasonable and fair figure."

Roger glowered and said, "What the hell's the matter with you? We build a better mousetrap and we shouldn't profit by it? Good God, we're in business to make money. We don't do charity. It's a good thing Dad knew better than to let you run Sunrise."

George said, "That's right. You don't do charity; you do robbery. And I hate to say this, but guys like you running big companies may someday ruin this country."

Roger shook his head. "George, you're nuts! Dad worked hard so that we wouldn't have to. Let's make the most of it. Don't forget, you're a stockholder too." He slammed down his cocktail glass. "I'm hungry. Let's go eat!"

Chapter Five

News From the War Front

Kim's friend, Hazel, had not heard from Douglas for several months since he transferred to England. She decided she could not stand it any longer and paid a visit to the Graf home. Mr. Graf opened the door and said, "Hazel, come in! I recognize you from a picture on my son's bureau that's signed 'Love, Hazel'. He showed her to the den and asked her to sit down. His face was drawn and lined. He said, "I think I know why you've come. I guess you heard about Douglas."

Hazel shook her head cautiously, eyes riveted on Doug's father. "Uh, no. What happened?" she whispered, lips quivering.

Mr. Graf quickly explained, "No—There's hope, at least. The Army notified me that Douglas is missing in action and may or may not be alive. He was flying in a group of P-51 fighter planes acting as shields between our B-17 bombers and German fighter planes. A buddy of his who saw the whole thing said one of the German planes was attempting to get at a B-17 behind my son's plane. Doug fired at the oncoming plane, hitting it, but some of the debris from the explosion took out the tail section of Doug's plane. His buddy saw the P-51 dive down, and Doug bail out. The parachute opened, but then he lost sight of it through the clouds. We haven't heard a thing about him since. I wish I had better news for you."

Mr. Graf sighed. "Hazel, I wish you could stay and meet my wife and daughter, but I am going downtown to meet them for dinner and a play afterwards. We must try to get our minds off our problems. This has been an ordeal for all of us."

Hazel was glad to terminate the visit. She was about to burst into tears and feared she might create an awkward situation for Mr. Graf, who appeared close to tears himself. She hurried to her car, drove to a secluded area, beat her fists on the dashboard and wailed. When she was all cried out, she headed home.

The next day she called Kim and retold the sad story about Douglas. When a letter from Carl finally arrived with his new return address, Kim knew where to send the painful news. She wrote:

> *Dearest Carl,*
> *Last month Hazel told me the bad news that Douglas was shot down in a battle with German planes—rather, the plane he shot blew up next to his plane and damaged the tail section. Anyway, Doug had to jump from the plane as it was falling. Another pilot saw Doug's parachute open and disappear into the clouds. He is listed as missing in action! I know I said at times that he was headstrong, but I like him. I like you both. Please be careful and let me know if you hear anything about Douglas.*
> *Love, and always thinking about you,*
> *Kim*

In mid October of 1942, on a foggy, damp day, Carl reported for duty at a barracks in sector 12, group headquarters near Nottingham, England. A portion of the barracks served as the office of Colonel Walter Stone, commander of U.S. Army

Air Force personnel. While approaching his destination, Carl noticed many fog-shrouded B-17 bombers parked in a field next to the black surface of the barely visible runway. This gave Lieutenant Emerson an eerie feeling and added to his uneasiness about the new assignment. However, his 201 file stated he was highly qualified to retrofit, calibrate and adjust Norton sights. His proficiency as a pilot and navigator with an IFR rating on a number of military aircraft was also cited. He was checked in by the officer of the day and shown into Col. Stone's office. After the usual military courtesies, Col. Stone studied Carl for a few moments, then looked out his office window and said, "It's gloomy out there, isn't it? Don't let it bother you. We're a happy bunch in here. The sun does come out, the fog leaves, and when you meet your crew things will look more cheerful."

Carl thought, *My God. The colonel's a mind reader,* but answered, "I look forward to meeting them."

The Colonel told Carl to take a seat. He said, "This evening you'll be settled and acquainted with our operation here. We have a small shop for your job, some good instruments, and two damn good technicians. And, Lieutenant, we aint too much on saluting and that regular army starchy stuff, except if there's some gold braid around." He called in the OD, Lt. Johnson, and told him to show their new man his quarters and surroundings.

Carl and his guide passed through a narrow corridor as an enlisted man exited an adjoining office. The man said, "Here comes that pesky Lieutenant Johnson again." Johnson replied smugly, "And there's that fat Sgt. Greg, always in the way and eating everyone's food!" The two jokers passed each other, their tongues protruding, as they jeered, "Nyah, Nyah!"

Carl was amazed. Such carrying on between an officer and an enlisted man! He said, "Lt. Johnson, what the hell was that?"

"Oh, just a little banter," Johnson replied. "Greg is our rear gunner when we fly at the Krauts. He's a damn good man. The captain and I love that guy. He saved our asses many times over Berlin. Has six known kills to his credit! We're glad he's on our crew."

"But you called him fat. He's not fat."

"That's true. But on a mission, none of us cares too much for food, except Greg; he eats all we leave."

After a few days on base, Carl realized the great respect these airmen had for each other. Their kidding was never malicious. It was an opiate for the terrible task that lay ahead.

That evening, Carl sent off a letter to his parents. He gave them a cheerful report, as they were no doubt worried, anxious to hear from him, and eager to obtain his address. He also wrote a comforting letter to Kim. An upbeat message would be good for both of them. After all, his job was not to be a combatant, but to assure navigation and bomb sighting equipment were in perfect adjustment for the B-17 planes—So he told Kim, though he knew it might not be completely true.

His shop was fairly well equipped with testing devices for navigation instruments: altimeters, gyros, IFF units, and two-way radio equipment. Leroy Stevens and Bob Helms, the two electronic technicians assigned to work with Carl, were in the shop at seven-thirty. They greeted Carl with a handshake when he arrived a short time later. They explained that some of the B-17's he saw yesterday needed extensive testing, repairs and replacement of various instruments.

Helms said, "You know, Lieutenant, a bombing raid sometimes beats the crap out of those goodies."

"Yeah," chimed in Leroy. "Some of those birds look like Swiss cheese when they flap in here!"

And so their task, awesome as it was, awaited them.

The maintenance advisor reviewed malfunctions written up by the captains of the B-17's scheduled to be worked on. He determined where and when a shop trained to repair or correct a malfunction could do so. If B-17 number 250 needed fuselage work, engine maintenance, and its radar repaired, it would be scheduled for work in the hangar adjacent to the shop specializing in fuselage work, then moved to the engine repair section. Finally, it would go to the electronics area. Unforeseen problems would of course change the lineup.

It seemed that most every aircraft had some form of electronic problem. The intercom system was the most frequent source of trouble. Fortunately, Carl's technicians were well versed in solving intercom problems. The electronic systems were more bothersome. For the most part, altimeters, airspeed indicators, and almost all of the cockpit indicators were replaced with off-the-shelf new ones. The Norton bombsight was Carl's most important instrument to calibrate, repair or replace. When one was repaired or replaced, the plane in which it had been installed would be flown over a pre-arranged target. Carl, as adjuster of the bombsight, would ride in the Plexiglass nose of the bomber and assume the role of bombardier during the equipment test. It was a strange and exciting feeling, watching the countryside slip by thousands of feet below, with nothing between him and the sky but a clear, thin shield.

During one of the early flights, Carl had asked the pilot a question about the apparent "frailty" of the nose and what would happen if the plane, cruising at 200 miles per hour, were to strike a bird. The pilot smiled and replied, "That depends on the size of the bird. But don't worry—Each tries to avoid the other as much as possible." Carl was not comforted by the answer.

When they reached the target area, dummy bombs would be dropped, and the accuracy of the bombing relayed to the plane from the ground crew. When the bombs impacted within a prescribed area, the bomber was declared combat ready.

One morning, Col. Stone came into the electronics shop and said, "Carl, so you're from Milford Connecticut! I'm from Saymour, but if the troops knew that, they would say, 'no wonder his briefings ain't brief!'"

Carl laughed and said, "Yes! Saymour—little town north of Milford. My friends and I used to go to Marlin's Dance Hall near there."

"Well I'll be damn, so did I, a long time ago," the colonel said in surprise.

Carl no longer felt like a stranger in a foreign country. Colonel Stone, his boss, was a neighbor. The feelings of loneliness he'd experienced despite being around others diminished. Talk about doings in Connecticut would help Carl's morale. Yet, the saying, "It's lonely at the top" applied to Col. Walter Stone.

Carl soon trained his senses to ignore the roar of B-17's taking off from the runway visible from the electronic shop, knowing the grim fact that some would not return. In time, he became almost completely oblivious to their noise.

One day, about a month after his job began, Carl became aware of a plane whose takeoff sounded far quieter than usual. He glanced out the window and saw what was surely the longer, slimmer profile of a German plane rising off the runway. He called out to his technician, "Leroy! What the hell? That's a German reconnaissance plane! What's it doing taking off from here?"

Leroy answered, "Sir, a few weeks before you arrived, that plane ran out of fuel on the other side of those trees beyond the runway. Lucky for him, there was a field to land on. The limeys must have spotted him and alerted a whole bunch of military and air raid watchers around here. What I hear, there was a bad fog. He seemed lost and headed inland. The fog started to break. He lucked out just in time over the field. When the Kraut landed, he had a welcoming gang that would make Hitler envious."

Carl questioned, "Why wasn't he shot down?"

The technician shrugged. "I didn't hear why."

Carl remarked, "Seems funny—a German aircraft with British insignias, and painted white. I sure would like to learn how to fly that bird."

Carl soon learned that Col. Stone knew how to fly the captured plane. Perhaps he would be lucky enough to learn it too. No harm in asking.

That evening Carl found two letters in his room. About time, he thought. Hope the home folks are OK. His parents' letters were cheerful, informing him his dad had received a substantial pay raise, and that their cat, lost over a month ago, was finally found by a neighbor. Carl wrote back:

Dear Ma and Dad,

I have a job here that I really like. My two assistants are right on the ball, which helps a heck of a lot. But the best thing about being here is that the base commander, Col. Walter Stone, is from Saymour, Connecticut! He sure is an officer and a gentleman. He used to go dancing at Marlin's, where my buddies and I went so often. We both have something in common, and unlike basic training at Devens and Wright-Patterson, you don't wear out your arm saluting or strain your back standing at attention because of the gold braid always

*around! I like it here, you two, so don't
worry about me!*

*Love,
Carl*

The next letter was from Kimberly Durand. When he read
Kim's account of Douglas's encounter during the bombing
strike, and of Doug's being listed as missing in action, a heavy
feeling sank to the pit of his stomach. Tears came to his eyes.
After an hour, he wrote back that he would try to find out if
Doug was imprisoned in Germany. He said he was sorry to hear
about his friend, and if Kim learned anything else, to please let
him know.

*Let's hope he is OK. Keep your chin up,
and tell Hazel I will try my damnedest to
get someone who can possibly find out
about Doug.*

*Love,
Carl*

A few days later, Col. Stone entered the shop. His eyes
appeared tired and bloodshot. He said, "Carl, we lost several
men in yesterday's raid." He paused, shook his head, and
continued, "Damn good guys. If their replacements, if they ever
get here, are half as good as them, we will be lucky."

Carl said, "Yeah, I see a lot of the big birds didn't get back.
And the ones that did look really bad!"

Stone nodded in agreement. Carl asked the colonel, "These men that don't come back, do you receive reports on them— whether they are alive, wounded, or dead?"

"Well, debriefing knows who gets back, and about reported parachute openings, but the count may not always be accurate. The Nazis sometimes report the dead, wounded, or captured by radio. The International Red Cross rarely gives us information, and British intelligence may come through with something. When we do get a report from the Red Cross, it is confirmation of a live prisoner of war."

Carl asked about the German plane he saw taking off a few days ago. The colonel answered, "That plane was spotted by British radar coming in over the eastern shore of England. It was identified as a reconnaissance plane. The meteorological people say he probably took off from Belgium early in the a.m., and soon after flying over England, a dense fog closed in. It was too risky to send fighters after him in that weather, and since he appeared to be lost, passing over this area several times, fighter command group 12 figured his gas would soon run out. Sure enough, he glided into a field over there."

Colonel Stone pointed out the shop window to the woods across from the runway. "We found out later that his direction finder failed."

Carl said, "I can fly a few of our American planes. I might be able to pilot that German baby, but someone would have to translate the German labels on the instruments and controls."

Colonel Stone's eyes lit up. "You want to fly it? I'll teach you how. I can read and write German, one of my courses at Yale. After we service and repair what's left after this last bombing run, when your work load permits, I'll get clearance to fly 'Snow White' and show you how. It's really a simple aircraft to operate. Just a matter of interpreting the German words, as you said. Group 12 command ordered that we do only touch and go with it, and limited the flight to within a five-mile radius of the control tower. That's just about eight kilometers on its air speed indicator in a no-wind situation." He added, "We painted it white because, if it wasn't, even with the English insignias, someone sure has hell would get the phones ringing at headquarters. Nazi planes always seem to be painted a dark gray."

Carl's opportunity to fly "Snow White" came a couple of weeks later. As hoped, interpretation of the words on the craft's instruments was really all he needed. After an hour of flying, the colonel said, "Let's land. You've got the hang of it."

Three months after flying the enemy plane, Carl answered all the letters Kim and his parents had written him. The last one from Kim was a bit more cheerful than the previous ones. Hazel had informed her that Douglas was alive—a prisoner in Germany. Douglas's dad said he was so happy to relay that news to Hazel. Kim added:

*Now all I have to worry about is you!
Carl, absence makes the heart grow fonder.
Does it do that for you? I hope so.*

*Love,
Kim*

The news about Douglas relieved Carl, as he had been frustrated about failing to uncover any leads or information about his friend.

On April 1, 1943, general headquarters (GHQ) informed Col. Stone that more strikes at enemy targets were planned:

Intelligence is evaluating reports from their
agents on selected targets. Coordinates on
the set targets will be transmitted to your
squadron. Action must be implemented as
soon as practicable. On receipt of
coordinates, you will have ten (10) fully
armed B-17 carriers with qualified
personnel.

Stone read the notice and thought, *wouldn't you know it.
On April Fool's Day!* He listed Lt. Carl Emerson as bombardier
on the manning list for the projected action, as the one assigned
to the last bomber in service had been hospitalized.

Carl's notification to attend the briefing had a chilling
effect on him. *My God, I wonder if this is it? Maybe I'll luck
out. At least half of them come back.* His thoughts raced on.
*50/50 odds. Damn this war! I hope it ends before they send us
out.*

Carl's efforts to focus on his shop work proved futile for
several hours. Finally, that evening at his quarters, with the
radio blaring loud jazz music, he wrote two cheerful letters—
one to his parents, and one to "my dearest, dearest Kim."
Neither letter mentioned his new orders.

Two briefings were canceled due to weather conditions in
the target area. On the 10th of April, forecasts were favorable
for the bombing mission. The target was defined as submarine
pens, shipping and dry-docks at Bremerhaven, 420 miles due
east of the base, ten miles from the North Sea on the Weser
estuary. The squadron commander was introduced to the group
and details vital to the mission were discussed. Carl was
assigned as bombardier of the last B-17 to leave. He was glad
Lt. Johnson and Sgt. Greg were assigned to his plane. Lt.

Johnson introduced Carl to their commander, Capt. Sterling. The captain's warm greeting coupled with the camaraderie of Greg and Johnson bolstered Carl's morale. The adrenaline flow in their veins stimulated the aggressive instinct to kill or be killed by a common foe, bonding them more closely than blood brothers.

Although Carl had flown onboard the E model numerous times, the takeoff set his heart pounding. The entire aircraft shook as Capt. Sterling throttled up the four 1200 HP Wright "Cyclone" engines. The vibration intensified as the flying fortress raced down the runway. Then came that moment when the great war bird reached 100 M.P.H. and left the ground. Despite the roar of the engines, Carl sensed a great calm as the craft climbed to its 15,000-foot cruising altitude. He left his seat and moved forward toward the cockpit.

Capt. Sterling looked over his shoulder and asked, "Carl, are you checked out on the 30 caliber machine gun?"

"Not yet," replied Carl, slightly embarrassed by his lack of training.

"That's all right," replied Sterling, who turned to the navigator. "Wilson, this is Carl's first time up on a mission, so you man the nose gun this time. Carl, you can sightsee up front and make sure our payload gets delivered on target."

The squadron reached Bremerhaven in a little less than two hours, their fighter planes escorting them. It seemed to Carl that the fast P-51s came from nowhere. In fact, they had taken off from the base an hour after the bombers already departed. Several minutes before they'd reached the target area, German fighter planes met the fleet of bombers and protective escorts, and a fierce air battle began. In spite of the action going on around him, Carl felt surprisingly confident. Keeping an eye on the bombsight, he moved the release handle from the "lock" position into "selective". When the targeted area positioned itself under the sights, he released the first rack of bombs, calling out, "Bombs away!"

Antiaircraft fire was heavy over the crucial area. The enemy fighter planes kept away to avoid becoming casualties of their own ground gunners. Beyond the targets, both ally and German fighting planes swarmed around the remaining airborne bombers. The squadron leader counted three B-17's missing from the group. Of the P-51's, one was seen to drop from the sky. Seven German planes were destroyed.

Another pass was made over the target, and more bombs dropped. The squadron departed for home base, still in a valley of fire. Carl heard Lt. Johnson yell over the intercom, "Good job, Greg. You got those three!" Greg's reply could not be heard, but Carl saw the Lieutenant grin and shake his head. As the plane banked to change direction, heavy smoke was observed rising from the ground below. No doubt the raid had been successful. However, as the last plane in the squadron headed westward over the estuary, a freight ship came into view.

As they approached the freighter, Carl could see flashes of fire coming from the deck as the crew manned the four twin antiaircraft guns. Puffs of black smoke appeared in the sky ahead of the bomber. *Flak bursts,* thought Carl. *Once we get through this it should be smooth sailing back to the base.*

Suddenly a powerful explosion, followed by a gut-wrenching jolt changed everything. Carl whipped his head around to the outer starboard engine. The prop was slowing, belching thick smoke that streamed behind.

Capt. Sterling yelled, "Carl, you better get topside. This may be a rough ride!"

Carl scrambled back near the two waist gunners as the fire spread to the inner starboard engine. Then he heard popping and crackling sounds, and the cockpit began to fill with smoke.

Sterling shouted, "Men, we're not going to make it. I'm going to try to set her down as close to the shore as I can. Johnson, keep the landing gear up. It's easier to belly in than take a chance on the wheels hitting something."

Carl felt a shudder go through the plane as it skipped once on the surface of the water. Then everything was lost in a blur as a wingtip hit a wave and the plane began to cartwheel. The next sensation Carl was aware of was water rushing into the plane.

Oh no! he thought. *We're sinking!*

He caught sight of a shard of light streaming in through a large tear in the skin of the aircraft and hurled himself through the opening. Carl plunged into the waves, scarcely aware of the frigid water temperature. He kicked his legs, hit bottom, and stood up, amazed to feel air blowing around his head. He opened his eyes to find himself standing not quite shoulder deep in water. As he stumbled toward shore, he turned back to look at the plane. The entire forward section was twisted rubble.

"Lt. Emerson, sir!"

Carl pivoted to see Sgt. Greg and the two side gunners standing onshore. Someone said, "Lt. Emerson! Where's the rest of the crew?"

Shock had numbed Carl's senses. "I, I don't know," he stammered. "You men—help me find them."

The group waded back into the surf and over the next half hour located the bodies of the remaining crewmen and dragged them ashore. As they stood, heads bowed in silent farewell, a roar sounded from further inland. Within moments, a fleet of military vehicles appeared, and they found themselves surrounded by German soldiers.

"Du zurückreicht auf," yelled one of the soldiers, pointing a rifle at them. Carl didn't understand German, but there was no

mistaking the speaker's intent. The men raised their hands in unison and were taken prisoner.

German radio broadcast for allied consumption the following news item:

> The cowardly Americans bombed the
> homes of innocent civilians in the
> Bremerhaven area. Many men, women, and
> children were killed. Our brave pilots
> destroyed a great number of their bomber
> and fighting planes. No damage was done to
> our military installations. . .

The propaganda continued:

> The great skill of our fighting men was
> evident when they fired and hit an enemy
> plane from a small freighter in rough waters
> off Bremerhaven. Four men from the
> crashed plane survived and were captured
> in Holland.

The broadcast provided names in an effort to make the whole account credible. Listed among the captured was Lt. Carl Emerson.

U.S. Army intelligence investigated and verified the personnel named in the broadcast. Relatives of the survivors were notified that their loved ones were now German prisoners of war.

One quiet afternoon, Tom Emerson answered the front door. A military officer said, "Mr. Emerson?"

Tom, cautiously eyeing the uniformed man, began to tremble in anticipation of the worst news. "Oh no! Yes I am Carl's father, Tom Emerson."

The soldier said, "I have a message for you from the war department. It could be worse." And he handed the telegram to Tom. Beads of sweat dropped onto the envelope as the father tore open the envelope and read:

> Lt. Carl Emerson was taken prisoner by German military following action over Germany on 10 April 1943. You will be notified of any further information we can report. Further details of the action are classified and cannot be revealed at this time. Lt. Emerson is believed to be uninjured.
>
> Sincerely,
>
> Col. William Bowen,
>
> Adjutant, U.S. Dept. of Information

The messenger said, "Mr. Emerson, we often get information about prisoners of war. When we do, we pass the word to the prisoner's parents. Take care and don't worry."

Mrs. Emerson had been working in the adjacent den and heard the news. She emerged appearing surprisingly calm. "Now he won't be killed," she told her husband.

An article soon appeared in Milford's weekly newspaper, telling of Carl's capture. Kim read the notice and gasped. She handed the paper to her mother and said, "I'm going to see Carl's mother. I must!"

Kim met Mrs. Emerson in the front yard and said simply, "I know." They embraced, sharing tears and gladness. They both loved Carl.

Roger Durand invited his brother and sister-in-law for a day of sun, fun, booze and good food at Golden Vista. Roger said, "They say Saturday is going to be great. One of those warm days we seldom get this early in May. So come early. The heat's on in the pool and it's time we used it this year. The Popes will be over a little later. We'll play poker and beat the pants off the women, eh?"

"Better watch it," his brother replied. "Laurie is a damn good player and so is your wife. I don't know about Grace, but we may have our butts out. We'll come early and you can update me on the latest about Sunrise."

Saturday was a fine day as predicted. The brothers went for an early swim, while their wives opted to chat in the library. After about 40 minutes in and out of the water, the men sat sunning themselves on the edge of the pool.

"So what's new at Sunrise, big guy?" George asked.

Roger glowed. "The money is rolling in. I don't know what the hell the Navy needs shovels for, but we signed a contract for five hundred of them."

"Well, my learned brother, there's a branch of the Navy called the Seabees. They probably need shovels to develop runways on some of those islands in the Pacific," George informed him, adding, "What's the contract worth?"

"Fifty dollars a shovel," Roger answered.

"That's highway robbery!" exclaimed George. "You used to make them for three dollars and sell them for eight. This war is making a few of us rich. I don't like it. Someday when they look into these contracts, there will be hell to pay."

"George, all the big boys are making it, so why not us? Hell, this other contract we got from the Army calls for 2,000 pairs of crutches. We'll get $80 a pair. A hundred and sixty thousand bucks!"

"Roger, for the love of Mike. If they start investigating, the crap will fly! I've tried to convince you to go easy on the markups. There will be a reckoning, and Sunrise may soon see the sunset. Some guys out there fighting this war will get a leg blown off and be issued your crutches along with a heap of praise from rich big shots like you, and it's not going to amount to a pile of crap."

In spite of the brothers' arguments, everyone enjoyed the day. The ladies walked away from the poker game with more than a hundred dollars each. George walked away with a plan: to add to his substantial shares in Sunrise Industries so that he could gain control of the corporation before his brother destroyed it.

It amused Roger to hear George pontificate on the evils of price gouging. That night in bed he told Sylvia, "Your brother-in-law takes after your mother-in-law. Ma was timid—so willing to give bargains to customers at that little paint store she and Dad owned. She even paid the bills before they were due."

"She's your mother, and he's your brother. You make it sound like they're not related to you," Sylvia remarked as she switched off the light.

Chapter 6

Prisoner of War Camp

After the four Americans were apprehended by the Germans, they were transported to a police station in Rotterdam, where they were locked in jail cells, Carl a good distance away from the three enlisted men. Early the next morning, Lt. Emerson was taken from his cell and led to an interrogation room. It was furnished with a table and two chairs. On the far wall was a large portrait of Hitler. A bare light bulb glared overhead.

The guard gestured toward one of the chairs and said, "Sit."

After a few moments, the door opened and a German officer came in and sat in the other chair. Carl said to the officer, "I must object to the way I have been separated from my men."

The officer jumped to his feet and yelled, "You object? I must object to the way your bomber killed innocent people! Now you will tell me the location of the airfield that your plane took off from."

Carl replied, "My name is Carl Emerson, First Lieutenant, U.S. Army Air Force. My serial number is 6063613."

His interrogator said, "Very well. We have nothing more to discuss. You will be transported to one of our prison camps today." He turned on his heel and was gone.

Moments later, two guards ushered Carl to a military vehicle where he was placed on a wooden bench in a dimly lit detention area in the rear of the wagon. After three hours of bumps, jolts, abrupt stops and starts, he banged on the small glass window at the back of the cab, through which he could see the driver and passenger. The guard turned to face Carl who began frantically waving his hand and pointing his finger downward. The driver stopped and the two guards led him outside the vehicle.

"Ya, sehr gut gehen schnell," one of them said to Carl. As they marched him at gunpoint to a wooded area, a truck full of German troops whizzed past, hooting. The guards alternately relieved themselves, and then watched Carl do the same. They returned to the truck, where Carl spent the remainder of the trip dozing and waking until they pulled in to the prison complex.

Stalagluft Number Five was built in early 1941 to imprison captured Russian soldiers; but no Russian was ever imprisoned there. The German war ministry had decided that the Russian prisoners would better serve the third Reich by working in factories producing weapons of war. The austere 200 by 70-foot wooden structure stood on a three-foot high poured concrete foundation. Three separate sets of stairs accessed the building, one opening into the German quarters on the south-facing façade, the other two entering the north side from the 200 by 100-foot prison yard, which was heavily enclosed by a 15 foot-high chain link fence topped with coiled barbed wire.

As the vehicle approached the complex, Carl was jarred awake from a fitful sleep by the sound of shouting. Bright lights appeared through the cab window. His captors opened the back of the vehicle and marched him into his new "home," escorting him by flashlight to his bunk.

The first morning of Carl's imprisonment, he awoke to the sound of a plane just as two guards arrived. They escorted him to the German prison commander, who said in heavily accented English, "Lt. Carl Emerson, I am Col. Karl Schneider. Carl, that's a good name. You may like it here." Then he delivered a stern lecture on the rules and regulations of the camp, making it clear that any infraction would justify severe punishment. He motioned to the guards to return the prisoner to quarters.

The bunk Carl had slept in was intended only for late arrival prisoners. He was re-assigned to bunk number 260, which was also his prison number. He was issued a tin cup and bowl, a flimsy blanket, and a shaving brush and razor that appeared used. He stashed them with his few belongings and gazed out the south-facing window next to his bunk, realizing this was to be his only view of the outside world for an indefinite period of time.

The guard introduced Carl to a Captain Smyth of the Canadian Air Force. Capt. Smyth asked Carl where he was from in the States, adding, "I visited New York City some time ago. It's a lively place day and night."

Carl answered, "You're right about that. I live in Connecticut, not too far from there."

"Then you must meet another chap from your state. Can't remember his name. Since you're new here, you'll be the last one served breakfast. Meet me here after chow and I'll introduce you."

The prison mess hall consisted of a bench on either side of a narrow 25-foot long table. It could accommodate only fifty inmates at a time, forcing the facility's maximum 300 inmates to eat in ten-minute shifts.

Carl learned that if a prisoner died or was taken away for any reason, the man with the next number would take his place, adopting not only the departed prisoner's number but his bunk as well. Since the bunks were stacked three high, the rotation meant a constant shuffling from top, to middle, to bottom bunk, then back to top, with no regard for the occupant's height.

Another result of the system was that if prisoner number 50, for example, was reassigned to number 49, he could now eat ten minutes earlier. The scheme was called Schneider's Folly.

As foolish as it was, it did lessen the brain-numbing tedium of captivity and fueled many a joke.

At lights out, one prisoner would loudly whisper to the man below his bunk, "Hey, don't fart in your bed, I might have to use it if they ship you out." This would set up a chain of similar statements through the barracks with so much laughter, the guards had to scream for silence. One time, prisoner 101 said to prisoner 100, "Hey, drop dead. I want to eat early tonight." Though the surface levity was contagious, inwardly the men were deeply troubled.

A Secret Committee

Carl's first breakfast was tasteless. The coffee was terrible, and his meager portion of dark grain mush tasted like rye bread soaked in something that barely passed for milk. His table companions told him that the "coffee" consisted of ground-up herbs that were roasted brown and brewed like coffee. But Carl was hungry and managed to finish the meal. He left his table in less than ten minutes, and observed Capt. Smyth talking to another prisoner whose back was to Carl. Smyth eyed Carl and said, "Here's your buddy. Don't drop dead like he did when I told him you were here."

The prisoner turned around. It was Douglas Graf. "Jesus Christ! I just don't believe it!" Carl yelled. Doug responded, "How the hell did you get here? I didn't know you were a flyboy!" They embraced and patted each other on the back. Smyth allowed, "Hey, I'll let you two talk."

Doug led his old friend out onto the steps of the complex. He appeared thin and tired. He said he'd been a prisoner since early October of 1942. After talking at great length about their mutual friends in Milford and all the good times they'd had at Golden Vista, Douglas lowered his voice and said, "You know,

Carl, I've been in this damn place seven months. I was the 125th prisoner when I got here. Now I'm number 120. You know why those five men aren't here anymore? Three of them went berserk, one died in his bunk, and the other was shot trying to escape from the yard when they opened the gate to let a supply truck leave. The guy's name was Graves. He was sitting right here. He waited for the front of the truck to pass by. When the rear wheels were even with the steps, he ran, crouched down, and actually made it out of the yard. He darted into some bushes on the west side of the building—too late. I think the driver saw him in his mirror. You know, the bastard stopped the truck, yelled, and marched Graves at gunpoint to the middle of the road outside the yard. Shot him point blank. A bunch of us saw the whole thing. That SOB turned and smiled at us after he killed Graves. Schneider of course was there right away. When he passed us he said, 'See what happens when you try to escape?'" Douglas dragged his hand down his face, as if trying to wipe out the memory.

"Carl, I want to tell you about our secret committee," he continued at a lower volume. "Captain Smyth and a bunch of us have been meeting by Smyth's bunk every Saturday after lights out. We discuss how we can get the hell out of here. There's only one guard by the entrance. He can't hear us. Carl, I hate this place. We need some fresh thinking on how to escape. Maybe if you look around, you'll see something we missed, or hit upon some new idea. I want out. They all want out and so will you." He scanned the surroundings for any guards, then continued, "When a new man joins, Capt. Smyth gives him a complete rundown on the structure of this place, how it's run, when guards go on or off duty, all that sort of thing."

Carl studied Doug's wan face as he spoke, thinking, *I guess I'll start to look like that, living under these conditions.* He decided to think positive and help his friend somehow.

Doug said, "Carl, I'm going to hit the sack. Someone will call me for chow. You should walk around our wonderful playground. A lot of guys will realize you are new here and want to talk to you. Don't mind the guards if they seem to size you up. We all went through that stupid stuff. I'm going in."

Carl slowly walked the perimeter of the yard, which extended north about a hundred feet from the northeast corner of the building, and west about twice that distance. The west side of the rectangular enclosure featured a ten-foot gate hinged to the south end. The prison complex lay in a flat treeless area. Short aircraft runways, with a windsock at the intersection, lined the south and west sides of the prison. Carl gazed up at the watchtowers located at the outer corners of the yard, noticing their height. He took note of the gate and how it opened, and thought about the placement of windows around the facility. He knew none existed on the west side that housed the prisoners of war, but the north and south walls of the prisoners' quarters each bore six barred windows, two feet wide by four feet high.

From the yard, he could not see whether the east end containing the German quarters had windows, but he supposed it did. He also guessed from the overall symmetry of the building that the south side of the German portion had three windows opposing the three unbarred windows visible on the north side from the prison yard. Carl took note of the bushes on either side of the step landings at the entrances to both the prisoners' and guards' quarters from the north side. It was safe to assume that the Germans also had their own private access to the building from the south façade, so that their personnel could avoid using the prison yard.

The new prisoner then turned his attention to the structure's foundation. He wondered if there might be an opening under the landing. Then he peered up at the sturdy chain link fence. The barbed wire on top appeared formidable.

The men he met were a mixture of friendliness and indifference. Some seemed sad, others, eager to talk. In a few days, he had the prison routine down pat. He knew when to get in line for meals, and that the best time for shaving or washing was late at night or very early in the morning, by the dim lighting in the latrine.

On Saturday, Carl was most anxious to attend the secret committee meeting. Nighttime couldn't come quick enough. A few scattered low-wattage lights illuminated the sleeping quarters, enabling the men to find their way to an area of 40 unoccupied beds, where Capt. Smyth would conduct the meeting. The captain sat on the most distant bed from the occupied section as the other men quietly took seats on adjacent beds, or stood clustered around the captain.

Smyth started the informal meeting by saying, "Well, we have a new man here now, Lt. Emerson. So I will go over the things he doesn't know yet about this place. If I leave anything out, just say so." Smyth scoped the room cautiously for any sign of the Germans, then continued, "As you've probably seen, there are three watch towers. They are all equipped with machine guns and rifles. Every tower has a high intensity spotlight, and we know there are phones in them too. There is a siren on the roof of this building. It can be operated from any tower. We learned that when Graves attempted his escape. We found an opening about 15 inches wide and about two and a half feet high in the foundation wall, underneath the landings to each of the two entrances to the building from the yard. Beyond the sill, the crawl space is about three feet high, I would guess."

Smyth leaned forward and gestured around the room. "As you can see, we are in a bar room without booze—I'm talking about the iron ones. Now let's see," he continued. "This whole place sits in a flat area. There are fields all around. One of our guys said they are potato fields. There used to be bushes scattered outside the fence but one man tried to hide behind them, so Schneider had them all removed. Now we've got a 20-foot grass border on three sides, and about a 2,500-foot runway parallel to the south wall of our country club, where the grass ends. This runway crosses another one going north and south about twenty feet beyond our west wall. You've probably seen the wind socks out by them. The Germans have a back entrance to their part of this place. It has a landing to a set of steps like the two in the yard. They have a walkway from the steps to the runway. There are two buildings and two fuel pumps behind their quarters, across the runway."

Smyth froze suddenly and put his finger to his lips. A door slammed. Everyone waited tensely until Smyth nodded, and the meeting resumed. "There's a railroad line somewhere to the west. When the wind is right, we can hear it. We just don't know how far away it might be."

The captain cleared his throat. "There is a small opening in the foundation, but it has an iron door with a padlock. Workmen crawl through it to get to the plumbing, wiring, or whatever. When our crappers overflowed, we could see them pulling pipes underneath us. That's it, unless anyone has any questions or information to add. Next Saturday I'll have 'Pee-on-it Campbell' tell you about his subterranean adventures. He's sacked out now. Let's go to bed." And the meeting ended.

The next day, Carl sought out Doug to ask why they called their fellow prisoner "Pee-on-it Campbell." Douglas said, "I'm not sure why he's called that. Let's find him. I'd like to know too."

They found Campbell resting on the entrance stairs. Doug said, "Ho, Campbell! Mr. Churchill wants to talk to you. I think he wants to make you a general."

A broad grin on his face, Campbell said, "Well, it's about time I get credit for my great ability."

After the laughter, Douglas asked about the nickname.

Campbell answered, "Lads, let's sit down. I just walked around this beautiful park eight times." He took in a lungful of air and began, "A while back, this pilot Graves of the Royal Air Force Spitfire—I flew the darn things too, only for Canada— Well, Graves despised this place with a hate worse than the devil could muster up. But he was like a little kid— fearless and naïve. He always said, 'pee on this,' or 'pee on that.' If a guard came near him, he would say, 'Pee on you.' Luckily the guard didn't understand. Well, one day, a truck came in the yard to deliver supplies to the Krauts. Graves told one of us that when the truck passed by the steps, he was going to make a run for the gate. Someone said, 'You'll get shot,' and he said, 'Oh, pee on getting shot!' As you know, Graves was shot dead when he tried to hide in some bushes on the outside perimeter of the prison."

Campbell wiped his brow, then continued, "The day after Graves got it, Col. Schneider ordered all those bushes removed. I was "volunteered" to do the work—under guard of course. Working on the south side of the prison, I noticed an opening for what could be a basement window. Instead of a windowpane, it had an iron cover hinged to the sill, with two slots to pull it open, except that a padlock secured it closed. The high German Krauts that come here to snoop use a set of stairs with a landing just like this one. There used to be an opening under those stairs but concrete blocks were cemented into the opening.

"In my bunk that night, I kept wondering, could there be an opening under our stairs too? You know, the landing? The foundation is only three or so feet above ground. I thought, if I could crawl, say, seventy or more feet to that iron window, then what? That damn lock is there. So the next day, I sat down by the bushes on the side of the landing. It's shady and they don't

57

mind guys sitting there with their backs against the foundation, talking or just goofing off. No one was watching, so quick as a rabbit, I went crawling through the bushes under the landing and sure as hell, there was a good opening to the crawl space. I kept crawling through the darkness, away from the steps. My hand hit one of the pilings supporting the building. Another ten feet, I figure, I touched another support. Pretty soon I saw two spots of light to my left. It had to be the covered window. I reached it and pushed. It moved out a little bit, but the lock stopped it from going any farther. Boy, I hurried back crawling like a scared snake! The opening under the stairs was faintly visible from the closed window, so going back was easy. No one knew I had left the prison yard. After all that, I thought of how desperate Graves must have been to attempt his escape. I tried to imagine what he would have done if it was him instead of me, crawling through that space to the unguarded south area. Then, just as plain as if he were still alive, I heard exactly what he would have said when he came upon that damn lock and hasp: 'Pee on it!' That's when the idea hit me like a ton of bricks."

Campbell turned to the two listeners and said, "Did you ever notice the urinals in a cheap barroom? How the screws and metal parts are all rusted and green from being pissed on? I thought, if I could get some piss on the hasp—the part with the lock loop—a whole bunch of times, the screws might rust out, or maybe the wood would rot in three or four months."

Carl interrupted Campbell and said, "Are you kidding? If they caught one of our volunteer lawn and weed cutters pissing against that window or anyplace, they'd cut his water off, and you know that would be bad."

"Oh, I know that. I mean soaking it from the inside," he replied.

This time Doug snickered, "What—a six foot guy pissing in a three-foot high space?"

They all laughed.

"Wait a minute. I'll tell you how I do it. See this?" said Campbell. He removed a flask from his jacket pocket. "Well, before taking off to fight our friends here, I used to fill this pal of mine with half coffee, half brandy. You know, it gets cold up there in the air. This flask was my buddy. When I became a guest of these goose steppers, I thought they would steal the flask, but they gave it back to me, I think because it's not real silver." Campbell leaned in closer to the other men and lowered his voice. "Now what I do—first I pee in that cup they gave us and pour it into the flask. When it's filled with pee, I crawl under, push the panel to make a crack, and pour the good stuff on, about in the middle. I've been doing it three or four times a week for the past month. A couple guys saw my latrine routine and started calling me 'Pee on it' Campbell."

Carl shook with laughter. "I hope you wash your cup after that."

Campbell replied, "Why? My wiz is better than their coffee."

Huddled together at the next secret meeting, Douglas asked Capt. Smyth if he thought Campbell's subterranean escape route really stood a chance of working. He said, "Emerson and I figure a daytime escape is almost impossible. Say we get the locked lid open? The next stretch of grass and runway is at least 50 or 60 feet—a wide-open space to run across, and if the grass in that south field is too short to lie down in until dark, well, we've had it. And say it's dark, we can't do it then. The guards keep us in at night. Unless we duck under the building during the day, and attempt the escape when it gets dark."

Smyth said, "You're right. It would be real lucky to escape, but there's still a chance it may work. It gives us hope—you, me, and the rest of us caged by these idiots. Goddamn it, we need hope or we'll go crazy." He scanned the surroundings and added, "And if no one happens to be looking from their end of this building, we may luck out."

Campbell continued the soaking routine. On the third month of treatment, Carl "volunteered" to cut weeds and mow grass around the prison. Two guards kept the lawn workers in a group. Six prisoners and the guards worked their way eastward from the gate, then south, and around the whole complex back to the prison gate. On the south part of the building, Carl was able to examine the hasp on the enclosed window. Sure enough, corrosion covered the screws and plate of the loop holding the padlock. The painted wood sill appeared blistered. He thought, *I'd bet my left arm it's rotting under that paint.*

After the job, the workers marched back to the prison yard and were dismissed. Carl sought out Campbell and reported the condition of the hasp and sill. He said, "I think your idea is working. Give it another month. I bet by August, a good push will pull the screws out, and the panel will open."

Campbell could scarcely conceal his excitement. Forcing a rhyme, he punned, "My urine did fine."

Carl said, "Oh brother!" and laughed.

Like a sedating drug, prison time and the men's meaningless existence often caused friends to avoid one another, or simply nod their heads in passing. Some even stayed in bed during their allotted mealtime. One morning Carl decided to skip breakfast and remain in his bunk. He hadn't slept well, and wouldn't miss that slop. He fell back to sleep but was awakened a few minutes later by the sound of a truck or some motorized vehicle running on the south side of the prison. He tried to look out the open window, but the bars prevented his head from extending far enough to see the source of the noise. He noted it sounded like a plane, and went back to bed. Later that day, he asked someone about the offending racket that had awakened him.

A short, balding prisoner replied, "It's a plane that drops in here once or twice a week. We think some fat Nazi and his aides come here for inspections or orders for his underlings. You can hear it loud and clear in the south yard. The bastards wake me up, warming their plane at my end of this hellhole. I guess you must be busy washing up or eating when they leave in the morning. You can't see it unless it flies north, but it don't go north much since I been here."

A plane, thought Carl. He skipped several breakfasts in order to go to the west end of the prison, to see if he could observe the plane. The fourth time he waited by the window, the aircraft taxied into view. A uniformed man stepped out and placed chocks against the wheels. He then walked to the entrance on the east end of the building. The engine idled a good fifteen minutes before two men appeared. One removed the chocks while the other boarded the plane. Chocks in hand, the second man also embarked. Engines revved up and the plane rolled west out of Carl's view. The windsock indicated the wind was from the south. After a few minutes, the plane was exiting the north/south runway.

Carl left the viewing place, hungry and excited. He kept wondering, is it possible? That afternoon, he ate his tasteless lunch, plus some left by his messmates. His fasting and mental concentration on the escape scheme had made him that hungry.

After the meal, Carl found Doug and said, "I saw the plane that we hear every morning. It's a Courier, used also for surveillance. They call it a Fieseler. I know how to fly the damn thing."

Doug responded, "Oh, so now you want to join the Luftwaffe and become a Nazi general? Where'd you learn how to fly a German plane?"

Carl told of his experience with Capt. Stone when he was stationed in England. He continued, "Seems to me, they warm up the motor at the intersection of the runways when the wind is from the north or south quadrant. Must be the pilot that taxies it up to our end, chocks it, and walks back to their hangout with the motor idling. I guess he doesn't want the racket near their place, so they bother us, the bums. It seemed to me, he let it idle fifteen minutes or more, then he came back with another man, removed the chocks, and the two of them got in, taxied to the intersection and took off toward the south."

Carl had piqued Doug's interest. He said, "You're thinking of hijacking it to get out of here? Say by the remotest chance you made off with it? This place must be in the central part of the country. They'd have planes shooting at you from above and below. Or, say you even made it to England? 'Hey, here comes a Kraut—Get the son of a bitch!' Carl, the English Channel is mighty cold."

Carl said, "Look, you and I want out. If we did get away with their plane, the two we took it from would be scared stiff to report it gone right away. They would try to convince Col. Schneider that his guards were lax and allowed two men to escape—these two escapees broke into the locked aircraft and were able to start the plane and take off in the full moonlit night. I bet you Col. Schneider doesn't have much use for the Nazis, and while they're arguing, we're heading west."

"OK," Doug said. "How in hell do we get to the airplane?"

Carl responded, "By our Mr. Campbell's subterranean escape route. We'll have a talk with him tomorrow. The both of us, Doug."

The next day, Carl and Doug found Campbell sitting against the foundation next to the stairs. Carl asked about his crawl to the blocked opening on the other side of the structure and told of the new plan. Carl explained, "When the airplane is in place, and the man starts to leave, Doug and myself will exit the building. We sit here a few seconds, then crawl under to the blocked opening, and try to force the lid open with a heavy rock. Either the screws or the wood must be corroded enough by now."

Campbell said, "I hope my sprinkling pays off, but would you take a suggestion from an old Canadian Air Force captain? You two should crawl under there three or four times, get used to the dark, the location of the pilings—the second one a little to the right of the first one. Keep going, and when two spots of light appear, you're on target. Don't use a rock—too noisy. There are a couple of planks about four feet long—not too heavy—to the left as you go under. Put some rags over one end and use it to batter the panel. Try to do the ramming when the plane is idling, to drown out the noise. Practice your moves. Don't be too hasty," he warned. Then he threw his hands up as if the whole thing were a fantasy. "Hey! Who the hell knows how to fly that Kraut plane anyway?"

Carl supplied the answer.

Within the next few days, both men made several excursions under the prison. After a few bumps from the pilings, they located the escape panel on the first attempt. They covered the end of a wooden post with rags and a couple of towels left by former prisoners, fastening them on with a piece of wire.

Capt. Smyth was informed, and expressed his belief that the plan was worth trying. He insisted on helping. Two extra men were included in the scheme. The next phase of the plan was accomplished. Carl and Douglas moved the battering ram up to the panel that was to be their escape hatch, and left it in place for future action.

One man went to the observation window every morning to see if the plane taxied to the usual area before take-off. Whenever the courier plane was heard or seen arriving, all participants were alerted. Five men were to loiter around the end bunk and wait for a signal from the observer, whose word "go" would set the plan in motion. At the signal, four of those waiting at the bunk would head down the corridor to the prison yard door. One man would station himself midway between those at the door and the one remaining at the bunk. When the chocks were in place and the pilot began walking toward the building, the observer would issue the go signal, which was to be relayed to the men at the door. Carl and Douglas would descend the stairs, turn left, and casually sit against the foundation beside the bushes next to the stairway. The remaining man on the landing would look carefully about the area. His turning to the right was a no-go situation. If he felt sure the would-be escapees were not under observation, he would descend the stairs and nod to them. At that point, the two men would dart beneath the building and commence their escape route. Upon reaching the locked panel, they would rap firmly on the sub-floor as an indication that they were ready to begin using the battering ram. If the observer above returned the signal once, the escapists were clear to batter the panel. Two raps meant stop pounding the panel immediately. If the escapists heard no further acknowledgement from above, it meant too late, try another time.

The plan was rehearsed several times, with the exception of the battering. They all felt confident that the escape, at least through the panel opening, was possible. Capt. Smyth suggested they batter the escape panel to loosen the screws or corroded hasp before their actual escape.

"When the panel is forced out about half an inch or so, leave it like that, to save time the next time you go. One hard smash and it should open."

Carl realized the captain was right. They might take up too much time trying to break through the barrier, and ruin the escape, or worse—get caught.

Two escape attempts were aborted. Early one morning in July, the escape plane taxied to the designated viewing area. The plane's chocks were put in place and the pilot walked back to the Germans' quarters. The attempt was launched on the word "go". When they reached the breakout area, Carl rapped the floor above him. Two loud thumps sounded from above. Both men muttered, "Nazi bums!" and crawled back to the prison yard where they discreetly brushed the dirt off themselves before returning to quarters. Their observer, Fred Williams, later explained that the pilot had turned and walked back to the plane, removed a briefcase from the cockpit, and stopped to read a paper.

"I knocked twice on the floor when I saw him returning. I almost told you to go. The jerk stayed by the plane reading until his fat-assed boss came. Sorry—the plane is gone," he said.

A second alert was called off when, after taxiing to the observation point, the pilot alighted from the plane and appeared to be undecided about something. He had the chocks ready to place under the wheels but was looking south. He didn't chock the wheels, but went back into the plane and taxied back toward the east. Williams could no longer see or hear the aircraft. The windsock showed a shift in wind direction. No doubt, the plane took off from the east-west runway.

Chapter 7

Flight to Freedom

On July 15, 1943, as in previous attempts, Carl and Doug said their good-byes to their accomplices, but this time they broke out to the south side of the prison. Douglas quickly pushed the panel closed and set the loosened screws and hasp back in place. Then they bolted full tilt for the plane, loping low to the grassy strip like a pair of stampeding chimpanzees. Carl slid into the wheels, removed the plane's chocks, and darted to the cockpit, where he noticed a white silk scarf draped over the back of his seat. Douglas catapulted after him, slamming the door shut. A hurried taxi to the runway intersection, a left turn, and the craft accelerated southward and ascended steeply. By 8:06 a.m., Carl Emerson and Douglas Graf were set on a course due west.

Seconds after the plane left the runway, the German pilot was leisurely descending the steps from the German quarters, the corpulent Nazi colonel following, when suddenly the superior officer shoved the befuddled pilot aside. Both stopped short, transfixed by the sight of the German plane clearing the runway. They rushed back into the building and the red-faced colonel burst into Col. Schneider's office screaming, "If that's one of your idiot guards deserting in our plane, you'll be court marshaled for not disciplining your men!"

"What the hell are you talking about? None of my men know crap about planes," responded Schneider.

The Nazi colonel roared, "I demand you hold a muster of your men immediately."

"You don't give orders," shot back Schneider. "I'm in charge around here. No fat, ass-kicking Nazi from Berlin tells me what to do. Why don't you pick up the phone and call Georing or even the Fuehrer. They would love to hear how you and your smart pilot left a plane idling unattended."

The visiting colonel realized he was in trouble. He called his pilot, who was waiting outside the office, and accused him of disobedience for not standing guard by the plane as ordered by a superior. Astonished, the pilot said, "Sir, you wanted to make sure the engine was warmed up good so it would not stall out at colder altitude. You said it happened to you once. You told me I could wait here until you were ready to leave and the plane was ready also."

His colonel bellowed, "Enough, you liar!"

Colonel Schneider shook his head and said, "God help Germany. The war is lost." Then he ordered a muster of his men and the prisoners. The result showed no Germans missing, but two American prisoners, lieutenants Douglas Graf and Carl Emerson, unaccounted for. When the Nazi colonel heard the result of the muster, his arrogance returned.

"Your guards should be shot. Didn't I see a supply truck leave the yard two days ago?" he boomed. "Yes, that's it," he continued without waiting for an answer. "Your men didn't spot those Americans jumping into the empty truck. Those swine leaped from the truck and hid someplace, snuck back here at night, and waited behind one of those buildings back there."

Colonel Schneider chimed in, "And they saw your unattended plane with the motor running. So like a lot of Americans would do, they stole the damn thing."

Mention of the unattended plane mollified the Nazi. In a civil tone he said, "You know, Colonel, we're both in trouble. I'll make a report that a person or persons unknown broke into the plane and somehow started it and stole it. Later on, you can report that your guards shot those two thieves when they tried to escape. We keep this whole thing quiet, OK?" He shook his head up and down persuasively and continued, "You know, those fools can't fly to Russia in a German plane. They sure as hell can't go to England with my plane, and France is under our control. The damn pigs!"

Schneider replied, "Ya, ya," thinking, *Rudolf Hess did. Still, this weasel from Berlin is right. I'd better keep my mouth shut. Damn those guards for not seeing those prisoners sneak into that truck!"*

An inspection team assured Col. Schneider beyond all doubt that the only way the two Americans could have slipped away was on the empty truck. All barred windows and padlocked places appeared intact, though in reality, Campbell's escape route was still usable, perhaps. The report meant no reprisals to others who would have been tortured for information on how the pair escaped.

The Nazi colonel called his superiors in Berlin and reported a fabrication worthy of a compulsive liar. Col. Schneider was relieved to hear him claim that the thieves were definitely not prisoners of Stalagluft Five. Their arguing, the muster, the cooked up story, and phone call consumed a good thirty-five minutes, Carl and his buddy soaring west, miles away.

The colonel's report to headquarters created a real problem. If the Luftwaffe was ordered to shoot down or simply interrogate the crew of any plane of the type hijacked, (several were flying on observation or courier duty over Germany, France, Greece, the Russian front, and the rest of the countries under their control) and some important Nazi were shot down by mistake, there would be hell to pay! Also, the Luftwaffe was hard-pressed to defend in combat the ever-increasing allied sorties over Germany. They really did not need this additional problem. If that plane were to come down on German soil or access-controlled areas, all well and good. A German aircraft flying for England or Russia would spell suicide for the hijacker or hijackers. Hence orders were issued to all commands to report any sighting of the plane in question, and to hold the pilot and anyone else on board for further questioning upon landing.

Ceiling and visibility were unlimited, so Carl and his co-pilot were able to avoid the few high hills on their planned mostly low-level flight westward. Carl maintained low altitude until he observed an increase in dwellings below. Then he would climb to see if a city lay ahead. That being the case, he would veer the craft north or south of the congested area and then head west again. After thirty-five minutes of flying in this erratic but necessary manner, Doug yelled out, "Carl, we're over Holland! I can see the North Sea!"

Carl replied, "Boy, that's right. I think this is near the place we cracked up. I didn't think we were this far north. I guess we've been in a southwest wind for a while." He corrected his direction to avoid the North Sea and aimed for England.

When Britain's high-level radar detected the plane heading for England over the North Sea, two spitfires were dispatched to investigate. Carl saw them bearing down and yelled to Douglas, "Get this goddamned scarf behind me and wave it out your window. Hurry! See if you can find these guys on the radio."

As he spoke, he rocked the plane and raised his hands in the air in a surrender gesture as the planes passed dangerously close. Douglas frantically spun dials with one hand, waving the scarf with his other, and finally raised the British pilots on the radio. He switched to "transmit" and blurted, "Hold your fire! We are escaped American prisoners."

Switching back to "receive" on the radio, the two ex-prisoners heard, "Say again your message."

Douglas repeated himself, adding, "Please guide us to any base you can. We are escaped American prisoners."

One pilot responded, "OK, Wilco, follow us," muttering, "Damn, I hope we don't have a couple more Rudolf Hesses."

The senior officer on one of the planes escorting the German aircraft informed Ipswich group headquarters that the occupants were not hostile, and were granted permission to land at that facility. Carl landed the craft as directed, minutes before the escort planes touched down. When the stolen plane coasted to a stop, two jeeps with three armed men in each screeched to a halt, one in front of the plane and one by its exit. Carl and Douglas emerged from the plane, hands raised above their heads as ordered, and were driven to headquarters in separate vehicles.

The two escapees were brought into an anteroom adjoining a Captain Jarvis's office. Guarded by two military police, they were told that the captain would see them shortly. While they waited, the two pilots of the escort planes were ushered past them into Jarvis's office. When the two British fliers left the captain's office and anteroom, a young lady in military attire indicated for either Carl or Douglas to follow her to Jarvis's office. Douglas went while Carl waited. Twenty minutes later, Douglas came out and told Carl he was to see the captain now.

Twenty minutes later, the captain emerged, Carl following. The captain spoke to the guards, then looked at Carl and Douglas. "You must understand you will be held in the lock-up until someone from Intelligence gets here. Sorry, fellows, but we must be careful. At least you'll eat better here," he said.

"Take them to detention. I'll call now so they can be checked in," he told the guards.

At the detention building, both men were ordered to shower and be disinfected. Seeing their soiled uniforms, the sergeant in charge of the jail said, "You Yanks been crawling around in a pigpen?"

Douglas responded, "No, we crawled around underneath a pigpen."

The puzzled sergeant responded, "Are all you Yanks daft?"

Carl laughed and said, "No, but where we came from the pigpens are elevated."

Serge shook his head and issued faded khaki coveralls to the new detainees. Printed boldly on the back of each pair was the word, "prisoner".

"Well, Doug, how do you like being a free man again?" quipped Carl.

Douglas responded, "Oh, this isn't going to be so bad. Jarvis is going to send his cute secretary here with a huge steak dinner and a bottle of champagne and after I eat she is going to enjoy the champagne with me, and then we'll make passionate love in my bunk."

"Hey! What am I going to do?" protested his buddy.

Doug said, "You can wash the dishes. There's the sink."

Carl mused, "Same ol' Doug—Just looking for a chance to push me in the drink, I mean sink. Say, I'm hungry." He grabbed the bars and yelled, "Yo, Serge! When do we eat?"

The serge snickered. "We don't feed Nazis around here."

Carl responded, "Vell, ven vee concah de khol vorld, vee vill take off your shtripes and kick you on de ass. Dat vill make Hitler happy."

The Sergeant appeared and said, "Sorry I was so rude. Take away my stripes, but don't hurt my ass. They had enough trouble finding pants big enough to fit it. Chow is at five."

He turned on his heel, muttering, "Dumb Yanks!"

When the tired and hungry former POW's arrived at their new quarters, it was three-thirty p.m. Carl said to his cellmate, "If you don't want the bottom bunk, I'll take it. And if you want the top bunk, well, heck, I'll take the bottom one. I'm a nice guy. Now let's get a little shut-eye before chow."

Douglas replied, "Your logic dazzles me. You must have graduated summa cum lousy from Yale. OK. I'll take the top one, you low-lifer."

The men were finally coming to the realization they were no longer prisoners of war. Before sleep overtook him, Douglas said, "Carl, I'm sorry I pushed you in the pool. And I'm sorry I let the air out of your tire."

His friend answered, "Is that all? When we get back to the States, I'll get even," and they both drifted into sound sleep.

At five p.m., the sergeant slid open the cell door, shook their beds, and yelled, "Slop's on. Come on, get up!"

He directed the men to a small mess hall where fewer than a dozen prisoners were eating. Carl and Douglas followed the sergeant to the serving table, and they received their allotment of food. The trio sat at a table selected by the sergeant, who said, "Capt. Jarvis called me a little while ago and told me you two will be questioned by someone from British Intelligence. They won't let you out of here until they know every damn thing about you—how you stole a Nazi plane seems to bother them. They will even want to know your mother's maiden name. I mean it. If they left it up to me, I'd hang the both of you."

Douglas said, "So you think we're Nazis!"

"No, I know you're Yanks. Yanks usually steal autos. You two stole a plane. I'd hang you both with the same noose." The sergeant laughed heartily.

Carl responded, "I see—guilty by association. We're in for it! When is this joker from Intelligence coming?"

"Day after tomorrow. Do you mind if I come to your hanging?"

Douglas chimed in, "You can if you bring Jarvis's secretary to our cell this evening."

The sergeant feigned a hurt look, and replied, "Shame! We British frown upon such carryings on. Anyway, she's coming to my room tonight."

After a satisfying meal, Carl and Douglas were walked back to their cell. Two days later, the interrogator from British Intelligence arrived. Carl and Douglas were transported back to Captain Jarvis's waiting room and questioned one at a time.

The official began, "I know the names you gave to Captain Jarvis and I saw the ID tags you claim are yours, but for all I know, they may belong to dead or murdered American servicemen. Now tell me, just how did you manage to escape?"

Douglas told as much as he could recall of the escape. Carl went into more detail. The interrogator spoke a few sentences in German to both men. Seeing Carl's confusion, he said, "You didn't understand when I asked you to name some of the instruments on the plane's dash panel. Explain how you were able to fly it."

Carl related how a similar plane had been available for him to fly under the instruction of Col. Stone. The interrogator wrote something on a notepad and continued, "When you were taken prisoner of the Germans, what did you tell them besides your name, rank, and service number?"

Both affirmed they had adhered to the rule that POW's provide no further information than the three items stated.

"Well then," said the official, "One last question, and then I'll need your fingerprints. Give me your home address, city and state where you were born, and your mother's maiden name."

This done, he told each man, "We can confirm your information in a day or two. If everything you told us is true, you will be confined to this base, free to use recreation facilities, and you will be quartered in another barrack away from the detention building. Your fingerprints must be verified in Washington, DC, which may take a week or two. So be patient."

Carl and Douglas were returned to the detention center. When they arrived back at their good sergeant's domain, he said, "You two back again? We were looking forward to your hanging."

Carl said, "We? Who's we?"

He answered, "I and that cute secretary that spent the night with me. We had it all planned—a picnic basket, the parade, and the gallows for you two. You Yanks spoil everything for us poor Brits." He tossed his head toward the cell. "Come now. Follow me. I'll let you into your beautiful apartment."

The cell door clanged shut once more. The sergeant returned a short time later with some tea and cakes for his charges. On leaving he said, "Lunch in an hour, gentlemen."

Carl said, "Too bad I don't have a watch. Doug, what happened to yours? I never see the one you got at Kim's."

Doug told him, "When I came down on that chute, it tangled me up in a tree near a farm. The farmer came and released me, so I gave him my watch. Minutes later, German troops picked me up. That was the only watch I never lost or broke. I'm glad those troops didn't get it."

After four days, both were released from the detention quarters and assigned to a barracks with all the privileges of other military personnel, except for off-base leave. They spent time at the base library, the recreation hall, or walking around the base. Being without funds, they obtained razors, razor blades, soap, toothpaste and other personal needs from the Red Cross.

One month after their escape, Capt. Jarvis informed Carl and Douglas they'd been certified as Lieutenants Douglas Graf and Carl Emerson. Accordingly, the Intelligence Department ordered they no longer be detained by the British military.

Capt. Jarvis congratulated the pair and said, "My country thanks you for the plane you stole, but we won't let Goering know about it. Now Miss Lawton will drive you to Major Breen's office. He's the U.S. Army's liaison for occasions like this. He has all the information on you chaps."

He handed a package to Carl and said, "You fellows may never forget this. Open it when you get back home."

Major Breen returned the salutes from the two happy and now free lieutenants. He admitted he was amazed by the report of their escape, and told them orders were cut for them to report to US Army Air Force headquarters within three days. Transportation was to be arranged by Maj. Breen's office. "You will report here at zero nine hundred. A civilian driver and one of our vehicles will take you there. It's a two-hour drive. When you get checked in, you will be paid enough to cover your subsistence and buy proper uniforms, until your pay records are checked. You should get a whole pot full. See you in the A.M."

They thanked the major, saluted, and left.

Before returning to barracks, Carl suggested paying a visit to that old codger, the sergeant of the detention building. They found him at his desk.

Douglas said, "Serge, we are so sorry you can't hang us now. We wanted to make you and Miss Great Britain happy, but Churchill said Yankees' asses are too precious for a fat sergeant to kick around. Besides that, your girl promised to marry both of us."

The sergeant put on a melancholy face and said, "Poor Churchie. You tricked him. You are nothing but plain thieves. I mean plane thieves." He slowly rose from his chair, raised his hand and said, "Go! And never darken my door again!" He laughed with the two Yanks and said, "Hey, good luck. Guess the war is over for you."

Back in Berlin, the Nazi colonel's friends believed his story and his position as inspector of prisoner of war camps continued. He became custodian of a new aircraft for his own transportation. As in the past, he kept the warm-up phase away from the German section of the building. "Let the prisoner of war suffer the noise," he often said.

Then it happened. A British plane flew over the prison compound and spotted the solitary plane parked some distance away—an excellent target. The pilot's aim was good. The plane exploded, and a full fuel tank, encouraged by a strong breeze from the south, set the adjacent structure ablaze. Prisoners inside the building raced to the only exit on the north side of the compound, to the prison yard. The guards in the three towers, confused by the men rushing out, the noise, and the huge explosion, opened fire on the prisoners, certain it was a mass escape attempt. Sixty-three prisoners were killed, twenty-four others wounded. Two roving German guards were also killed by the panicked machine gunners.

The Nazi propaganda report was broadcast the next day. It stated:

> *The allies paid dearly for bombing a prison of war camp conspicuously marked with a red cross on the roof of the building. The bombing killed seventy of their own men and seven of our brave soldiers trying to rescue some of their own people in the deliberately targeted building. We will show no mercy to*

*these degenerate people when victory is
ours.*

All the information major Breen had given Carl and Doug turned out to be fairly accurate, but their pay records had still not arrived after several weeks. They were bored with meaningless paperwork, filing, and record reviewing tasks. One evening, Carl lay on his bunk listening to a German radio station. The broadcast featured the usual propaganda to discourage English or American listeners. Just as he was reaching for the dial, he was amazed to hear:

*Two American prisoners of war were shot
dead as they attempted to escape from
Stalagluft Five. They were identified as
Douglas Graf and Carl Emerson of the U.S.
Army. Harsh treatment must be used on
such depraved criminals.*

The song "Lilli Marlene" followed the announcement. Douglas had been in the latrine when the broadcast aired. When he returned to quarters, Carl was pointing to the radio, screeching, "We're dead! We're dead! They just said you and I are dead!"

The door opened and two officers barged in. Both exclaimed, "You guys hear that? Kraut radio says you're dead!"

One of the officers commented, "We have two Mark Twains here."

Neither Doug nor Carl had written home recently, as they could not be sure of their location from day to day. Douglas remarked, "I hope none of that crap gets back to the folks at home."

The urgencies of the war further delayed travel orders for the two friends. On the first of September 1943, Carl was reviewing the record of a recent air strike in Eastern Germany when he read:

> **August 29, 1943:** Capt. Sikes, pilot RAF Spitfire, 071, on strafing mission--target: railroad and vehicular traffic. Mission: successful. Three trains with military equipment hit, several lorries destroyed. Small stationary aircraft adjacent to military compound strafed. Aircraft exploded. On reconnaissance, compound seen engulfed in flames.
> **Aug. 31, 1943:** Building destroyed on 29, August 1943 identified as POW camp Stalagluft 5.

The report horrified Carl. He shoved his chair back from the file cabinet and raked his hands through his hair. Then he buried his face in his arms, muttering, "My God" over and over again.

When Douglas heard about the report, he was likewise stunned. That evening he said to Carl, "Good God, I hope the ones who helped us get out of that hell hole made it out of there alive."

Carl nodded and said, "You know, Doug, most of those older guys broke their asses helping us. Why would they put their lives on the line for us? I'll bet Capt. Smyth or maybe Campbell was afraid a couple rash young guys like us might try a stunt like Graves did. I sure hope they escaped that God-forsaken place with their lives."

Douglas added, "If they did, I wonder where they are now?"

Chapter 8

Homecoming

The long-awaited pay records finally arrived, along with a set of orders for the two lieutenants. They were granted a thirty-day leave, after which they both were required to report to Elgin Army Airfield on 12 October 1943. On the tenth day of September 1943, a MATS plane transported the two jovial, well-groomed and well-funded officers to its third stop, New York's LaGuardia airport.

When Douglas called home, his father answered the phone. Douglas said, "Hi, Dad! I've got leave. Can you pick us up at the train station in two hours?"

Mr. Graf shouted. "How? When? Yes! My God, yes! Two hours, all right. Who's with you?"

Douglas answered, "I don't want to give you a heart attack, but Carl Emerson is with me. I'll tell you everything when we get together. He doesn't think his ma would be in any condition to drive. You know how shocked you are. The train leaves here in about six minutes. Gotta go."

"OK, son. Don't miss your train. We'll meet you."

On another pay phone, Carl was saying to his hysterical mother, "Calm down, Ma. We can talk for 30 days! I'll see you in a couple hours. Uncle Sam said I was a good boy and could go home now. Ma, we don't want to miss the train. So long for now."

For the next several days, Doug and Carl were met with hugs, tears, kisses, and requests for detailed explanations of all that had happened to them.

On the fourth evening of his leave, Doug pulled into a secluded oak grove after a movie and told his lady friend, "Hazel, I've missed you so much since I went away, and the

81

thought that in a few weeks I'll be gone for God knows how long again, and not being with you. . . Well, I love you. Will you marry me before my leave is up? My orders are for duty in Florida. We can live there and come back to New England when the war ends."

Hazel threw her arms around Doug's neck and said, "Yes, yes, Douglas! I love you and want to be with you always."

Doug and Hazel were married in a quiet ceremony with a few friends and relatives at the gazebo in the back garden of the Graf home. The minister from Hazel's church performed the ceremony. After the vows were said, Douglas thanked the best man and maid of honor and asked them, "Kim, Carl, when are you two going to tie the knot?"

Kimberly replied, "I only wish we could."

Carl jumped in, "Maybe some day," and he clutched Kim's hands. He turned to Douglas and laughed. "Why? So you can be best man?"

The newly married couple circulated among the guests and informed them they would spend their honeymoon in Florida. But they had no intention of living on an Army base after the war, that was for sure. As soon as Douglas had written proof of their marriage, he mailed the information to the personnel department of the Army.

Kimberly did not have to return to her second year at Yale University until late September. She would be leaving a week or so before Carl, when Douglas and Hazel were due to leave. When she asked her parents' permission to throw a party, they suggested that it would tie in nicely with an informal meeting Roger had planned with two CEO's of other corporations, since the hired help was already planning quite a spread for them.

At last the day of the celebration arrived. It was Saturday, and the last weekend before Kim was to resume classes. Gilbert drove his employer's limousine up to the main entrance of Golden Vista. He stopped the vehicle and quickly stepped out to open the rear door for the two visiting CEO's. Roger Durand opened the main door and greeted his guests. He instructed Gilbert to bring in their baggage. Martha would show them the guestroom for their weekend stay. Sylvia made her appearance as the businessmen were telling Roger the details of their flight from Chicago to New York.

Roger said, "Sylvia, I want you to meet Clyde Wilson and Alfred Blake. I've talked to both of them on the phone several times, but now we get to meet them in person."

Sylvia welcomed the men and asked, "Why didn't you bring Mrs. Wilson and Mrs. Blake? We would love to meet your wives."

Clyde shrugged and said, "My wife hates to fly."

Blake told them, "My wife came with me from Kansas City to Chicago. We have a daughter there, so this was a good opportunity to stop and see her. When I return to Chicago, my wife and I will stay with her a few more days."

He turned and winked at Roger. "But right now, I've got a little freedom."

Roger asked whether his guests wished to rest up or go to his study for a cocktail. They chose the latter. Sylvia stopped at the study entrance and said, "You must excuse me. Our daughter is entertaining some of her friends in the rumpus room. Two of her guests are handsome army officers. I must protect them from the girls." She laughed and walked away.

The men chatted about the best restaurants in Chicago and Kansas City. At the mention of food, Roger informed his guests that perhaps the lobster dinner being served that evening would make them rethink where the finest food might be found.

The small talk ended when Clyde Wilson, Chief Executive Officer of Magnetic Motive Company, Inc., said, "We all know why we are here, Roger, so lets begin. As I told you, Blake here is the president of our parent company in Kansas. As you know, the plant there manufactures all types of electric motors, generators, and related items. I've seen many large orders from your company for our small electric fan motor. I've read several government proposals, for which contracts were awarded to Sunrise Industries, Inc. Now here's what I'm getting at. A friend of mine in Washington tells me on positive knowledge that the Navy will very soon need a large quantity of generators and electric motors. This could mean a $20,000,000 contract."

The executive leaned in and straightened his tie. "Roger, here's my proposition," he said. "You bid $25 million on the proposal. My Chicago company, Magnetic Motives, bids 23 million, and our parent company, Kansas Electric Products, bids 20 million. Kansas gets the contract. Blake here, an electrical engineer, tells me the whole job can be done for about 30 percent of that. That's six million dollars, leaving us with a tidy 14 million-dollar profit. You get one percent of that just for making the high bid. How's $140,000 sound for an hour's work by one of your secretaries?"

Roger pursed his lips and let out a long, low whistle. "That's well thought out," he said. "I assume there are future contracts we may collaborate on as well?"

"You got it," Clyde responded, nodding enthusiastically. "As future prospects come up, we can swap around. I'll be the high bidder next time, for example. Whenever you make the low bid and win the contract, Blake's plant will transship the finished products to your plant for final shipment to their destination by your people. We'll pay for all the shipping and the one percent is still yours. Likewise if I'm the low bidder."

"Sounds very workable," Roger said, and they all toasted to the scheme's success.

Clyde set his glass back down and said, "And to be on the up and up, your payment will be a personal check from me to you, not to Sunrise."

Roger brightened and said, "Beautiful!"

After a few more cocktails, Blake suggested they visit the party in progress. "Let's show those love-starved girls a couple he-men from the west," he said.

The three executives invaded the dance floor and amused the young girls with their own renditions of the Jitterbug, the Suzy-Q, and something they called "trucking." As they flounced about, the music abruptly stopped. Roger told the two Midwesterners he wanted them to meet a couple handsome and intelligent officers.

Carl grinned at Douglas and said, "Which one am I? Handsome or intelligent?"

After a round of handshaking and a hero's welcome, Roger addressed Carl. "Say, I ran into your dad at the country club. He told me you have a habit of losing watches. You remember the last time we had a party here? We . . ." Roger hesitated, looked at Douglas, then back at Carl. "Uh, no, you must be the Emerson fellow—oh hell, I meant Graf's son."

Kim witnessed her father's confusion, took Douglas by the hand and said, "He didn't lose the watch, Dad. He gave it to a German farmer." Then she nodded pointedly toward Doug, and said, "Isn't that so, DOUG."

Her dad muttered, "Yes, of course. Never could tell one uniformed man from another."

Mr. Wilson took a step toward the two young officers and held his drink out. "I am proud of you two," he said. "When this war is over, if the government doesn't do something for you guys, by God I'll get on some people in Washington, and by God, they'll get those fat Congressmen off their duffs."

"Damn right," chimed in Mr. Blake in a righteous tone, his florid face matching that of his associate.

In due time, dinner was announced. The guests found the meal sumptuous beyond belief. Mr. Wilson said, "I'll never again say the food from my hometown is the best. Mrs. Durand, my compliments to your cook."

Sylvia responded, "Thank you. I'll pass that along."

Not to be outdone by his boss, Blake spoke out, "Thank her? Why, I'll marry the gourmet cook who prepared this lobster!"

Sylvia, Kim, Roger, and the maid broke into loud laughter. As the three Durands exchanged glances with Martha, Blake assumed she'd prepared the meal. "Martha, marry me!" he blurted.

Martha replied, "I'm afraid if you wish to marry the cook, you'll have to wed my husband, Gilbert!"

When the laughter subsided, Roger explained that their multi-talented chauffeur was a down-Easter, and knew more about cooking lobster than his wife, Martha, or any chef at the Waldorf. And they had to be Maine lobsters. He beamed with pride for his hired help, certain that their skills reflected on him personally. "Martha, more champagne all around!" he ordered.

The Monday following the festivities, after all the guests had gone, Roger felt like staying home. As he prepared to roll out of bed, he began telling his wife about the wonderful deal he made with Wilson and Blake. He said, "And you know, this money is not going to our corporation. I'll get a personal check from Mr. Wilson every time I bid on contracts that they alone will fulfill! Just think, our first check may be a hundred and forty thousand dollars. Hell, that's almost as much as I make now in a year!"

Sylvia sat up on her elbows and stared at Roger for a moment. "Why should you get money for doing nothing?" she said. "Are you sure you're doing the right thing?"

He replied, "No doubt in my mind. Other companies are pulling the same stunt. Can't wait to call George and share the good news."

His wife said, "You call it a stunt. Stuntmen often get hurt. Anyway, you can't call George. They'll be in Maine the next couple of weeks to catch the fall foliage. They don't have a phone at the cottage. Wish we could have gone with them. Write to him and see what he thinks of your stunt."

"All right. I will write to him," he replied. Roger threw his arm around his wife. "My brother is living in the dark ages. Why he doesn't get a phone up there beats me. I'll tell him to get a damn phone, the tightwad."

Roger's letter began:

Dear George,
*   I've made a wonderful deal with the head of Magnetic Motive Company that should benefit you both as my brother and as a stockholder in Sunrise . . .*

It ended with:

*   To be fair, since the money is not going to our company, half of what I get is yours. George, when the war ends, the gravy train*

ends, and we'll have to work our butts off
to meet payroll.
    Sylvia sends her love to Laurie as do I.
George, the foliage here is great also.

Love,
Roger
PS—Get a telephone!

The following Thursday evening, Sylvia accepted a collect telephone call from George. "Sylvia, if Rog is home, I'd like to talk to him. And I won't mind if you listen in on another phone!"

Sylvia called her husband, who answered the phone in the library. She quietly sat in the parlor and listened, her hand cupped over the mouthpiece.

"Hi, George. How are you?" began Roger.

"Never mind how I am. What in hell are you thinking of? Are you out of your mind? If you go through with that agreement, you're a candidate for Leavenworth. The government would have you and your buddies up for fraud and collusion. All your previous government contracts would be scrutinized and re-evaluated for their fair cost. Dad's wishes for the firm would be down the tubes."

Roger broke in, "Hold on, damn it! These guys know what goes on in other firms. Would they stick their necks out if they thought they'd get caught? I don't think so. With the great demands of this war, the government can't look into who did what. What's a million dollars here or there in cost overruns? A war costs money. Always has. Anyway, I shook hands with them."

"You shook hands with the Devil and his brother. Now listen some more. This war can't last much longer. The

Germans are losing in Russia. Italy is just about done for, and we're bombing the hell out of their war production factories. After the war, some ambitious federal prosecutor will look into these unreasonably high costs and go after suspected fraud, collusion, or price-fixing cases like a bloodhound after a scared rabbit. He nabs a couple or three crooks. They go to jail. He gets elected to the Senate as a great public servant and Sunrise is history. Roger, think of what you have now. Think of Sylvia; think of Kim. Remember Dad. Forget the money. We don't need it. I'll see you later."

Sylvia carefully set the phone back on its cradle and dragged herself to the library. She hunched over a book, pretending to read.

Roger studied her for several minutes, then said, "Oh, so you listened in. Well, don't let it bother you. George is a worrywart, afraid to take a chance on anything."

Sylvia lowered the book and turned to her husband.

"You know, Rog, you referred to this arrangement as a stunt, and now you say you're not afraid to take a chance. Well, show-offs try stunts, and getting hurt is the chance they take. Rog, listen to your brother. I hope I didn't marry a crook." She clapped the book shut.

"Wow," Roger exclaimed. "You think that?"

Sylvia took in a deep breath. "A man steals a loaf of bread and he's a thief. You and your friends steal thousands. What does that make you?"

Roger scowled at his wife and said, "You remember, dear, at a board meeting just before we got into the war, my associate, Higgins, said, 'What's the matter, Roger? Afraid to make money?' Now my brother tells me to stop making money, and my wife calls me a thief. What is this, a conspiracy?"

"Yes, dear," she answered. "It's a conspiracy to keep you out of jail, because we love you."

The next morning, the chief executive officer of Sunrise Industries awoke in a cheerful mood. He told his wife she was just as pretty as the day he married her. He praised Kim for her good marks at college, and before departing for the office, embraced Sylvia with more than the usual degree of affection. He said, "Hey, don't worry, dear. See you tonight."

When he arrived at the office, he called Clyde Wilson and informed him that Sunrise Industries would not be participating in the plan. Wilson responded, "Roger, are you afraid to make money?"

Roger recoiled but regained composure and calmly stated, "No, I'm afraid of going to jail."

"Are you a blind fool?" Wilson yelled. "This is the modern world. Big bosses of corporations, businesses, and railroads have been fudging their books and flimflamming the government ever since the Revolutionary War! They'd fill a phone book the size of Milford's. You think you're above them? But hey, if that's your decision, you're stuck with it. Goodbye!"

That evening Roger related the conversation to his wife. "So that's it, Sylvia. I guess I'll just watch over Dura-best Paints with a sharp eye like Dad wanted. It was his pet business. Of course, I'll run Sunrise Industries, same as always."

Sylvia scarcely dared blink, lest she awaken from a wonderful dream. After dinner that evening a calm atmosphere once again prevailed over the Durand household as the family digested the news.

Chapter 9

Friends and Fortune

On the sixth of October, Douglas made a phone call to Carl's home. He said, "Carl, you won't believe it, but Hazel and I will not be going with you to Eglin. I sent the Army a copy of our marriage certificate a few weeks ago and today I received a set of orders amending the original one. I'm to report to Hanscom Field in Bedford, Mass., the same day we'd planned to be in Eglin. Hell, I thought we would spend the winter in Florida."

Carl said, "Don't knock it. You're both lucky. Bedford is near Boston, which is close enough to us here. I think it's great! How does Hazel feel about it?"

"Actually, that was our first little disagreement. You see, my Dad gave us a nice house in Milford for a wedding present. She's eager to start commuting from Hanscom to Milford, to start furnishing and decorating our home."

"Your dad gave you a house? Holy Cow!" Carl exclaimed.

"Look, my dad is in the real estate business. Now and then a real bargain comes along, that's all," Doug explained.

Carl repressed a pang of jealousy, saying, "Good luck. Hope you two make out OK. I have to get cleaned up. Going to see Kim this evening. Hey, I'll see you after they surrender, or maybe before."

"Yeah, OK Carl. Best regards to Kim. Good luck the day after tomorrow."

That evening, Tom Emerson offered Carl his gasoline ration book to purchase fuel for his vehicle. "Happy to let you use a few extra coupons," he said. "My car pooling might as well benefit you too." Now Lt. Emerson could afford to pick up his girlfriend, treat her to a meal at a decent restaurant, and dancing at an upbeat nightclub. Then they would drive to the beach to enjoy the moonlight. They would talk openly of their love for each other, and the hopes they had for times ahead, after she graduated college and he was discharged from the service.

It was four a.m. when Carl brought Kim home. He kissed her one more time and said, "Kim, I hope you had as wonderful an evening as I had. Please thank your ma and dad for all the good times. I'll write to you, and see you when I get leave. When the war ends, I may become a pest. Goodbye for now." He studied her face at arms length for several moments, then turned away quickly and left.

On the train ride to Eglin Army Airfield, Carl reflected on all that had happened over the past few years. Somehow, he felt lonely and dejected, even though the coach was filled with passengers. He wondered—if he had not become a prisoner of war, had not encountered Doug, would Doug be dead now, or perhaps so badly burned in the fire, he might as well have perished? Even when Carl first arrived at Stalagluft Five, Doug seemed on the verge of a mental breakdown. Maybe he would have tried an escape sooner or later. *Would I have tried if Douglas hadn't been with me? Did I save his life? I think so. Maybe we saved each other's. But he's lucky. Always got anything he wanted. Sure, he beat me at tennis. No wonder— with two tennis courts in his backyard. He got that nice watch from Kim's old man that was supposed to be for me. His Dad buys a house for Hazel and him for a wedding present. And now he gets a beautiful job close to home with his wife living right there. He can give Hazel the best of everything, and he tells me to marry Kim. What the hell can I give Kim if we get hitched? A two-room shack, for all I have in the bank! Her old man—that pompous blowhard—would laugh me out of the house if I asked for his daughter's hand in marriage. Of course, Mrs. Durand is nice enough. How the hell she and Kim can stand him is beyond me. That watch would have been mine if he wasn't so boozed up. I think Kim would marry me, but how long could it last, on the crummy pay of a grease monkey?*

Carl yawned. *Crap, I'm feeling sorry for myself.* And he nodded off to sleep.

The next day, Carl's morale improved, thanks to a good rest and a pretty girl seated beside him. She had boarded the train in Washington DC while Carl was asleep. She was happy to talk to him, and he was charmed by her southern accent. She was from Mobile Alabama and had been visiting her aunt and uncle in Virginia. She told Carl that her aunt was so sorry to see her leave, because her uncle Herman, a colonel in the war department, was so busy, he scarcely had any time for socializing. With her niece returning home, she would feel like a lonely widow. "But I can't stay with her. I have college to attend. Why, you young lieutenants have it easy," she said, looking straight into Carl's eyes.

Carl responded, "You know, you're right. If they don't send me to battle soon, I am going to quit the Army and do something useful!"

The young woman glanced at Carl's uniform. "Oh, my lord. My big mouth!" she said, pointing to the bars on Carl's chest. Carl laughed at her embarrassment, and felt more like a hero than he'd felt since he'd enlisted. They both enjoyed the balance of the trip. The young woman disembarked at Mobil Alabama and the next day Carl reached Eglin.

He was assigned to base supply. His job was to maintain a supply of aircraft parts for the extremely busy airbase. He liked his assignment and found time to write to Kim, his family, and others back home.

Kim's letters always expressed her deep affection for Carl. She said she was happy about her grades thus far. She had received a letter from her good friend Hazel, now Mrs. Douglas Graf, stating that Doug had been promoted to captain and was now in charge of personnel for the reserve training attachment at Hanscom Field. Once again, Carl felt a fleeting resentment at Doug's promotion. He thought, *son of a gun, he beat me again!* But the feeling fled when he was informed that his own captaincy was forthcoming in thirty days.

Carl did his job well. Time passed quickly. Then, on the sixth of June 1944, the allies established a beachhead at Normandy France. Thereafter, the news became more and more encouraging. On May 7, 1945, Germany surrendered. And finally, September 2, that same year, Japan surrendered. The war was over.

War's end resulted in high unemployment due largely to two factors: the return of thousands of military personnel to civilian life, and the discharge of thousands of factory workers no longer required to produce war goods. Carl was without employment for three months after being discharged. His friend, Douglas, was immediately employed by his father's real estate firm. Real estate was in an enviable position, as the government aided veterans in purchasing homes at reasonable terms. It seemed Douglas had lucked out once again.

Carl's father was able to get him a job as a switchman in the railroad yard in New Haven. Mr. Emerson had been reluctant to tell Carl about the opening, as it was at night and rather dangerous. However, his son wanted work. He needed money and was tired of hanging around. His girlfriend was in college and other friends were either away, working, or looking for work. So Carl became a switchman with the railroad.

His new job was in no uncertain terms an arduous one, especially in the winter. One slip from a moving freight car or a careless coupling procedure could result in serious injury or death. He was careful and alert, and managed not to get hurt. However, he never cared for the job. He would keep looking for employment more to his liking.

On weekends, Kim was almost always at home, unless a special lecture or event kept her on the Yale campus. She was pursuing her masters in Economics. Kim and Carl sometimes went to beaches and various places of entertainment with their mutual friends, but more often than not, they dated alone.

One weekend evening Carl dropped his lady friend off at her home. When she entered the house, she was surprised to see her mother in the sitting room adjoining the entrance hall. "Ma," she said. "It's after one a.m. Why are you still up?"

"I started reading this book in bed but Dad began to snore. I knew I wouldn't get any sleep with that racket so here I am. How was your date?"

She needn't have asked. Her daughter glowed with brilliance beyond anything she'd seen on her before.

"Ma, just spending the evening with Carl, walking, holding hands and talking, is as wonderful as anything I can imagine. He is so interesting. Not shallow like some of the guys I know. He is pretty well versed in Economics, too. And he's got a sense of humor. It tickles me, the way he pokes fun at himself. There hasn't been a date we've had that wasn't fun."

Sylvia Durand smiled. "Sounds like you're in love. Are you two getting serious?" she asked.

"Mother, I think I am. But when Carl and I talk about other people getting married, he says he believes a man must be in a position to give his bride a life as good as she was accustomed to, or better. I asked him, 'If a girl had all the things she wanted, but was not smart enough to know that real happiness is not achieved by material possessions but by the love and sincerity two people have for one another, would that marriage last?' He looked at me and said, 'I wonder how long such a girl could give up so much for one who could give so little. A short time, maybe.'"

"My, you two are philosophers. Just what kind of work does Carl do for the railroad?"

"He's what they call a switchman. He helps assemble freight trains in the New Haven yard. The job is dangerous and the pay is so-so. Anyway, he told me he's looking for a better job. I told him Dad could get him one with good pay."

"I am sure he can," said Sylvia. "Tomorrow I'll ask him to place Carl in a good position."

Kim quickly responded, "No, Ma. Don't ask Dad a thing, please. Carl said he could never take a job in one of Dad's companies. He said if he did, his boss would feel uncomfortable, knowing Carl was a friend of the big boss. Either the guy would show him favoritism, which would be embarrassing, or he would go out of his way not to, and Carl would end up in trouble for every trivial mistake. No, he couldn't do it. He said thanks for the offer."

Mrs. Durand said, "Well, dear, I guess Carl's right. I admire him for his principles. Hope your Dad has stopped snoring. I'm going to bed now. Aren't you going too?"

Kim replied, "Yes, I'd better. I have a lot of studying tomorrow." She kissed her mother goodnight.

Carl answered a help wanted ad for a position with the Everbright Paint Company in New Haven. His experience as a supply officer in the Army and his high marks in chemistry helped cinch the job for him. The manager told Carl, "Andrew Higgins, the big wheel, likes your résumé. I have been promoted to manager of our company's Connecticut and New York sales district. My job will be contacting building contractors in the region for their paint requirements. The house-building industry is going wild now. You'll have an office upstairs next to mine." He added if Carl proved he could handle supervising two clerks, ordering supplies, doing the accounting and payrolls, and assisting at the counters, he would become manager in three months. "You'll get help from me, but after three months, you're either in or out. Good luck."

Carl gave two weeks notice to the railroad company and commenced his new job in early September 1946. The postwar surge in home building carried Everbright Paints to record high sales. The company's excellent performance proved an asset to obtaining the necessary funds from its holding company, Sunrise Merchant's Trust. Five new stores were added to Everbright's chain of seven.

After two years, Carl was appointed manager of the five stores in the New Haven area—a testimony to his excellent record as manager since he started with Everbright. The home building boom continued and his wages increased considerably.

Chapter 10

Blinding Sunrise

Meanwhile, Dura-best Paints were plummeting. Roger Durand attributed the drop in sales to the lingering effects of war's end. He dismissed reports in newspapers, magazines, and technical journals that warned of the hazards of lead-based paint. "Dura-best Paints are the finest and will always dominate the paint market," he retorted. He charged that the manufacturers of cedar shingles and clapboards concocted the notion of lead paints being hazardous, or perhaps it was "those idiots trying to push asphalt siding."

One day Carl was driving into the parking lot at work just as another employee happened to pull in. He parked an impeccable 1938 Chevy next to Carl's old Ford. Carl's eyes lit up. "Morning, John. Boy, that Chevy looks brand new. Who did the paint job?" he asked.

John answered, "I did. Painting old cars is a hobby of mine. Good way to take advantage of our employees' discount. Let me tell you, our paint is really tops."

Carl said, "Would you paint my old jalopy? I don't want any favors. Charge me the same you would a stranger."

John handed him some business cards. "Sure," he said. "Call me when you want it done and we'll talk."

Two weeks after Carl had his car painted, he drove to Kim's for their usual Saturday date. He parked in the guest parking space while Gilbert was washing one of his boss's cars outside the garage. He stopped what he was doing, and said, "Hey, your car looks like it just came from the factory. Who did the great paint job?"

Carl retrieved the painter's business card from the glove compartment and handed it to Gilbert. "Yeah, I think it's pretty good too," he said. "Keep the card." Then eyeing a wall clock in the garage, he said. "I wonder if Kimberly is waiting for me. I'm a little late."

Gilbert chuckled. "You know women. Men do the waiting. Got to get the inside of the limo clean. See you, young fella."

Carl waved and ambled to the front entrance of the Durand house where Martha welcomed him. He told her they planned to attend the local theater to see "Gone With the Wind", which Kim had seen before but really wanted to see again. Carl hadn't seen it yet, so it was perfect for them both.

After the movie, they intended to go dancing at Marlin's, but the evening turned out so pleasant, Kim suggested they return to Golden Vista to sit and talk at the gazebo. "You know, Carl," she said. "In the moonlight, with the flowers in the garden."

Carl said in his best Rhett Butler impersonation, "Frankly, Kimberly, I don't give a damn about the flowers in the garden. The moonlight and you will most certainly do."

"Ouch!" was Kim's response. "I hope your poetry goes with the wind. But that's a nice thought."

The gazebo proved every bit as romantic a setting as they had anticipated. Carl snuggled up to Kim and said, "Here we are, alone with only the moon and the flowers. You're so beautiful. If I were to ravish you, no one would hear your protests."

She giggled and said, "Are you certain they would be protests?"

He answered, "It's true you are ravishing, but I, like Rhett Butler, am a gentleman."

She responded, "I, unlike Scarlet, am a lady, but ravish could be interesting. Anyway, I'm not sure Rhett was a true gentleman. He had other women. Do you?"

Carl stroked his lady's moon-drenched hair. "None. No one but you," he murmured. She turned to him, eyes glowing softly. All joking ceased. Suddenly, words leapt from his mouth: "I can't think of ever being with anyone but you, Kim. I love you. Will you be my wife?"

Kim's breath caught in her throat. She squeezed her eyelids shut and dropped her head onto his chest. "Carl, Carl, I love you too," she gasped. Her eyes rose to meet his. "Yes. I will marry you," she said, tears glinting off shards of moonlight.

The two embraced, awhirl amid the stars, clutching each other tightly as if the gazebo had somehow transformed into a merry-go-round, and if either were to let go, the other would be hurled off into the night. They kissed with restraint so tender it only stoked their passion. Finally, Carl said, "I almost asked you to marry me a couple of times before—once when I came home from the Army, and the other time when I started working for the railroad. Both times I thought I had nothing to offer you, Kim. Now I am doing OK. I feel even if we both have jobs, the marriage can work."

They agreed to keep their engagement a secret for the time being, as Carl wanted to feel more secure in his employment and their financial situation. "But I want to buy you a ring next week. Keep it out of sight, and when we get ready to announce our engagement, you can wear it."

"We'll invite your folks over and surprise our parents with the news," Kim said excitedly.

Carl's enthusiasm flared for a moment, then dimmed. "I hope your Dad approves of our marriage," he said.

"Don't worry. He will. My mother loves you, and that will do it."

A singular chime from the village clock drifted faintly through the still air.

Carl responded, "It's late—or early morning, I should say." He walked his fiancée to her front steps, kissed her again, and drove home, spirits soaring as if he were back in the cockpit of Snow White, this time charting a new course for the rest of his life.

As the months passed, sales from the Dura-best Paint subsidiary lagged increasingly. Roger Durand focused his attention on the earning reports of this, his favorite company. One morning he read an article in the New York Times stating that the building industry had reached unprecedented housing starts, and builders were hard-pressed to meet the demand. The publicity about low revenues coming from the only branch of Sunrise based on the Durand name affronted the CEO's pride. In the past, Dura-best Paints had been the star of Sunrise. Roger vowed they would rise again to that zenith. He called his secretary to his office and told her, "Miss Saltmarsh, I want you to obtain sales records of our subsidiaries from the accounting department for the following items: lumber, hardware, plumbing supplies, and paints. I want these figures submitted to me once a week for the next six months. You and I will go over these reports to find out just what items are selling fast or poorly, or whatever they are doing. Stir them up at accounting—my orders. I want to know who's goofing off in sales. They may have to be replaced. Paint should be selling like mad right now."

Miss Saltmarsh said, "Certainly, Mr. Durand. I'll have the first tabulations by next Monday."

Her boss replied, "Excellent. This will shed some light on which Sunrise member salespeople are not shining." He laughed at his pun and Miss Saltmarsh forced a grin.

On the second week, the records revealed excellent sales in lumber. Hardware and plumbing were also faring well. However, Dura-best Paints showed no gain over the previous week's report. Records of the third week showed plumbing supplies and lumber still excelling, and hardware improving, but paint sales had declined further.

The end of that third week, the Popes arrived at Golden Vista as guests of the Durands for their usual Friday bridge tournament. John Pope was aware of Roger's efforts to ferret out sales problems at Dura-best Paints. He asked his host, "Roger, how are sales in plumbing?"

Roger answered, "Oh, kitchen sinks were strong this past week. Looks like they may replace commodes next week."

Sylvia and Grace exchanged bemused looks and laughed. Grace jested, "I doubt a kitchen sink could replace a commode."

Roger smirked and said, "Come on, ladies. I'm talking sales inventory. John, tell me why women must be so picayune."

John answered, "Beats me, Roger. But I don't think I'll buy a commode from your company. It would look funny in our kitchen."

"Wise guys," said Roger. "Let's play bridge! . . . But seriously, my concern is about our paint outlets not doing so well in the midst of a building boom."

Sylvia blinked slowly at her husband and said, "Dear, don't bring your work home. As you said, let's play bridge. It's time we made the Popes host a party at their place. Oh, by the way, the Kemptons are joining us for bridge tomorrow."

The card game ended at 2:30 a.m. The Durands won, meaning if the Popes lost the next game, they would host the quarterly IRS revenge party. Roger, elated, teased: "I know you're heartbroken because you lost. Here's a nightcap to soothe you. Now wipe those tears and go to bed. You'll feel better in the morning."

Grace, feigning a sob, said, "Oh, thank you, kind sir. But before I retire, may I use your commode . . . I mean, kitchen sink?"

Grace's husband said, "Hmmmm. Wonder where they wash dishes in this house!"

Roger flung out his hands at the couple. "Oh, good night. Sylvia, let's leave these uncouth people alone." They all retired in good spirits.

At half-past noon the next day, Ed and Gladys Kempton arrived at Golden Vista. The Kemptons were pleasantly surprised to see the Popes again. They all had much to talk about. Roger and the two male guests had cocktails in the library. The women retreated to the sunroom to discuss window treatments. As usual, the men inquired about each other's health and their respective occupations. John Pope asked Ed if he was still teaching Business Administration at Windsor College in Hartford.

Professor Kempton answered, "Yes. We have a huge influx of veteran students because the government is paying their tuition. It sure has helped colleges. In fact, we are adding another building. It will mean more classrooms and labs. I hope we can meet our need for additional instructors."

Roger listened with interest and said, "Ed, maybe you can tell me why some products crucial to the building industry would be selling like gangbusters while another, just as critical, would be lagging behind?"

The professor answered, "Yes, the home building industry is booming like mad. What isn't selling?"

"Dura-best Paints," Roger answered. "Not just standing still, but declining every day."

The professor peered at Roger over the frames of his glasses and said, "That's odd. Paint should go along with the rest of the building needs." He paused to sip his drink and continued, "That reminds me of something that happened to a grain and feed supplier in Maine. They'd been doing a good business every year, but suddenly their livestock feed sales really dropped. This continued for several months until someone in the sales department advised the management to lower the price of feed. Well, they lowered the cost of the 100-pound bag by one dollar. Guess what? They got back all their customers and became profitable in a short time. The solution was that simple."

"Hey, that's interesting. A reduction of one cent a pound made the difference," exclaimed Roger.

John Pope said, "I guess a dairy farmer buying in large quantities could save a lot. Sure. Two hundred bags, two hundred bucks. Makes sense to me."

Professor Kempton beamed, grateful to be discussing his area of expertise. He leaned in closer to the other men and added, "Here's another company's solution to overcome a drop in sales. A pretty big tire retailer in Hyannis, Mass., had been doing a brisk business—One of those shops that replaces worn out tires while the customer waits. The retailer had five men just replacing tires all day long. Well, one of the workers incited his coworkers to slow down, take more time on each job. It was a ploy to force a pay increase. As a result, the manager had to tell customers to wait a couple hours, or come back another day. His customers went to the competition instead. After three months of low revenue, the big boss hired an efficiency expert to discover just what the problem was. The expert posed as a mechanic and helped with the tire work. He befriended the employees and soon learned about the scheme and its perpetrator. The troublemaker was fired, and a new mechanic hired in his place. Efficiency improved, and business returned to its previous level.

Pope remarked, "I suppose if they had a union shop the guy wouldn't be fired."

"That's probably right," said the professor. "But what I am pointing out is that an efficiency expert can be helpful in discovering what ails a business. It may seem unethical, but I guess that depends on what the problem is."

Roger was intrigued by the professor's stories. He decided on a similar course of action for Dura-best Paints.

After an hour of conversation, Martha announced it was time to meet the ladies in the dining room, as the meal was ready. As usual, the Durands' food proved excellent. The conversation ranged from world affairs, business, art, and education, to the latest on the couples' offspring. Professor Kempton inquired, "Has Miss Durand finished college at Yale? We thought she might be here for this wonderful meal."

Sylvia said Kim had received her master's degree in Economics in June. "But she has a boyfriend she likes to see on weekends, so we hardly ever see her."

Prof. Kempton cupped his jaw. "Interesting. As I told these gentlemen, the college I work for is expanding. More instructors will be needed soon. If Kim is interested, I suggest she submit her résumé and I'll see that they act on her application right away."

Roger responded, "That would be wonderful. If she got the job, all that studying and time at school would not be wasted. If she marries that fellow now, all that education is kind of pointless."

"Is that so?" Gladys Kempton piped. "You mean he doesn't want her to work after they get married?"

Roger answered, "I don't know if he does or doesn't. It's what I think. A woman wants to get married, she stays home. If she's after a career, no marriage. Simple."

Grace Pope knew Roger well enough to poke fun or criticize him when given good reason to. His last statement brought a loud protest from her. "Simple?" she remarked. "Roger, you're simple, or blind, or both. This is the 20th century. More and more married women are working, and a lot of married couples both work—some to make ends meet, others to better themselves. Wake up, man! You get bored with eight hours at work. Don't you think a woman gets bored staying home 24 hours a day?"

Roger questioned his wife, "Are you bored staying at home, dear?"

Sylvia answered, "Of course not. But I don't do any cooking, cleaning, laundry and other things. She's not talking about wives in my situation. Grace means women who don't have one tenth of what we have. I have a wonderful flower garden to tend and I can leave here anytime I want without having to worry about feeding you or Kim or any guests we may have."

Professor Kempton said, "Folks, during the war, women worked in factories doing jobs that were always considered men's work. They did welding, machine shop work, toiled on assembly lines making trucks and tanks, plus did a host of other jobs previously unheard of for women. And I'm sure Roger here had women replacing men in his factories. But a sad practice began that exists now, and probably will continue for years to come. Women were paid far less than men for the same work. This double standard is being exploited in every industry, big firms and small companies alike. You see women doing plastering, painting, roofing, plumbing, you name it—but always for smaller wages. Why, a few days ago I had an eye examination. It amazed me to see a listing of the staff they had: Four doctors, all men, and thirty-one technicians, all women. You hardly ever see male clerks in department stores any more. It's almost always women. But the thing is, the women get less. Maybe one day women will grow tired of getting the short end of the stick, and say 'to hell with this. I'll go home and be bored, and let my husband be the wage earner.' Roger, you do pay your women employees less, don't you? Are you sure you want them in the home and not working for you?"

Roger was taken aback. "Well hey, they all pay women less. Why should my company be the exception?"

"Ahah!" was Gladys's retort. "So you now think it's OK if a married woman chooses to work, as long as she works for less. Roger, you're guilty of two double standards!"

Roger cried out, "Martha, Martha, more food! More liquor! These guests are killing me. Get them in a good mood!"

After dinner, Roger showed his guests around the estate. Then they all marched to the rumpus room, to watch a home movie of a trip Roger's brother and his wife had filmed in Alaska.

During the showing, George and Laurie arrived for an unannounced visit. Laurie noticed the vehicles in the guest parking lot and said, "That's the Popes' car, but I wonder who owns that other vehicle?"

Martha greeted them at the main entrance. "You two come in. I'd call Mr. and Mrs. Durand but they are in the middle of showing the Popes and the Kemptons a five-star production of a travelogue in Alaska, produced and directed by George Durand and his talented wife, Laurie!"

Laurie said, "For those kind words, you shall star in our next production. The contract will be in the mail tomorrow!"

Martha replied, "Alas, I am under contract with the other Durands. They may frown upon your offer to me! Oh, I hear talking. The movie must be over. Follow me."

She led them to the rumpus room and called out, "Mrs. Durand, you have more guests."

Sylvia came out, followed by Roger, who yelled, "By George, it's my kid brother, George, and his beautiful wife. We just saw your masterpiece. What a life of leisure you two lead!"

George quipped, "That's right. And soon we are going on a safari to Africa. Maybe do some big game hunting. Want to come?"

"What? With your marksmanship, I wouldn't dare!"

They ambled to the rumpus room, where George and Laurie were introduced to the Kemptons. The ladies decided to stay and use the exercise equipment to work off some of the calories they'd ingested from the Durands' rich food.

Roger served the men drinks in the library, while they conversed about sports, travel, teaching, their younger years, money, and the people they admired.

Roger recounted his early working experiences when he was attending high school in Hartford. He told his friends, "I had a job at a gasoline station during the summer, after school let out. I worked for a Mr. Sam Porter. I really admired the guy. He knew how to make the money. At first, my job was just pumping gas, cleaning windshields, and checking oil or fixing flat tires for the customers. Then he had me changing oil. He told me when I drained the oil from a customer's car, if the engine required five quarts of oil, just put in four quarts of new oil and put back one quart of the used oil. The customer paid for five quarts of oil. He showed me how to clean off the old oil filter without removing it. Then he charged the customer for a new oil filter they didn't get. Another good trick he had was a real moneymaker. Often when a customer needed an oil change, he had me loosen the wheel nuts just a little on one front wheel and give it a hard kick to throw it slightly out of line with the other front wheel. The customer was called from the waiting room to view the misaligned wheel, and told he or she should have the alignment corrected right away, while the vehicle was over the pit and his mechanic could fix it for half the cost that alignment specialists charged. 'A 60-dollar job for only 30 dollars!' he'd say. More often than not, they paid the 30 dollars. So Sam got 30 dollars for four quarts of oil on several occasions! He sold fan belts by the dozen, simply by loosening the idler and calling the owner's attention to the loose fan belt.

"Another neat trick he had that always worked—He would stick a thumbtack in the tread of a tire and let a little air out. The tack was too short to actually puncture the thick rubber, but he would show the customer the head of the tack and say he or she better have the tire fixed before driving off. Then he'd present the customer with a nail that he claimed had come from the tire. He was careful not to pull those tricks on the same customers. He had a good memory for names and faces. One time he told me, 'I can't make money selling eight gallons of gasoline for a dollar!' He even charged people for the water he put in, or sometimes didn't put in their car battery, and most of the time it was plain tap water. Now there was a guy who knew how to make a buck! I learned a lot from him!"

Roger's astonished guests stared and shook their heads in disbelief. George simply continued thumbing through a magazine. He had heard enough about Sam Porter in the past, and was embarrassed about his brother's lack of ethics. Finally he looked up and said, "Roger, you know damn well you didn't like his rotten tricks."

Roger retorted, "Well, damn it, he did make money, and a lot of businesspeople use tactics a hell of a lot worse than what Sam did. George, we had robber barons in the past. Today they're called entrepreneurs, tycoons, or captains of industry, and are very well respected."

Professor Kempton tried to ease George's irritation by saying, "It's true that many fortunes have been made in this country through the unsavory practices of unscrupulous men who enjoy a good reputation in spite of it."

John Pope changed the subject by suggesting a golf match at a later date.

Another month passed, and Dura-best Paint sales remained poor. Roger decided to boost sales by implementing one of the methods that professor Kempton had spoken of. He called his secretary to his office and said, "Miss Saltmarsh, no need to bring the sales reports to me for a while. Keep them on file as you get them. Now this is what I want you to do: Find a couple companies that are in business management and get the names of their efficiency experts. Tell them we need one for at least a month. We will interview several candidates and work out a contract with the best one."

A few days later, Miss Saltmarsh called her boss on the intercom and said, "Mr. Durand, a Mrs. Hoffman from Northpoint Management Corporation is here. May I show her in?"

Roger assented and a neat but plain-looking woman entered the office. After she was seated, he asked if she'd be willing to travel.

Mrs. Hoffman replied, "Certainly. I travel a lot in this business, often for months at a time."

Hoffman appeared alert and capable. Roger thought, *this girl might uncover the reason for our slumping sales.* He said, "Mrs. Hoffman, we have ten stores that the company wants investigated for clues as to our slumping sales. I don't know if it's the fault of our managers or the sales personnel, but something is going on. As an efficiency person, perhaps you can find out. How would you go about finding the cause?"

She said, "You must start things going from your office. Send a letter to each store you want me to check. Tell the manager that the accounting department of Sunrise Industries needs an update on the capital equipment of all its stores. Capital equipment only—items necessary for the store to function, not your retail inventory. Mention desks, chairs, cash registers, counters, delivery trucks, shelves—anything valued over ten dollars. The managers should be told that a Shirley Hoffman from your accounting department will be there sometime within the next month. I'll need a letter of introduction, of course, with your signature. I'll have inventory sheets made up to make it look official. Do you have a company car I can use?"

Roger felt this lady knew her job. He enthusiastically praised her idea. "Yes, we have a car for you with our firm's name on the doors," he said.

"Good," she answered. "Get those letters out and tomorrow I'll have a figure for my fee."

Two days later, Mrs. Hoffman left to investigate the ten stores Roger had selected in the New England area. In spite of the high price of her services, he felt certain he'd made a good investment.

On the evening Mrs. Hoffman embarked on her first assignment, Roger arrived home in high spirits. He swept Sylvia into his arms, soundly kissed her, held her at arm's length and said, "Woman, I have the prettiest wife in Connecticut."

Sylvia gasped and managed to say, "Well, whatever happened to you at work should happen more often!"

Kim witnessed the greeting and said, "I saw Daddy kissing Mommy. Guess I'd better leave the room."

No, you don't," he said. And he reached for his daughter's arm. "Do you know why you're so beautiful? It's because your mother is so beautiful!" and he kissed Kim on the cheek.

Martha appeared and said, "If you three love birds care to eat a lovely dinner, made by their lovely cook, it awaits you."

At the dinner table, Roger's family wanted to know what had triggered his jubilant mood. He told them, "Today I hired an efficiency expert that really knows her stuff. Name is Hoffman. I am sure she will find out why the stores are losing money. She is ostensibly there to check the firm's fixed property like desks, chairs, and cash registers—not our merchandise. In reality, she will be watching the employees. Are they doing their job for Dura-best Paints? Giving good service? That sort of thing."

"Gee, Dad," Kim said. "I don't think I would like a job like Miss Hoffman's, spying on people."

He replied, "In today's world, some people think they never get compensation enough for the work they do. So they loaf on the job, take long lunch hours, come in late, don't treat customers right. An efficiency person can find out who they are and the problem can be corrected. Anyway, it's Mrs. Hoffman, not Miss."

His wife said, "Well, that's a switch. You hired a married woman. What happened to 'the wife stays at home' nonsense you told our guests? If this Mrs. Hoffman brings back information you don't like, it's back to 'stay at home, you married female.'"

Kim exclaimed, "Right! Isn't that the wrong attitude, Dad? I went to college for years to learn something useful. To get a job that's both interesting and rewarding. Are you saying I shouldn't get married because a married woman must stay home? Dad, women vote these days. And I bet you will see more women governors and senators as time goes on. If you told Mrs. Hoffman married women should stay home, she would tell you to open your eyes, get with it. You're not keeping up with progress in the paint business, just as you don't keep up with the fact that women have progressed from homebodies and baby makers to persons with equal rights that men enjoy. Your old ideals belong wrapped up with yesterday's garbage!"

Roger's face reddened. "Now Kim, I have a right to my opinion. About you going to college, you should know that you didn't have to. You will never have to work. You could have traveled all over the world for those four or five years you spent in college. Seeing the world could have been your education. With our money, life can be one sweet song. Why the hell work when you don't have to?"

Sylvia turned and spoke to her daughter as if Roger weren't present. "Often in the past, your father has spoken of his mother's death at the early age of fifty-six. He told me how difficult it was for her to bring up two boys in the storeroom of their little shop, waiting on customers, cooking meals for four people on a small gas burner, even helping her husband whenever he needed a hand with painting jobs he took at night to make ends meet. While she worked with your grandfather, your dad was left at home, that is, the backroom of that little shop, to care for Uncle George and him. All they had was a small kerosene burner to heat the shop and the wash water. She died of consumption. Your father used to say if his mother had had a normal home life and hadn't worked so damn hard in that miserable backroom, she may have lived longer. A college education would have helped her earn a decent living without killing herself. Your dear father clings to the past. He doesn't accept the fact that this is a new era. But we love him dearly," she added, eyeing her husband.

Kim said, "Oh Dad, I love the work that is available to me because of my education. I would like spending the day teaching others what I know, and after the day's work, meeting my husband at a restaurant, or going home to cook a meal together. That would suit me just fine. Carl thinks it's a great idea too. We could better ourselves, have more money to travel and so forth, and every weekend would be like a honeymoon."

Roger responded, "The day is coming when the man stays home and the woman works. Well, my two critics, I'm through eating and listening. Care to join me on the porch?"

The phone rang. Martha called out, "Kim, a call for you."

Kim dashed to the den and picked up the phone.

"Fine, Hazel. You bet Carl and I are still holding hands. But my love life is none of your business, you old married woman!" Kim said with laughter. "And to what do I owe the honor of your call?"

She listened as Hazel's voice came back, "Douglas and I would like to have you and Carl as our guests for dinner this coming Saturday. Doug thinks I'm a good cook, but of course he's biased. You two can be the judge. Come about fivish if you can. Call me when you find out, and give Carl a hug and kiss for me."

"Thanks, Hazel. I'll call you. But Carl will get his hugs and kisses from me, thanks. You're married, remember? Say Hi to your handsome husband. Gotta go. My aunt and uncle just arrived."

Kim heard her mother say, "Well, this is a nice surprise. Had you two arrived an hour earlier, we would have had you for dinner."

George saw an opening for a pun and said, "I'd be tough, but Laurie would make a nice dessert."

"Very funny," Roger remarked, adding, "So, little brother, you came calling without calling. What's up?"

"Little brother, hah! I might be younger than you, but I'm bigger," George said. "We want the three of you to come to our cottage on Sebago Lake in Maine for a couple weeks. The foliage is at its peak the last three weeks of this month, and even into early October. Roger, the fishing is super and we can visit the harvest festivals and fairs they have this time of year. Don't say no. I'll do the driving and a lot of the cooking."

Laurie interjected, "Yes, do come. George makes a better cook than bridge player."

George smirked and said, "Just because I trumped her ace the other day with our neighbors."

Roger exclaimed, "Hey, you don't have a phone there. How am I to get news from work if we go?"

George offered, "If you want, I can take you to the general store in town so you can call your secretary. But I suggest you forget Sunrise for a while."

Sylvia said, "Roger, let's go. We have been homebodies long enough. It will do both of us good."

Kim added, "Yes, Dad. Let's go! All you have talked about is Dura-best Paints. Let's see some real painting—the fall foliage!"

Roger agreed. "OK, OK. I'm outnumbered. But we can't leave until Monday. I have an important meeting coming up."

That Saturday, Carl picked up his future wife at Golden Vista. They drove to the end of a curved, tree-lined driveway that secluded the beautiful home of Hazel and Douglas Graf. It impressed Carl. He said, "First Golden Vista, now this beauty. Boy, do I hobnob with the Nah bobs! People will think I'm a social climber. Kim, I'm a peasant. And still, you'll marry me?"

She answered, "Dumb dumb, of course I will marry you. My aspirations are not so lofty as you may think!"

The car stopped at the front entrance. Douglas's sister opened the door even before Carl was able to ring the doorbell. She exclaimed, "Hi! I'm Freda Graf! And you must be my brother's guests, Kim and Carl. My brother appointed me the official greeter because he knows I love to welcome people. Please come in." She called out, "Hazel, Doug, your Army buddy and his girlfriend are here."

Hazel gave a tour of the home. Later, drinks were served in the den. While the ladies were conversing about Hazel's decorating feats, Douglas took Carl to his well-equipped basement workshop to show off his latest woodworking projects. Carl was surprised at the quality of Douglas's workmanship. He remembered his friend had been a poor shop student in school. Carl congratulated Douglas on his fine work. Doug shrugged and confided, "Carl, I do this stuff—It keeps my mind off that crap we went through in POW camp."

Carl nodded and said, "I'm glad it helps you forget. You were in that hellhole a lot longer than I was."

Douglas sat on a stool and motioned for Carl to do the same. "I wish we could find out where some of our cellmates ended up. Sometimes I can't sleep worrying about who made it out of that fire."

Carl thought a moment and said, "Campbell and Smyth were Canadians. I wonder if some government agency in Canada could give us any information about its WWII veterans, living or dead?"

Doug slapped his knee. "I'm going to find out," he said just as Hazel yelled by the basement door.

"Hey, you guys. Time to eat!"

When the meal was over and the dishes cleared from the table, they all gathered in the den. Freda said, "Kim, my brother never talks about how they escaped from the POW camp. Did Carl ever tell you how they did it?"

Kim shook her head and turned to Carl.

A chorus of three women pleaded, "Please tell us!"

After a couple more cocktails, Doug said, "It was a simple matter of 'urine and yer out,' right Carl?"

Carl smirked. "Let's just say we were able to escape because the urine worked fine," he said, elongating the "i" sound in the first word to force a rhyme.

Their host offered, "He peed, we fleed."

The ladies squealed and giggled, demanding, "What the hell are you guys talking about?"

At last, Carl sighed heavily and began: "There was a crawl space under the prison". . . And he told the story of the escape.

"So that's why we are here now—half nuts, maybe, but alive," he concluded.

The room grew quiet. No one moved. Then Hazel blurted, "In a crawl space, how the heck did you . . .I-I mean, I don't get how you . . . well, you're so tall and . . ." She blushed and everyone laughed.

Doug said, "Honey, shhhh. I'll explain after the company leaves." The women did not pursue the subject further, at least not then.

When the glasses were empty, Hazel suggested the women come to the kitchen to talk while she stacked dishes in the dishwasher. Doug and Carl took a walk around the premises, and out onto the country road beyond the driveway.

Kim couldn't stop complimenting Hazel on the décor of her home. "Hazel, I love your furniture, and this is a dream kitchen."

Hazel responded, "Yes. Doug is doing so well in real estate with his dad, we have the means to buy right. Did you know he sold some property in New Haven that netted him $20,000? We thought it best to invest in the stock market. And guess what? We put it all into Sunrise Industries. He calls it our bird nest."

Kim laughed and corrected her. "You mean nest egg! Anyway, I hope Sunrise doesn't disappoint you, so we can still be friends."

Hazel turned quickly toward Kim and caught her winking at Freda. She said, "It's a good thing you are kidding. We are friends, no matter what happens."

On the way home, Carl commented on his Army buddy's nice home and his topnotch shop. He told Kim, "Doug's a lucky guy. But, then, I'm lucky too. I have you, and that's better than anything."

She said, "I'm lucky also," and she kissed his cheek. She knew how it disturbed Carl not to have the means to provide as nice a home as their friends had. She changed the subject by saying, "Guess what? My uncle invited Mother, Dad and me to their cottage on Sebago Lake for a couple of weeks. This time of year the foliage is so beautiful, and there will be harvest festivals and fairs all over the place. Don't fool around while I'm away!"

Carl said, "Two weeks? How will I get along without you? Just watch out for those slick farm boys if you go for a hayride, and don't forget to call me once in a while."

She said, "I won't fool with the farm boys if you don't sit on your cashier's lap. Promise me?" He promised to be good. They arrived at Golden Vista and said their goodbyes.

Chapter 11

Durands' Retreat

At four p.m. on Tuesday, the Durands arrived at George's cottage on Sebago Lake. Four hundred feet of driveway wound through the woods to a clearing where the house stood. The driveway extended from the main entrance on the north to a perimeter road serving several other cottages around that end of the lake. From the house, a cement walk led to a sandy beach and the dock belonging to Durands' Retreat.

The place was somewhat larger than the average summer camp or cottage in the area. It had an emergency generator for power failures, and an electric heating and hot water system. It contained three bedrooms, each with their own bathroom, plus a kitchen and one huge room equipped with comfortable chairs and a large table used for dining, playing cards, and other games. A fireplace nestled between bookshelves was straddled on either side by two enormous picture windows overlooking the lake to the west.

George readied the cottage for occupancy by opening windows and turning the electricity on. When he completed the routine, he said, "Kim, take any room you want, but you'll have to sleep alone. I forgot to tell Wilbur you were coming."

Sylvia's ears perked up. She said, "And just who is Wilbur? I'll pass judgment on who my daughter sleeps with."

Grinning, Kim said, "My mother still changes my diapers."

George said convincingly, "Oh, it's not Wilbur. He has three handsome sons. She can choose whichever one she wants."

Sylvia said, "Then tell Wilbur to send his sons here. You and Roger can sleep in a tent outside!"

119

Roger remarked, "There you go, George. Getting us in trouble the first thing."

George replied, "All right, all right. I won't call Wilbur, but speaking of sons, ladies and gentlemen, it's time you saw a sun you will never forget. Come outside with me."

Laurie said, "Humor him. It will be a full moon tonight and he gets like this."

George led them out of the house and onto the beach. He told the ladies to sit on the sand facing the lake. Kim snuggled up between her mother and Laurie. Then Roger settled down beside Sylvia, and George squeezed in next to his wife. As the sun pressed into the horizon, George said, "There's the sun I meant." The group sat riveted to the spectacle: vermillion shards of light slashing through purple clouds edged in gold— the colors deepening, merging, transforming dramatically, yet imperceptibly before their eyes. They uttered not a sound, dazzled by this daily reenactment that has inspired and humbled mankind for eons. The silence prevailed for several minutes. Then the earth turned and bade the sun goodnight.

A fish surfacing after an insect broke the spell with a splash, prompting George to say, "Roger, let's go fishing in the morning."

Laurie's cooler of food provided an ample evening meal, tiding them over until they could drive to the small town of Windham to stock up on food for the two-week vacation. The elder Durands spent the remainder of the evening playing bridge while Kim curled up in a comfortable chair reading a book selected from the loaded bookshelves. The long ride from Connecticut had been more tiresome than they'd realized. The players retired at 10 p.m. Kim read for another hour, then closed the book and rolled into bed, thinking of Carl.

Fishermen are early birds, and George was no exception. At five a.m., he pounded on his brother's door, calling, "Get up, lazy bones. Let's get those fish before they die of starvation."

George heard Sylvia say, "Roger, get up so that pest will go away." Then to George she whined, "Go fishing and let me sleep. You two had better come home with some fish or I'll make bait out of you both."

Roger carried his clothes out to the great room and dressed. Then he grabbed a jacket and they left. Just as he was about to step into George's boat, he said, "Boy, I've got to piss."

George said, "Well, go in the woods, and hurry. We haven't got all day."

When Roger trudged back to the boat, he told George, "You know, getting up so early to catch fish is a lot of crap. We could just drive to Portland and get good fresh-caught ocean fish. If we are lucky enough to catch anything, I'm not going to clean them. I may not even eat them, no matter who cooks them."

"Damn it!" George said. "Can't you relax? What you need is a big mean bass fighting on the end of your fishing line, running like hell with your leader. Outwitting the sucker and tugging him in gets your adrenaline pumping. Then you get a big thrill when you land him in the boat. I'll take you to a cove that's a favorite spot for bass. Let's see if we can outsmart them."

George maneuvered the boat to the cove and cast his line to commence fishing. Roger cast clumsily, but managed to land his hook in a few good spots. Luck was with them. In two hours, Roger had caught four bass, and his brother, three. Both men's stomachs were growling. Roger said, "I'll bet the women are up and the coffee is almost ready."

"OK, OK. You won't let me get another fish. I'll never hear the end of this. You caught four and I only got three," ranted

George. "You are going to have bass for breakfast! I'll clean and fillet these, and Laurie will cook them. I promised her last night, 'Fish for breakfast.' Come on. You take the tiller while I clean the fish."

By the time they reached the dock, the fish were ready for the frying pan. On their arrival, a chorus of "Who caught the most fish?" greeted the fishermen.

Roger asserted, "I did. My younger brother was lucky to catch one more just as we were getting ready to come back, or else he'd have caught only two."

"Me, lucky? Why, the way you were casting, those bass laughed themselves silly. They knew they were going to die laughing anyway, so they took your hook and went with a smile on their lips. You saw how they danced around in the boat!"

Kim said, "Uncle George, I guess they didn't learn much in school."

Laurie groaned, "Oh my God. The fish tales have begun. Next thing you know, they'll be talking about the big one that got away. Come on, throw them in the pan so we can eat."

Everyone said how delicious the fish was except Roger, though he enjoyed it as much as anyone. Instead, he said, "Why don't you have a telephone, George? What would you do for help if there was an emergency? Or what if your car won't start?"

George answered, "You think we're isolated here? Well, when we drove in yesterday, I'll bet all the people around here knew about it. You'll see. Sometime today, Wilbur—he's the farmer with the three sons—will show up. He comes every day except Sunday. There's a claxon horn below the peak of this roof. If we needed help or the car wouldn't start, I'd press that button by the door. The darn horn could wake the dead a couple of miles from here. I sure would have help then. Anyway, the phone lines end at Windham. They may run them this way in a couple of years. If we go shopping today, you can call your office. I have a feeling that's why you asked about the phone."

Roger replied, "I do like to keep in touch with the office, but it can wait."

Sylvia said, "Good for you, dear! Tell you what—When we ladies go shopping today, I'll get you the New York Times and a Portland newspaper." Roger agreed.

After breakfast, Kim spotted a vehicle winding up the driveway. She called out, "Uncle George, someone's coming."

George pulled the drapes back and said, "Oh, that's Wilbur." He rushed to the door, flung it open and shouted, "Wil! Glad to see you. Come on in."

Wilbur parked his small pickup truck behind Durand's car. As he stepped out, George noticed he was carrying a package. Wil arrived at the door and shook George's hand. "Glad tah say ya," he said.

George led Wilbur to the great room. "Thanks, Wil. I want you to meet my sister-in-law, Sylvia, my brother, Roger, and their daughter, Kim. Folks, this is Wilbur Mayhew. He has a farm about a mile down the road."

"Well, I'm sure happy tah meet you folks. And Laurie, you look prettiah than evah, and that's a fact." Wilbur handed Laurie a box of eggs and added, "I must go back tah the truck. Excuse me for a minute." He came back with another dozen eggs, saying, "T'won't do to have jist a dozen. Take these. I'll bring more by 'n' by."

Laurie protested. "Wil, thank you, but you needn't do this."

He responded, "They's lots o' things I needn't do, but givin' a little somethin' to yah, —ahm mighty happy that I can." Wilbur turned to George and said, "Ahm also happy tah tell yah, the bahn is finished. You come this Sunday—the whole bunch o' yah. We ah havin' a little shindig fuh all the nice folks that helped us build the new bahn. Agnes and the boys want you folks tah help us celebrate. Come early. Now I gotta go and delivuh a few mowah eggs." He winked and shuffled out the front door, saying, "Nice meetin' yah kin folks."

Sylvia asked about Wil's boys. George said, "Otis is the youngest. He's 14. Tom's a year older, and I think Bob is 17."

Sylvia remarked, "My lord, they're only youngsters. The way you talked, you made them out to be men."

George laughed and replied, "Hey, they're all taller than me."

After the laughter died down, Kim said, "What's the story about Wilbur's barn?"

He told her, "This summer, his barn was struck by lightning. It burned to the ground, and his farmer friends helped him rebuild. They help each other in many ways. He was lucky his hen house didn't go too, or he would have been ruined."

"And how did you help?" she persisted.

George covered his mouth with a napkin and coughed. "Well, uh—we buy eggs from them. Have been for a long time. Roger, let me show you some handiwork the glaciers did around here before even you were born."

Roger thought his brother's answer evasive, but said nothing. Laurie diverted Kim and Sylvia's attention from the conversation by saying, "Come on, you two. Let's go shopping." The women piled into the car and drove off as the men set out on their hike.

George had always been curious about a wooded knoll he could see around the other end of the lake. He pointed across the water. "Rog, I want to see what that hill north of here is like. Are you game to hike that far? It looks like maybe a couple miles through pretty thick woods. The lake skirts that high part."

Roger said, "OK. Let's do it. Those pines look nice and shady."

The trek took over an hour. As they trudged nearer the high ground, shrubs and trees became less evident. Soon the soil gave way to bare rock with patches of earth here and there, supporting tufts of grass and brush. Suddenly they came to a promontory high above the lake, with an awesome view of the water below. The brothers sat on a warm, flat rock and contemplated the view in complete silence. After several minutes, George said, "I'm glad we came here. This will be my thinking place."

Roger remarked, "Yeah. It sure is tranquil. Conducive to reflecting on what life is all about."

George turned to Roger, a curious expression on his face. "Do you do much of that kind of reflecting?" he asked.

Roger said, "Sometimes. Like yesterday, I had a flashback to the time I was about six years old."

George said, "Oh? What about?"

Roger leaned over to brush an ant off the rock. Then he resettled and responded, "Remember when you mentioned Wilbur's three sons, and the girls said, 'Tell Wilbur to send his sons here. You and Roger can sleep in a tent outside'? Well, it got me thinking about young boys and how they discover the facts of life. I remember when Mother used to go with Dad to help paint apartments. They would take you with them. I guess they figured the two of us together would get into mischief, so they asked our neighbors—Remember the Cataldos? —if their daughter, Helen, would watch me. She was sixteen, and home alone most of the time, because her mom and dad worked. Well, Helen took care of me several times, but not like you think. Some girl!"

George looked at his brother. "What do you mean?"

Roger hesitated, turning his face away. Finally he sighed and began, "George, I never told anyone about this, but my first day at Helen's house, I told her I had to go to the bathroom. She took me there and pulled my pants and underwear down, and told me to do what I had to do. I said, 'But I only have to pee. How come you pulled my pants down?' She said, 'That's all right. Pee with your pants down,' and I did. When I was done, she said, 'Look. Girls are different from boys,' and she pulled her dress up. She had no underwear on, and I was surprised to see hair where her legs came together. I thought that must be how girls were different from boys, because you didn't have hair there and neither did I. Helen then put the toilet seat down, sat on it, spread her legs and pulled me to her. As she hugged me tightly, I thought it was because she liked me, but after a while, I realized she was hugging me for herself. Finally she let go of me and pulled my clothes up and we went back into the living room. She read me a story, and just before it was time to take me home, she gave me two pennies and told me never to tell anyone what she did. This happened many times when I stayed there. One time when she was hugging me like that, she cried out, 'Oh, I wish you were like the milkman!'"

George exclaimed, "My God! And Ma thought Helen was such a nice girl! If she ever knew about that—oh boy." He shook his head, flabbergasted. "You know, I often wondered how you were able to buy candy. You used to tell me you found the money!"

Roger said, "Hey, I was a dumb little kid and I think I was afraid to let you or anyone know what Helen did. I guess I was afraid it meant I was a bad boy, but I really didn't know if I was."

George responded, "No. There was something wrong with her. There are people like that—some in professions requiring morals above reproach."

Roger kicked a small stone over the ledge and watched it plummet down the side of the hill and splash into the water. "Damn!" he exclaimed. "I'll never let anyone overpower or take advantage of me like that again!"

George studied his brother thoughtfully for several seconds. Then he threw an arm around Roger's shoulders and said, "Life is crazy, Brother. Let's head back." And they left the thinking place.

For four days, the Durands attended all the fairs and harvest festivals within a reasonable drive. Each morning, they pored over the local newspapers for times and locations of the events, and planned a new excursion. Roger wasn't too impressed with the crafts and agricultural exhibits. He was more interested in building exhibits, such as one panorama he saw illustrating the process of making shingles, clapboards, and plywood from log to finished product. George noticed his brother's preference and said, "Roger, man does not live by building alone."

His puzzled brother shot back, "Just what the heck do you mean by that?"

"Roger, your focus is so narrow," his brother replied. "Can't you see anything besides building stuff? Look at how people grow food. Look at how cloth is woven. Come and watch how these Penobscot Indians used to make their moccasins and clothes. They actually have a replicated village we can walk through to see how they once lived in wigwams and longhouses, made cook fires using a bow and a stick. Damn interesting."

Roger followed them to the Indian village, and was mildly impressed. But what intrigued him the most were the pigments the men used to paint their faces.

Sunday evening, all the Durands were convinced they had attended sufficient fairs to last them until next harvest season.

Upon their arrival at Durands' Retreat, they had cocktails. Kim returned to her reading, while her parents briefly resumed their bridge game. Soon the strain of the day's activities took its toll. They had walked most of the day. The games could wait. As George fell into bed, he said to his wife, "I must get Roger off his constant fretting over the firm. Can't get his mind away from his work. Today, at the Penobscot exhibit, he said, 'George, do you think the paint these Indians put on their faces is much different than our paint?' I told him, 'Don't compare their paint with Dura-best Paints. Theirs is made from harmless vegetable dyes.' I'm not sure he caught my drift, but you see where his mind is. I think he took Dad's last wishes too seriously. Dad did work hard, but he was a bitter man because of the lousy life he had when he was young. I think it adds to Roger's hostility. I had hoped this diversion from the damn office would help him relax a bit."

"Oh well, we have another week to try," said his wife.

They kissed and fell into a deep, restful asleep.

Sunday morning the group had a light breakfast and put on their blue jeans. It was Wilbur's party day. On arriving at the farm, Wilbur greeted the Durands and introduced them to his neighbors, some of whom George and Laurie knew. Three picnic tables, placed end to end, seated 25 guests. The women were setting tables, and children were running in every direction. George and Roger joined two other men on a team playing horseshoes. After their team lost, the opponents paired off to play two against two. The two members of the winning team then challenged each other in a final match. The winner was awarded a gallon of hard cider. Each loser was handed an ice-cold glass of the same good stuff.

Roger downed his drink and wandered over to inspect the new barn. A man was busy painting a section of bare wood on the structure. Roger saw two paint cans on the floor, one with its cover removed. He was puzzled that neither bore a label. He looked closely at the closed container and was surprised to read the words, "Sunrise Industries Inc." embossed on the lid. On the rung of a small ladder rested another lid bearing the same inscription. He called to the young man, "Hi, I'm one of the guests at the party here. Are you Wilbur's son?"

"That I am. Name's Otis. Told muh brothahs I'd be done b'fowah time tah eat. Fraid uh might not make it."

"Roger Durand's my name. I'm staying a while at my brother George's place."

"Gladja could make it," Otis responded as his brush slapped against the wall.

Roger said, "Why are the labels off the paint cans?"

Otis explained, "Dad bought 15 gallons of this heah paint at a real bahgain. He paid $60 for the lot. Mr. Clough, he owns the general stowah in Windham, bought quite a few gallons of this heah discontinued oil paint from a contractah ovah in Pohtland. Guess the guy figyahed that new latex stuff is a might less messy and a tad mowah convenient. Clough had the paint out undah a tahp on a flatbed truck ahind his stowah that night and a bad stohm blew the tahp off and soaked the cans. That's why they ain't no labels."

Roger scratched his head. "With no labels on the cans, how did you know the color of the paint?" he asked.

Otis turned his head slowly and stared at Roger, baffled. Speaking slowly, he replied, "Took the lids off and looked inside, that's how."

The slight rebuff didn't affect Roger. He was elated that they were using Dura-best Paints. He returned to the picnic area, muttering, "Smarter than those idiot contractors. Latex doesn't hold a candle to our lead-based oils."

During the fabulous feast, Wilbur stood up and asked for the guests' attention. When all was quiet, he announced, "This heah pahty is to show owah appreciation for the good neighbahs that helped in rebuildin' this heah bahn." He extended his arm toward the new structure as though presenting a dignitary. "Without yaw help I don't know how long we coulda kept goin' heah, because we ah still beholdin' to the bank. Now, my friends, I want all uv yah tah know, the bank in Pohtland plum refused tah loan us any mowah money fuh the fahm. But Geawge and Laurie Durand, sittin' right heah next tah me, gave us Mayhews $4,000. T'weren't a loan or a mawgage, or nuhthin' like that, but a gift. It paid fuh evahthin' we needed tah build the bahn."

Wilbur's neighbors applauded, uttering "ooohs" and "aaahs," and "How wonderful!"

Kim and Sylvia yelled, "Good for you, George and Laurie," while Roger sat quietly, his jaw unhinged.

George arose from his seat and said, "Wilbur, please sit down. I have something to say." He turned to the group and stated, "I had a selfish motive in giving Wil that 'gift', as he calls it. For the eight years we've vacationed at this beautiful lake, Wil has supplied us with fresh eggs, chicken, vegetables, and the delicious pies that you people make so well. Wil never charged nearly enough. We didn't give the Mayhews a gift. We owed them that money, and we want him to continue selling his milk and pies to us. Now, we're even. So no more about gifts, Wil."

Wil said, "Well, I'll be danged." He patted his wife on the shoulder and said, "Agnes, would yah make some uv yuh peach cobblah fuh the Durands, afore they leave fuh Connecticut? You know, that dessert I married yah for?"

Agnes sighed and said, "That proves the old sayin'—'The way to a man's haht is through his stomach!'" More cider was passed around, and good food and conversation abounded.

When Roger had the chance, he asked Wilbur if he used much turpentine to thin his paint. Wilbur responded, "No suh. We nevah use turps. Costs too much. Kerosene works just as good and 'taint half as expensive."

Wil's statement startled Roger. He said, "So that's what I smelled when I was talking to Otis. I think you're making a big mistake. Don't you know how flammable kerosene is?"

Wilbur gave Roger the same look Otis had given him when he'd asked about the paint cans. "So's turpentine," he said flatly.

Roger simply swallowed with an exaggerated gasp and said, "Mmmm. Good cider!"

On the ride back to Durands' Retreat, Roger said to George, "Don't be surprised if they elect you mayor of this place, or whatever they call the guy who runs the town. And don't be surprised when the next place burns down, they ask you for money like Wil did."

George said, "Hey, he didn't ask me for a cent. Laurie and I went to Windham to get some postcards at the general store. Wilbur and his son, Bob, were buying something, so I walked over to say hello and ask if the insurance on his barn came through, and whether it was enough. Bob didn't wait for his Dad to answer. He said they had insurance on only the house. The barn wasn't covered. He also told me they just got back from Portland, to try and get a loan from the bank to rebuild the barn. The bank refused, as they didn't have enough equity in the house or land.

"The kid even said that without their milk business, if they didn't get work somewhere, they would be living out in the woods. His father said, 'Bob, hush. Mr. Durand shouldn't be bothered with our problems. I'm sorry, George. Bob sometimes talks out of turn.' I told them I was glad he'd spoken up. So Wilbur didn't ask us for a damn thing. When Laurie and I discussed his problem that evening, we decided to mail them money to rebuild the barn, and we did."

Sylvia and Kim praised Laurie and George for their generosity. Roger said, "George, you can carry generosity too far. Other people might play you for a sucker. They'll think you're an easy touch and beat a path to your door. Need money to pay a bill? —Let George do it." He shook his head. "Don't be a fool, Brother."

George retorted, "Roger, these people are not connivers or crooks. Remember your executive friend, Al Blake, and his buddy, Clyde Wilson? You almost went along with those two crooks to screw the government. Never mind a path to your door. They were paving a highway to your door, and you almost let them bulldoze right in."

Roger didn't mention the subject again.

That evening, all grudges aside, the vacationers made plans for their remaining days at the lake. Laurie suggested a trip to Portland to board the ferryboat to Chebeaque Island, to feast on the scenery and the super meal described by a friend. They were not disappointed. The seascape proved spectacular, the food scrumptious and plentiful. That, plus the exhilarating air, worked wonders on Roger's morale. He asked Sylvia, "Do you think Gilbert and Martha got their cooking experience here? The food here reminds me of the seafood dinners they prepare when we have special guests. I never asked what part of Maine they were from."

She replied, "They did come from Portland, but Martha and Gilbert worked in a cotton mill that produced towels and fabrics. Gil was a mechanic and Martha operated some machine. When the mill moved down south, they lost their jobs. Martha told me that the factory owner asked her and Gilbert if they would prepare a clambake with all the fixings—lobster, clams, chowder, and blueberry pie, for an outing at some beach. This was for his loyal help, an affair they had every summer. The boss gave them time off and money enough to buy food for 30 employees. Well, they did a great job, and were hired to do that every summer for eleven years. When the owner died, his son closed down the plant. Martha and Gil came to New Haven to find work. We were lucky to get them when we advertised."

Roger mused, "Maybe I should give them a raise."

George said, "By gosh, I'm glad to see you so expansive and happy. We have another five days before you go back to 'worry incorporated,' so let the fun continue. Those in favor of going deep-sea fishing tomorrow say 'aye'. Those opposed, shut up." Without waiting for an answer, he injected, "The 'ayes' have it! Tomorrow I'll hire a boat with fishing gear and a skipper who knows where the big ones are. Rog, you may have caught more fish from our lake, but I bet I'll beat you and the girls at ocean fishing."

Sylvia said, "OK, George. If you catch more fish than the four of us, we owe you five dollars each. And if we catch more than you, you pay us $25. Agreed?"

George agreed. When they returned to Portland, he made arrangements to hire a boat fully equipped with fishing gear, along with the owner as guide and pilot. The ferry slip was next to several wharves berthing fishing boats for hire. He picked a craft that looked to be in good shape. He paid a deposit to the skipper and stated his party would be there at nine a.m. They returned to the cottage in time to view another spectacular sunset.

As forecast by the Portland radio station, the next day dawned cool and clear, a perfect October day. The Durands boarded the fishing boat and the captain headed for the cold, deep waters off Casco Bay, two miles east of Cape Elizabeth. He said he always had luck fishing in that vicinity. Thirty minutes of angling yielded several tugs on their lines. Kim was the first to land a striped bass. Soon, her luck rubbed off on the others, and they hauled in a sizable catch. By lunchtime, Kim had caught two good ones, her mother and father one each, Laurie two, and her husband, three. George grinned about his achievement all through lunch, after which they resumed fishing. At three p.m., the captain advised heading back to Portland. The final tally of fish caught was three for Kim, two for Sylvia, three for Roger, three for Laurie, and five for George, who bragged about being the winner. After docking in Portland, they thanked the pilot for finding such a good spot and gave him all but three bluefish. The fish were placed in a cooler packed with ice, stowed in the car's trunk. George told Laurie he would fillet them when they got home.

They stopped at a quaint 18th century inn for dinner. At the table, George said, "Now I hate to bring up bad news during mealtime, but you guys owe me five dollars each." He beamed and held out his palm. "I should get more, but I can't expect you landlubbers to know anything about catching fish."

His family chimed in, "Oh no you don't!" Laurie explained, "You owe each of us five dollars. The agreement was you would catch more fish than we did. But we caught a total of eleven, and you caught only five. So pay up, my dear!"

"What a bunch of thieves! My wife and my own brother and his family cheating me! Just for being so crooked, only two cocktails when we get home. Now I hope I won't embarrass you while I cry at the table in front of our waiter," said George.

Roger said soothingly, "George, please don't cry. I'll let you pay the bill for this meal and, to make you feel even better, you can pay the tip too!"

Kim shouted over the laughter, "Uncle George, don't worry. One of the first things we learn in Economics is 'always give a receipt when getting and get a receipt when giving.' We'll give you a receipt when you pay the $5 you owe us. Then maybe you can claim it as a charitable donation."

George, shaking his head, said, "Drat! My niece is getting too smart for her own good. Ah! Here comes the food. Laugh and talk all you want, you guys, I'm going to eat!"

When the meal was finished, George doled five dollars out to each relative and said, "There. Pay your own tip with this, and I'll pay for the meal. See how you like being cheated!" The waiter walked away a happy man.

The Durands spent the final days of their vacation visiting antique shops and scenic areas typical of the aptly named Vacation State. George hoped that his brother was at last learning to relax and forget his worries about Dura-best Paints, as Roger had managed to refrain from calling his secretary.

Kim's use of the pay telephone at Windham's General Store was another story. Over the twelve-day stay, she had made seven phone calls to her fiancé. A shortage of coins always seemed to interrupt their conversational lovemaking. One time, in a teasing mood, Kim said to Carl, "And then we went on a hayride, and this handsome farm boy leaned over and kissed . . ." Suddenly the telephone operator cut in and said, "Please deposit two more quarters." Kim began frantically shaking her purse upside-down, but only bills dropped out. The line went dead.

The next time Kim called, Carl was ready with a fabrication of his own. "Kim, it was so nice of that farm boy to kiss you. That made him happy, so I'm making our little cashier happy. She sits on my lap every lunch hour. You and I are doing our part to spread happiness."

Kim responded, "Darling, I'm so glad you're being nice to that girl because I've lost so much weight pining over you, you will have enough room on your lap for two. You can marry both of us. We'll call it a double wedding."

He responded, "Wonderful! After the ceremony, we'll dance the two-step!"

Kim replied, "Oh lord! And I thought all the corn was up here! Carl, when I get back, you're going to get it!"

Carl lowered his voice. "I can't wait," he said. "I miss you so much I. . . "

"Please deposit fifty cents," said the operator.

Kim growled in exasperation and clunked down the phone.

Roger made only one call to his office, thanks to George, who chided him every time he mentioned calling Miss Saltmarsh. On the last day of the vacation, George said, "For God's sake, Roger! You pay managers to run things. Leave the poor girl alone. When you get back next Monday she will give you all the details about anything that may have gone wrong. Come on. Let's explore that island I pointed out the other day."

The brothers boarded George's motorboat and explored a tiny, enchanting island covered with blueberry bushes. Though most of the fruit had gone by, the ladies were able to make pies that same day from wild blueberries the farmer's wife had preserved. When Sunday came, the Durands scurried about, making sure the house was clean and secured, and they returned to Milford Connecticut late that evening. Laurie and George yielded to Sylvia's urging they spend the night at Golden Vista.

The next morning, Kim shuffled through the stack of mail that had accumulated while they were away. In it was a reply from her application to Windsor College, requesting that she appear at Dean Cronin's office any weekday between the hours of nine and five.

Later that same morning, Kim jumped into her car and drove to Windsor College. After an hour-long interview with Dean Cronin, she was accepted to teach a freshman class in the Fundamentals of Economics. Kim was told to report for orientation the following Thursday and Friday. Her position would commence November 1.

She was assigned her teaching schedule, which would occupy eighteen hours a week, for an annual salary of $6,240, plus health benefits and three weeks' vacation. This liberal schedule pleased Kim, and the 38-mile commute did not bother her. At last, her many years of studying and "burning the midnight oil" were paying off. She could impart her knowledge to others. She dropped in on Professor Kempton and thanked him for expediting her résumé and for his recommendations, which no doubt led to her acceptance. She added, "And, Professor Kempton, you might be interested to know that my Dad has hired an efficiency expert to determine what's ailing one of his outlets. I think you gave him the idea."

Kempton replied, "Oh yes. I remember—At that nice dinner. I hope it works." Then he laughed and said, "I hope he won't be mad at me if you get married and still work here afterwards."

Kim said, "Oh, I think we've got that straightened out. We'll see what the future holds. Anyway, thanks again, and do visit soon. I am honored to be on the faculty with you and will try my best to make you glad you vouched for me."

That evening, Kim called Carl to tell him she had returned from Maine. She did not want to mention her position at Windsor College until she was firmly established teaching there.

Carl said, "Gee, honey, I'm glad you're home now. It seems like a month of Sundays since you left! It's a good thing you called me those times you did. My folks said I looked like a lost soul the rest of the time. I was even getting jealous of the farm boys!"

Kim responded, "I missed you a whole lot too, but Uncle George really kept us going. We were doing festivals, fairs, plays and picnics. I enjoyed myself, but Carl, I missed you when evening came. The nights were lonely."

He teased, "Oh. Were you lonely for me, or that handsome fellow on the hayride? You said he kissed . . . and then that pesky operator cut you off. Would you care to finish what you were going to say?"

"Yes, dear. The handsome farm boy leaned over and kissed the horse!"

"Strange people, those Maine-iacs!" said Carl.

Kim said, "Speaking of strange, how about your affair with that cute little cashier? Is she coming on our date Saturday night?"

Carl responded, "You'll see."

"OK, Sweetie," she said. "Do some arm stretches so you can embrace both of us. And come over early. I love you."

Chapter 12

Fires

When Saturday finally arrived, Carl opened his arms to his one and only love, Kim. The sweet talk came in stops and starts, interrupted by kisses so urgent they found themselves speaking quickly, breathlessly, between waves of passion. Finally, Carl said, "Kim, a while ago when I was still in the service you wrote me a letter, asking if I believed that absence makes the heart grow fonder. At the time, I thought the answer was yes, but now I realize I've loved you for a very long time. It wasn't the absence that was making my heart grow fonder. It was the love—the total, enduring kind that only grows with time. I sure missed you these last two weeks." As the morning sun intimidated the night sky, Carl reluctantly tore himself away from his fiancée and headed home. It had been a splendid reunion.

Monday morning two cars left Golden Vista. One, driven by Gilbert, was headed for the local train station with Roger, who was to board the early train to New York city. The CEO was setting out to prove that only he could correct the problems that Sunrise Industries was experiencing. His daughter drove the other car north to Hartford, to her first place of employment. Her only hope was to meet the demands of her job and be the best instructor she could be.

At the end of Kim's first week of teaching, one student remained in the room after class. He appeared older than the average freshman. He approached Kim's desk and said, "Miss Durand, I'm Cliff Gardner. I'm really not a student. The college always monitors new instructors to see if they have good rapport with the students, are coherent, able to deliver the subject matter in a satisfactory manner, and so forth. Dean Cronin indicated to me that you were quite knowledgeable in your subject. I am going to report that you also know how to teach. On behalf of the college I apologize for what may seem a little—how shall I put it—underhanded, but it really is in the best interest of the students. I enjoyed playing a student of yours, and congratulations. You may scratch my name off your roster."

Gardner left the amazed and jubilant teacher. She hummed for most of the drive home, planning just what to tell her parents and future husband.

It was Friday, the last day of Mrs. Hoffman's contract with Sunrise Industries. Miss Saltmarsh answered the telephone at 4:30 p.m. and said her boss had already gone home. Mrs. Hoffman said, "Please tell him my report is complete. I think we have some helpful information for him. I plan to bring it by on Monday and we can discuss it. I'll call before leaving."

Monday morning Roger arrived at his office, cheerful and eager to receive Hoffman's report. Upon receiving her message from Miss Saltmarsh, he thought it strange that she had used a plural subject. "Are you sure she said, 'We' have some important information?" he asked his secretary.

Miss Saltmarsh nodded confidently and said "Yes, sir." Accuracy and attention to detail had always been her strong points.

Mrs. Hoffman called at 9 a.m. and was informed that Mr. Durand would meet with her at any time. She said, "Fine. I'll be there about eleven."

Roger told his secretary to call his favorite restaurant and reserve a table for two at 11:30. A leisurely lunch would provide ample time to disclose the cause of the slumping sales that vexed him. *She'll tell me what is wrong, and I will make it right,* he thought.

Mrs. Hoffman arrived promptly at eleven. Miss Saltmarsh called Durand on the intercom. "Hello, Mrs. Hoffman. I'll be with you in a minute. Keep your hat and coat on and we will meet over lunch at Romano's. The food there is very good."

Roger emerged from his office dressed for the cold. "We can walk, if you don't mind. It's only a couple of blocks from here."

Mrs. Hoffman nodded. "The walk will do me good after all the driving I've been doing. It was a nice, comfortable car, though. I hated to turn it in!" She laughed.

During the meal, Roger said, "I noted your message said 'we' have some helpful information. I wasn't aware you had a business partner."

Mrs. Hoffman replied, "I did say 'we,' meaning my husband and I. He helped do some research on weekends, on your behalf."

"You mean he accompanied you to the stores you checked on?"

"No, not at all. I had already observed enough at your various retail paint outlets to conclude that the problem was not in personnel. Your clerks and store managers attended to business, were courteous, and willing to assist customers. I saw nothing but good, honest workers, and topnotch salesmanship. I still had a hotel room in Boston for the weekend, so I called my husband to come and join me. We own a small plane that he loves to fly. He flew into Logan and I met him there."

Roger began drumming his fingertips on the table, obviously losing patience with the woman's story.

"Mr. Durand, let me tell you how my husband helped me zero in on your problem. Saturday morning, a copy of the

Boston Globe was delivered to our hotel room. I noted a huge section devoted to new homes in the classified advertisements. We wrote down their locations and my husband and I spent the weekend driving around, inspecting these new housing developments."

Mrs. Hoffman paused as the waiter took their order. Then she resumed, "My husband asked the builders about the construction and other questions a prospective buyer might ask, including what brand of paint was used."

Roger sipped his coffee and motioned for her to continue.

"At a big new development in Avon, Mass., the painting contractor said, 'We use only latex paint. It's just as durable as lead based oil paint and a hell of a lot easier to clean up. All you need is water—keeps our brushes clean, and we can thin the paint with it.' Those were his exact words. On Sunday, we saw some real expensive places in Lexington, and guess what? All those lovely new homes—sixteen of them—were painted with latex.

"Mr. Durand, your help is doing the best they can with the product they have to sell. Other stores that sell latex are taking business away from you. Since the war they have been going great guns in this building boom. Miss Saltmarsh has my written report and recommendations. I'm sorry. This probably isn't the kind of news you had hoped for."

Neither one spoke during the rest of lunch. Finally Roger pushed aside a half-eaten plate of food and stood abruptly. "I'm sorry, Mrs. Hoffman, I must run. I'm due at a meeting pretty soon. I'll read your report and forward your check per our agreement." He dropped a $20 bill on the table and left.

Mrs. Hoffman was astounded. *What the hell ails him? she thought. His business is lousy so he takes it out on me. Poor Miss Saltmarsh—working for that kook.* She gathered her purse and hat and automatically reached for her car keys, quickly realizing she no longer had use of the company car. *Damn! That. s.o.b. left me stranded, too!*

The disgruntled CEO of Sunrise Industries bolted into his outer office, startling Miss Saltmarsh. He ordered her to retrieve the Northpoint contract and mail a check to them for services rendered by Hoffman. Then he had her mail Hoffman's report to his home in Milford. His secretary said, "Don't you want to read it now?"

He responded, "No. From what she told me at lunch, I know it's going to be a bunch of rubbish. I don't want it in this office. The idea of that woman taking her husband on a fact-finding mission instead of following my orders. No wonder she charges so much!"

Miss Saltmarsh averted her eyes. She had already studied Hoffman's report.

Roger Durand felt he was back to square one. He pondered the slump in sales, recalling Professor Kempton's tale about the grain and feed store in Maine that had overcome a drop in sales by undercutting its competition with a price reduction. That afternoon, he sent out directives instructing all Dura-best Paint stores to reduce the price of a gallon of paint by one dollar. Independently owned hardware stores were granted an equal wholesale cost reduction, and encouraged to pass the savings on to their customers. He told Miss Saltmarsh to be sure to obtain sales reports from the accounting department one month after the notices were sent out.

After a month of teaching, Kim felt comfortable at her job, and confident about divulging her secret to Carl—that she was gainfully employed. She phoned him and said, "Tell you what—Tomorrow, instead of you taking me to dinner and the dancehall, I insist on driving to your house, picking you up, and taking you to the Brahma Restaurant in New Haven for a sumptuous meal. Then we'll set off to Marlin's Dance Hall, where Gary and his orchestra are performing. We can dance the night away. Later, Sweetie, maybe I'll even take you parking. And I will pay for everything! I have something to tell you— but not over the phone."

Carl slapped his forehead and said, "Wow! I feel like we've swapped genders! Why should you pay for my pleasure of having a date with you?"

She answered, "They say it's the woman who pays and pays, but I haven't paid yet. Just let me do this. You'll understand when you hear the news I've been saving for you."

"All right, I'll go under protest because I love you."

The next evening turned cold, with a few snowflakes wending their way to the ground. Kim picked up her fiancé and drove to New Haven, where they enjoyed a fabulous shrimp dinner at the Brahma. After they ordered dessert, Carl leaned in close to Kim and said, "So what is that special something you wanted to tell me?"

Kim squeezed her palms together and smiled brilliantly. Then she took a deep breath and began, "A while back, we had some friends for dinner—the Kemptons, Ed and Gladys. Ed is a professor at Windsor College in Hartford. When he found out I have a degree in Economics from Yale, he suggested I turn in a résumé to the college. I did that a little over a month ago. After an hour-long interview with the dean, I was appointed to teach there. I've been teaching Economics for just one month yesterday. I didn't tell you because I wanted to be sure I could do the job. Now you know!"

Carl gazed off and said, "Really?"

Kim raised her eyebrows. "'Really'? Don't you approve of my working? I thought you would be ecstatic, or at least say 'that's wonderful' or 'great!'"

"Oh no, I didn't mean to sound negative," said Carl. "I am really thrilled you have that position. It just made me think about how fast American culture is changing. I understand that a majority of doctors in Russia are women. Russian women do lots of men's work. Real hard work. During the last war they actually had female tank commanders. Now that culture is becoming more prevalent here. We never had women in the military service before WWII. Sure, we had nurses in WWI, but they were not military people. In the teaching profession, women did most of the teaching in the lower grades, but men teachers took precedence in high school and college. A female professor was a rarity. Now lots of women are doing what you are doing. More and more, we see women chemical, electrical, you name it, engineers. What was inconceivable a few years ago is fact now."

"Sure," responded Kim. "It's about time. There are women generals and high officers in the Army and Navy today. I have a friend, Catherine Brice, who's in the Air Force. She had duty at Alamogordo, New Mexico. One day a rocket launch was scheduled. The colonel and a staff sergeant drove out to the launch to act as observers. Well, Catherine was working around the rocket, high up on an access platform when a gust of wind blew her skirt up for a second or two. The colonel saw it and said to his aide, 'Call the Air Police. We can't have exhibitions like that. Those airmen on duty won't know what the hell they are doing with a sideshow going on. Tell them to come to this staff car and I'll give them orders to haul that woman to my office.' Well, his staff sergeant did as he was told. The Air Police escorted Catherine to the colonel's office and they arrived just after the colonel. She walked into his office and asked what the problem was.

"The colonel said 'Tell me your name, and then we'll talk.' She told him, 'Catherine Brice', and the colonel said, 'I'm Col. Brennan and the sergeant here is my secretary. We went out to observe the launch of the rocket and saw how your skirt hiked up. My men are trying to work out there. I won't have a woman working on this field if it's going to create problems. You know what I mean.'

"She said, 'Well, I'll be damned. I wasn't doing a strip tease out there. I'm sure your men cross the border on their time off to see real strip shows. If that's what bothers you, issue me a pair of coveralls in your smallest size and I'll go back to work.'

"The colonel looked taken aback and was about to give her a lecture when she said, 'By the way, Colonel, I outrank you in two ways. I'm a civilian and my grade is GS-16. Also, I'm in charge of this project, and if the lab gets word of this delay the fur will fly. So get me those coveralls and get me transportation back there, and I won't report you!'

"Miss Brice was a physicist for the Rocket Lab at Hanscom Field. She graduated summa cum laude from MIT and, to her credit, perfected a rocket propulsion system that was much less prone to explosion on ignition than previous designs. The colonel later apologized to Catherine. She said the men didn't seem as anxious to work at the rocket site after she donned the coveralls, though!"

Carl laughed and shook his head. "Yes, things are changing—women rocket scientists, women generals, college professors, doctors, lawyers, bankers, and women doing every kind of manual labor. Fifty years ago, those positions were for men. Now it seems men are making a mistake that could land them at the bottom of the pay scale. I hope I'm wrong, but I believe men are foolishly avoiding professional occupations that require hours of studying and burning the midnight oil. I think a lot of us are being deluded by the fanfare and ballyhoo good football and baseball players get. Many colleges these days give preferential treatment to good athletes. Low grades are overlooked because the players draw big money-paying crowds to the stadiums. I think in the next century, women will domineer in all professions and men will have the crappy jobs, or serve as grunts in the Army. Many will be taking care of the kids while their professional wives are away at work. I'll even bet some of these professional and workingwomen will choose to be single mothers. Then you will see childcare businesses springing up all over this country. I hope I'm wrong about that."

An agitated Kim responded, "Then you do object to my working at the college, don't you?"

"Hell no!" he answered. "I'm always happy when women who study and sacrifice like you did get what they strive for. It doesn't make them any less feminine." He paused to lightly trace the contour of Kim's cheek with his thumb.

"But do you know what rankles me?" he added suddenly.

Kim smiled adoringly and simply shook her head.

"It's the insidious suggestion by ignorant people that if a male is lousy in sports or can't drink a keg of beer, or always has his nose in a book, he's not a man. When the macho pressure is on, many men say to hell with learning, and end up poor slobs!"

Kim said, "Carl, you're right about that. I've watched football games at Yale. I can imagine how the player felt when he made a touchdown and the spectators and all those pretty cheerleaders screamed for joy. And I can imagine how his teammates felt when they didn't get that attention. Carl, the male ego may be his downfall. But you, dear—you're different."

Carl smiled modestly and turned his face to the window. "Yikes! Speaking of downfall!" he exclaimed, pointing outside. White crystals were pelting the glass, filling in the corners of the windows with cottony webs. The leisurely meal had allowed the snow to accumulate unnoticed. Now the trip to Marlin's Dance Hall seemed out of the question. "The best laid plans of mice and men oft go astray, as the saying goes, but in this case it's the woman's plan that's gone astray," said Carl. They agreed to drive to Carl's house to pick up his jalopy. Then Kim would follow her fiancé in her car to Golden Vista, where they could spend the balance of the evening.

They arrived at Kim's to a relieved Sylvia who had been worried about her daughter's lack of experience driving in a bad snowstorm. She exclaimed, "Come in, you two snowbirds. Martha just made a pot of hot chocolate. We were hoping you wouldn't travel halfway to Hartford to dance. Besides, you'd catch your death dressed like that in this weather."

Carl kidded Sylvia, "Why, we were going to dance naked in this weather, but Kim got cold feet. Just ask her." He nodded to Kim.

Kim's eyes twinkled. "No, mother. It wasn't my cold feet at all. It was Carl's rear end. After he took his clothes off, he tried to do the two-step and slipped and fell on his buns. He has a hard enough time dancing, let alone when his rear end is frozen."

Sylvia smirked and told them, "You kids are terrible! Why, in our day, Dad and I never had such problems. We knew the right thing to do. We always wore snowshoes when we danced naked in the snow!"

Just then Martha bustled in with a tray of steaming mugs of hot chocolate. Head shaking, she muttered, "Evil family. They'll never go to Heaven. Gilbert and I will. We dance naked only in summer. Now have some of this heavenly cocoa. It will warm all those cold places!"

Carl said, "Thank you, Martha. You're an angel."

Sylvia excused herself to join Roger in the study. "Maybe the hot chocolate will calm his nerves after reading that crazy business report he got from, as he puts it, 'That dumb Hoffman woman.'" She bade the couple goodnight and left them alone in the den.

Carl asked Kim if she knew who the "dumb Hoffman woman" was. Kim answered, "I haven't met her but I'm surprised Dad called her dumb. A month ago he praised her and hired her as an efficiency expert to find out the cause of some troubles in his paint business. He believed his employees were goofing off, interfering with sales at his stores. She was to find the loafers so Dad could fire them. I guess he's been reading her report."

Carl put his arm around Kim. "Hmmm. A woman efficiency expert. That's something. Goes back to what we were talking about earlier."

They chatted for another hour about the effects of women's progress on the male ego. The next time Carl glanced out the window, he saw snow drifting at an acute angle under the lantern at the outer corner of the house. A peaked white cap atop the wrought iron fixture had grown at least three inches since they'd arrived.

"Kim, speaking of ego, I go—home," he said.

Kim pouted.

Carl tried for more humor. "If I no go now, I need snowplow. So perhaps I stay and sleep with you, eh?"

She laughed. "Nay, nay. Not today. Ask again another day!"

She kissed him on the nose and said, "I love you, clown!"

Carl said, "Kim, I'm sorry I was on my soapbox so long. I must have bored you. If I ever start going on like that again, please stop me."

He stood, clasped his arms around his sweetheart and lifted her to his face. Then he kissed her and bade her goodbye until the next weekend.

Miss Saltmarsh delivered the first month's sales records reflecting the reduced price program that Mr. Durand had formulated to boost sales for Dura-best Paint products. Several stores in rural areas showed a moderate increase in sales. However, rural areas never produced volume sales, as compared to those in the suburbs, where new homes were sprouting up like mushrooms. The lower prices failed to sway contractors and builders in suburbia. They simply preferred the trouble-free latex paint. Some urban do-it-yourselfers did purchase Dura-best Paints at the reduced price, but their impact on the total sales picture proved miniscule in light of Roger's expectations. He told his secretary that sales were always off during winter months, and would increase substantially when warmer weather came. With his new price structure, Dura-best Paints would soon be back in the driver's seat where it belonged.

Miss Saltmarsh replied weakly, "I certainly hope so, Mr. Durand." Her mind was muddled with facts she had read in a recent trade magazine, stating that lead based paint was toxic and could cause brain damage to children who ingested it in the form of dried chips or paint dust.

The following week, Roger brought the regular monthly board meeting of Sunrise Industries to order. After reading the secretary's report and approving the minutes of the previous meeting, he opened with, "Well, here it is—Friday again, another month and another opportunity to advance our corporation. If there are no requests to read the complete minutes of last month's meeting, we shall begin our discussions." The CEO then made his customary request for suggestions on ways to increase business or decrease expenses, or to present new manufacturing techniques for the corporation. Roger glanced briefly around the table. "The Chairman recognizes Mr. Harris. Let's hear what you have to say, John."

John Harris offered, "Roger, I read of a company, one of our competitors. They're copper plating the bottoms of the cooking utensils they manufacture. This really improves the heat distribution, and prevents burning in fry pans or cook pots, due to uneven heating from gas flames or electrical heating elements. It also reduces cooking time, which translates to fuel economy. Copper plating is not hampered by any patent rights, so I suggest our utensil plant begin copper plating its cookware."

"Good idea, John. I'll forward your suggestion to our research department. Anyone else?"

Mr. Beckhart addressed his superior, "Mr. Durand, I respectfully offer this as a cost–saving idea for Sunrise Industries. As you know, we spend many thousands of dollars to purchase paper stock for the fabrication of our line of paper plates, cups, and other picnic ware, and to manufacture shipping boxes—a big seller. Since we have hundreds of acres of pine trees in the South, I suggest we make paper pulp instead of turpentine from our own trees. By retrofitting our turpentine manufacturing plants, we can make enough paper to meet our own needs, and sell the surplus. This country's use of paper has more than doubled over the past few years. There's a huge market out there."

Roger Durand wet his lips and smiled condescendingly. "Well, Bob," he replied. "Your suggestion has its merits, of course, but I cannot not go along with it because turpentine is one of the most important products in the paint industry. For every gallon of Dura-best Paint that's sold, a can of turpentine is also sold. I don't have to tell you how effective it is as a paint thinner, and how well it cleans up paint spills and all that. No, Bob. I won't have our pinewoods decimated to make paper. It would be detrimental to sales for our paint outlets. Sunrise will always buy its paper stock, and that's that."

Board member Roland Powers rose without being recognized and blurted out, "Roger, what the hell is this fixation you have about turpentine? Bob's idea is a damn good one and should be looked into. Why, there are synthetic paint thinners on the market today that work just as well with your precious lead paints. And speaking of paints, I see the profit margin for your damn Dura-best Paints is so small that funds from our other products are being used to meet its expenses. In fact, the future of the entire lead paint business stinks. Why in hell do you sell only lead-based oil paint? Companies that have gone to latex are giving Dura-best Paints a kick in the ass—pardon, Miss Saltmarsh—but that's what's happening."

"Just a damn minute," Roger yelled. "Who asked you to comment, and how dare you criticize me? I'm running this firm and I know what I'm doing. Miss Saltmarsh, delete Powers's remarks from your notes. Powers, another outburst like that and I'll convene the board members and have you kicked out."

A chorus of "no" rang out from the members.

Once again, Powers shouted out of turn. "Mr. Chairman, you need a two-thirds majority as per the company's by-laws to do that and the 'no's I just heard seem to indicate that won't happen."

Roger looked as if someone had thrown hot coffee in his face. In a moderated tone, he said, "OK. So right now, paint sales are down. But I reduced the cost of our paint, and you'll see, as the good weather comes, our sales will become competitive with that of latex. You know, this watered down stuff is just a passing fancy. When users find out it doesn't protect wood and other surfaces like lead based oil, they will come back to Dura-best Paints."

This time, Powers raised his hand, and Roger said, "All right, Roland. What now?"

"I hope what I say now stays in the record book," Powers said, glaring. "Everyone is looking for convenience and lower costs. Well, sir, latex paint can be cleaned up with water, thinned out with water, and applied to damp surfaces. Now, let's see, does anyone here know what a gallon of water costs? How about the cost of that stuff you need to clean up or thin out oil-base paint—our good friend turpentine? It's not only high in price; it's high in flammability. And another benefit: use it in a confined space and soon your workers are floating to la-la land on the fumes!"

"That's enough, Powers. Miss Saltmarsh, I order you to strike those remarks. At our next meeting, I intend to show an improvement in sales. Then Powers will have nothing to be so riled up about. This meeting is adjourned."

Roger left the boardroom immediately. Miss Saltmarsh remained seated to rewrite the minutes, omitting Mr. Powers's comments. As Powers lingered over the coffeemaker, he eyed the crumpled sheet with his original statements written on it, snatched the paper off the table, and vacated the room.

As Murphy's Law would have it, the short but stormy board meeting was followed by a crisis. The phone in Roger's adjacent office was ringing as he entered the room. The call was from the plant manager of the company's turpentine refining plant near Jessup Georgia. A fire had broken out in the main plant. It was extinguished, but enough damage had been done to curtail production of the solvent until repairs could be made and new equipment procured. To Roger's relief, no one was injured.

He told the plant manager to secure the area as best he could, and to expect a team of engineers and workers he would be sending in a few days to rebuild the destroyed portions of the plant. Roger would inform the engineering department on Monday, as they had already gone for the weekend. He made a note also to check about insurance coverage for the Jessup facility.

Roger set the phone down and picked it back up. He dialed home and arranged for Gilbert to meet him at the train depot. No point compounding his frustration with an onslaught of heavy Friday evening traffic. Besides, the train ride would give him time to sort things out in his mind and plan resolutions.

On the train that evening, Roger reflected on all that had transpired. *That damn spook, Powers,* he thought. *He had just mouthed off about turpentine being flammable. This guy is worse than Higgins. What the hell can I do about him?* As the train rumbled along, Roger's mind began pulling things together. *Maybe I can entice Powers to start an unlisted affiliate of Sunrise Industries with funds from our bank, the same way Higgins did. If he fails, the bank takes over his enterprise. Boy—that would tickle me. But if he succeeds, we make money on it. By God, I'll demand he keep me out of this too, just like Higgins. Then Powers will be out of my hair, and I won't have to listen to his crap at board meetings.* As Roger's thoughts spiraled, his spirits soared. By the time he stepped off the train, he felt a major thorn had been removed from his side.

"Hi, Rog. Over here!" called Sylvia from the train station.

Roger hurried to his wife, gave her a bear hug and a kiss, and asked, "Is Gilbert paying you for this? Or are you just anxious to meet your handsome husband in this romantic setting?"

Sylvia shook her freshly coiffed hairdo and said, "I guess this place might look like a tunnel of love to someone with a one-track mind like yours!"

"Oh, Lord," he gasped. "Sarcasm at work, sarcasm in the tunnel of love. If I run into any more sarcasm, the sarcaster will get the Higgins-Powers treatment."

His wife said, "Oh oh. Another sour board meeting? Let's go get the car and you can fill me in on the drive home." She took his arm. "As for whether Gilbert paid me—No. I paid him not to come. I bribed him with all your fancy liquors and favorite wines."

"Sylvia, you were very thoughtful to do that. Gilbert is much too sober when he drives us around. No excitement in that."

Sylvia purposely swerved the car. "Thazz right," she slurred, weaving her head side to side, making Roger laugh for the first time all day. "Now tell me about this Higgins-Powers treatment," she said.

Roger gave his wife all the details of the fiery board meeting. He characterized Powers as "that spook" who talked about the dangers of fire from turpentine. "The next thing I know, the plant in Georgia burns down."

Sylvia listened sympathetically, then said she would beg Gilbert for a little wine for poor Rog.

When they arrived home, the Popes had already arrived, and Martha had cocktails waiting prior to a tasty meal. Kimberly joined her parents and guests. During dinner, Grace inquired whether Kim had a date with Carl. Kim answered, "Not tonight. I have several examination papers to correct. But he'll probably call and we'll make plans for the rest of the weekend."

Her dad said, "Kim, your boyfriend sure is taking his time about getting engaged. If he doesn't ask soon, a pretty girl like you could be snatched away from him by one of her students. I stole your mother away from a bashful boyfriend she had, but of course, I was a lot more handsome."

Kim responded, "Oh, Dad, don't embarrass me and don't rush us to the aisle."

Sylvia interjected, "Roger cried so much when I went out with other men that I married him out of pity. And he wasn't that handsome."

They all laughed and the small talk escalated. Kim bade everyone a good evening and retired to the little anteroom next to her bedroom. She slid open the cover to a small roll-top desk and commenced correcting examination papers until Carl called.

He said, "Hi, beautiful. I won't keep you. I know you're busy now, but tomorrow evening Doug and Hazel want us over for dinner. He didn't mention the occasion, but he sounded rather mysterious and insisted we come. Anyway, we can spend the day together, and then drive over there. Is that OK?"

She replied, "Swell. Come over around eleven. I love you."

About 10:45 the next morning, Carl parked his car in the guest space at Golden Vista and walked to the garage and living quarters for the Durands' servants. Through the open garage doorway, he noticed Gilbert dusting off one of the vehicles. The chauffeur looked up and beckoned Carl to come in. Carl said, "Morning, Gilbert. I see you're shining Mrs. Durand's wagon."

"Morning, Carl," said Gilbert. "Take a look at this." He pointed to a dusting of paint flecks on the garage floor, then to several bare spots on Sylvia's favorite car.

"I can polish the metal parts of this baby, but look what happens when I just barely wipe the dust off the wood. I've oiled the bare spots, but they keep increasing. Hope Mrs. Durand buys a new car one of these days."

Carl said, "Oiling the bare spots will help for a while. Maybe one of these days she will have it refinished. Kim says her mom loves this station wagon better than she loves her own daughter."

Carl glanced up at the wall clock. "Hey, speaking of Kim, I've got a date. Take care, Gilbert."

Chapter 13

Deep Space

Kim and Carl never had problems finding interesting things to do. They pored over Kim's stack of newsletters about weekend college lectures, symposiums, and celebrity appearances until they hit upon an event that intrigued them both. Later that afternoon, Yale University was to present a lecture titled, "The Astronomy of Deep Space," by an astronomer they'd both read and admired.

Carl said, "Let's head out there. You buy lunch, or I'll let you pay for lunch—your preference. Then we can go to the lecture and drive to Doug's afterwards for dinner. How's that?"

Kim answered, "Good. Since it's at my Alma Mater, your lunch proposal seems very fair. I will also leave the tip. I know a bargain when I see it."

He said, "Fine. My generosity knows no bounds."

Kim's mother overheard their chaffing from the adjoining room and couldn't help saying, "Carl, make sure she thanks you. And try to keep all the spooning on the table."

"Oh, of course, Mrs. Durand," Carl said wryly. "Anyway, the lecture is about astronomy. Kim will catch on soon about moon and spoon."

As they started toward the door, Sylvia thrust out her right arm and pronounced, "Go forth, my children, and acquire knowledge to fill the voids behind your foreheads."

Giggling, Kim said, "Carl, let's leave this nuthouse."

Mrs. Durand called back, "Carl, we love you because you're daft like us. Have fun, and goodnight."

Carl and Kim were captivated by the astronomy lecture. The speaker's well-chosen words and his extraordinary slide show cast them into a deeply pensive mood that contrasted all the earlier banter and silliness. On the drive back to Milford, they fell silent. Both were contemplating the vastness of space, the lingering effects of the lecture propelling their minds to higher realms than either had dared venture to before. Finally, Carl said, "Kim, what we saw this afternoon would humble the haughty, confound the atheist, and comfort the meek. I'm not much on religious stuff, but delving into the mysteries of outer space makes the notion of a creator or supreme being more believable. I guess you could go crazy thinking beyond the physical, wondering about the nature of such a creator. Did you ever ask yourself how the creator was created?"

Kim's face softened. She placed her hand on Carl's arm and said, "Don't dwell on that. You put yourself in the category of an atheist, but you are as awed by this deep space concept and the creation of stars as I am. Just believe, Carl. Just believe. I do, and it's a lot more comforting than being an atheist."

Carl shook his head and said, "Yes, I know."

When they arrived at Douglas's home, they were not surprised to see Freda Graf open the front door. She yelled out, "You remember me—the official greeter for my brother's friends? Come in, come in!"

As she ushered them into the entry hall, Carl asked, "So what's the occasion? I know Doug well enough to detect when he's got something up his sleeve."

Freda put her fingers to her lips and said, "Shhh. They told me not to tell." She pointed to the doorway of the family room.

Carl peered in to see Douglas talking to a man whose back was to the doorway. He noticed the left sleeve of the man's jacket hung limply by his side.

Douglas greeted his guests as they entered the room, and said, "I hope you're not easily shocked." Then he turned to the man and said, "Captain, here's my buddy, Carl, and his girlfriend, Kim."

The man turned and faced the couple.

"Carl, remember our prison mentor, Captain Campbell?"

Carl's face turned ashen. He finally managed to say, "Good God, you're alive!"

The two men embraced, then pushed apart to study each other's face at arm's length, shaking their heads and laughing all the while.

Finally, Carl said, "Kim, this is the man who made it possible for us to get away from the Krauts. My gosh, I'm so glad you're alive! Doug and I read a report about that place burning down. Did many get out? Your arm—what happened?"

Doug interrupted, "Hey, let's sit down, have a drink and relax. Capt. Campbell needs to catch his breath and fortify his stomach."

After his wife served cocktails, Douglas told his friends how he and Hazel had taken a trip to Boston. While there, he'd gone to the Canadian consulate to request the address of a Captain Campbell who had been a P.O.W. in Stalagluft Five. He told the consulate only that the captain had been in the regular Royal Canadian Air Force. The official expressed doubt about finding such a person, but the Canadian Air Force came through with a Capt. Percy Campbell who was at one time a P.O.W. in a camp destroyed by fire. They believed it was Stalagluft Five. "The consulate sent me the address of our friend, here, I invited him for a stay, and here we are," exclaimed Doug.

Capt. Campbell said, "Damn. They gave out my first name. Yanks used to poke fun at 'Percy'. They'd stop when I poked them back, but I guess I'd better behave now that I have only half a left arm." He laughed.

Carl asked what had happened.

The captain answered, "Well, it isn't a happy story, I'll tell you that from the beginning." He paused to light a cigarette, showing off his developing one-handed dexterity while his friends shifted uncomfortably, wondering whether or not to assist him. He completed the task, inhaled deeply, and blew smoke toward the ceiling. "About a month after you two escaped, I was sitting outside by the prison stairs, with my back to the wall. I thought I heard a plane flying around to the south of our cozy abode. Damn Krauts coming in with another inspection team, I was thinking. But then I heard shots. I thought, the fools are target practicing in the field. A sudden blast woke us up to the fact that something was amiss. That's when all hell broke loose. As I said, I was sitting on the ground by the stairs. I heard the exit doors smash open and Capt. Smyth came running out yelling, 'Come on! Get the hell out of here!' I saw smoke pouring out the doorway. He kept screaming, 'Everyone into the yard! Don't block the exit!' Well, the German guards thought it was an escape attempt and started shooting as the men poured out. Smyth yelled for them to hold their fire—the goddamn building was ablaze, and men were going to be roasted alive. Capt. Smyth spoke German so he was our go-between when we had to ask them certain things, but he wasn't able to stop the slaughter. The confusion was terrible. Capt. Smyth yelled down to me, 'Help me get these men away from the exit. Pull them down to the ground.'

"Just then, a shot caught him in the head. He toppled over the railing and landed on the bodies that were heaped all around me. Through all this shooting I saw Col. Schneider screaming at his guards, telling them to hold their fire and let the men escape the building, that it really was ablaze. He was frantic, but finally gained control and the shooting stopped—a little late for me. I caught a bullet in my left elbow." He shrugged his right shoulder. "Next thing I know, I'm waking up in some German hospital, minus one arm. Anyway, over 60 of our men were either killed by gunfire or burned to death. Some Germans were also shot by accident in that mad confusion."

Campbell paused to scratch his left sleeve at the severed end of his arm. He remarked, "It still gets itchy there."

He continued, "One of our buddies in the hospital was one of the first ones out. I think you two know him. He's the one who tapped on the floor to let you know if the coast was clear for your escape. Anyway, he described to me exactly how the building had caught fire. His bunk was next to a window overlooking the south area. He was trying to catch a few winks after breakfast while that Nazi plane was parked on the taxi strip across from his window. The engine noise teed him off, and he looked out just in time to see some aircraft sweep down and fire shots at the idling plane. A huge flash went up, and flames swept toward his open window. He ran like hell for the exit, yelling, 'Get out! Get out!' to the guys goofing off on their bunks. He stumbled down the stairs and broke his arm, but he got up again and ran into the yard. He sat there watching from a safe distance as they all streamed out of the building and the shooting began."

"My God," Carl said, "We read a report from a slightly more clinical perspective: Around August 29, '43, an RAF pilot strafed a small aircraft with German insignias on a taxi strip near a military compound. The pilot stated the plane was hit and exploded with a flame that spread to the adjacent compound." Captain, I feel terrible that you and those others who helped Doug and I get away from there are either hurt like you, or dead, while here we are . . ."

Capt. Campbell interrupted, "That's just what your friend Douglas said. Don't think like that. What you guys did was such a long shot that no one thought you would make it. Capt. Smyth told me he hoped we hadn't sent you fellows to your maker. I myself wondered what the hell I was thinking, to risk such a damn fool idea—two young guys wasted by a crazy old army man. None of us tried to escape through that sealed window. Not one of us had the guts to try fleeing at night when the chance of getting away was better. But, by God, you did it in broad daylight! For a short while I convinced myself your chances of getting away weren't so bad. Then Col. Schneider told me you were shot down and crashed into the English Channel. Those of us involved in your escape felt guilty as hell—like accessories to your murders. When Doug here sent a letter inviting me to visit him and Hazel, I felt that a burden I was doomed to carry for the rest of my days was lifted. I was overjoyed. I bowed my head and did what I should have done long ago. Thank you for finding me, Douglas!"

Carl admonished Campbell. "You had no cause to feel guilty. Why, Capt. Smyth and you agreed that we prisoners needed hope to somehow escape. It grieved you and Smyth to see a desperate man like Graves risk his life when his chances were absolutely nil. No sir, you gave Doug and me hope and a plan that worked. I thank you, Doug thanks you, Hazel thanks you, and my girlfriend, Kim, thanks you, as do our families. We love you. Because of your scheme, we are alive today!"

Douglas clamped his hands onto his knees, stood up, and proclaimed, "War stinks! Let's go to the dining room. I guarantee the food is a wee bit better than prison chow."

Hazel and Freda, hands on hips, responded, "Only a wee bit, eh? No second helpings for you."

Hazel added, "Yes, my cooking is so bad that poor Douglas has gained only 65 pounds since he left the service."

It was a joyful gathering around the table that evening. After dessert, Douglas asked Campbell, "Captain, what ever happened to your flask?"

He responded, "I had it in my jacket pocket when I got shot. When I woke up in the hospital, the jacket was gone. If someone took that flask, I hope they washed it good. I never had enough hot water in that place to clean it right."

Campbell wondered why the women were laughing along with the men. Douglas had told Hazel what the flask was used for, and Hazel had passed the information to Kim, her sister-in-law, and who knows how many others. When dinner was over, host and guests gathered in the family room where the men shared several details of their military experiences. The ladies listened with rapt attention, for neither Carl nor Douglas had been very talkative about that part of their lives. Capt. Campbell's presence served as a catalyst to revealing the untold mysteries their loved ones had kept bound up inside them. As the evening wore on, the secrets unfolded one by one, until weariness set in.

Carl and Kim thanked Doug and Hazel for the reunion, which had eased so many troubling thoughts. On leaving, Kim kissed the unsuspecting captain and said, "Thank you. You may have saved two people a lot of grief. Because of you, Hazel is not a widow and perhaps I won't become an old maid." She flashed Carl a coy smile. "Give us your address. Who knows? We may have to send you a wedding invitation one of these days!"

Carl embraced Campbell and bade the Grafs goodnight. Driving Kim home, he entertained kinder thoughts of Douglas than he'd ever dreamed possible.

Chapter 14

The Decline

Roger's plan to offer an affiliate business to Roland Powers in order to spare antagonism at future board meetings failed miserably. Roger settled back in his seat, awaiting Powers's grateful acceptance. Instead, he heard, "Durand, I don't give a hoot about starting a new business. You can get a lot more mileage out of me in an advisory capacity. Perhaps you don't know that I am on the board of directors of General Motors, Bell Telephone, Dow Chemical Co., and a couple other firms. They value my criticism. When I think someone's got a good idea, I tell him so. If I think it stinks, I advise him to toss it. I don't do this because of arrogance. I have a hobby of digesting every article published by a dozen or more trade magazines, which gives me the knowledge to evaluate an idea. I'm neither your friend nor your enemy. I just want the companies I have an interest in to make money, not lose it. When they make money, so do I. Mr. Durand, read some articles comparing lead-based oil paint and latex paint, and give some thought to manufacturing paper. It's white gold today. Now if you'll excuse me, I have another appointment." He hurried out of the CEO's office.

Roger sat immobilized for several minutes. Then he thought, *He can go to hell. I'll run this firm my way! When Dura-best paint sales regain a profit, I'll embarrass him before all the board members for his know-it-all attitude.*

Miss Saltmarsh interrupted his train of thought with a call on the intercom. "Mr. Herbert Worthley on the line for you."

Worthley, president of Sunrise Merchants Trust, said, "Roger, I'm calling you about the reserve funds we hold for Dura-best Paint stores. No doubt you are aware that moneys from these stores are falling short of covering payroll. This has been going on for some time. At this rate, the reserve funds will be exhausted in a few more months. Now I need some input from you. Shall we take money from Sunrise's general fund to meet these payrolls? As you know, the corporate bylaws state if a subsidiary's funds drop below $150,000, that branch must be closed down and its employees terminated. Shall we keep funneling money from the general fund to keep Dura-best afloat before it hits that level?"

Roger answered testily, "Yes, of course. I know the situation, but this is only a seasonal thing. Keep the money coming from the main fund. You will see the trend reverse itself in a short time. Keep cool, Herb. The building boom projected for the coming good weather will save us. Thanks for calling, and don't worry."

Worthley's secretary, Miss Chadwick, informed her boss that Mr. Higgins was waiting to see him. Before getting down to business with him, Herb said, "I want to tell you about a phone call I just had with our CEO, Roger Durand. I called to caution him about the reserve fund for Dura-best Paints approaching the cut-off point for those paint stores he cherishes. You know, we have been sending payroll money to these stores in excess of the revenue they generate for us. So I asked him if we should keep taking money from the general fund, or shut down his pets. He became cantankerous and told me to keep the funds coming. He claims the slump is a seasonal thing. When the building boom resumes in the spring, profits will reappear. What do you make of his reasoning? I think he is throwing good money after bad."

Higgins answered, "That guy isn't keeping up with today's technology. He thinks the name Dura-best automatically lends an aura of excellence unmatched by any paint on the market. The truth is, chemists have developed enamels and finishes far superior to those formulated just a few years back. I took advantage of their technology when I created Everbright Paints. The military has bought tons of our synthetic coatings. You mention throwing good money after bad. Do you remember the board meeting we attended before the war? I suggested we branch out into additional businesses that would be moneymakers, producing materials crucial to the war effort. He was cool to that idea. When I said, 'What's the matter, Rog, afraid to make money?' he got miffed, and you know what happened after that. I'm making money for Sunrise, but Dura-best Paints is losing it. He's not just afraid of making money, he's not afraid of losing it!"

"Yes, Andrew. I remember that meeting very well. You pointed out that military equipment, especially Navy stuff, needs coating impervious to salty environments and you were right. When your business was booming in the war years, I questioned you about competing with the big guy's pet project. Dura-best sticks to house paints for the most part. Of course, Roger never once inquired as to the nature of your business. All these years, I haven't told him, and he hasn't asked. He just wanted you off the board, and out of sight. He is aware that more money is going into the General Fund, but never questioned its source. I often wondered, if he found out you created Everbright Paint Company, would he have the bank terminate it? He probably would think, how dare he compete with me? Roger can't stand anyone disagreeing with him. At the last board meeting, Roland Powers told our boss he was wrong to throw out Beckhart's suggestion that Sunrise manufacture its own paper for the products we punch out. This galled Durand so much that he offered the same deal to Powers that he gave to you. But I understand Powers told the CEO to stuff it. He's still a board member."

Higgins responded, "Good for Powers! What a horse's ass that Durand is! Let me tell you, Herb, if he ever tries terminating Everbright, I would campaign like hell to get the stockholders to vote Roger out of office and keep my robust business. Have his sick pet, Dura-best Paints, euthanized. Imagine hanging on to something that loses money for all of us. What a blind fool!"

Herb added, "Roger is lucky, all his corporate managers are tops. That's what keeps us going. Andrew, if he is ever voted out, how would you like to become CEO of Sunrise Industries?"

Higgins eyed Worthley, shrugged his shoulders, and said, "Yeah. When they get a man on the moon. Anyway, if you would, please have your secretary make a copy of our account from your ledger. I'd like to see the quarterly report on funds remitted by our company to your bank, and a record of funds remitted to Everbright exclusive of payroll moneys. I know you mail them to my office but I like to get word on what's going on in our conglomerate, since this bank is the recipient of communications from all members of Sunrise."

Herb smiled and said, "Certainly. I reviewed the ledger yesterday, and your company's earnings are sure impressive. You've exceeded the previous quarter by more than fifteen percent, and ten percent of the profits will put your holdings in the five million dollar bracket!" He chuckled. "Don't be too surprised if they get a man on the moon soon."

The bank president called his secretary and instructed her to make a copy of the quarterly report for Everbright Paints. A few minutes later, Miss Chadwick handed it to her boss. After a quick glance at the papers, he handed them to Higgins. As he was preparing to leave, Miss Chadwick announced a call for Mr. Worthley from Roger Durand. Herb lifted his eyebrows. "What, again?" he muttered, and pushed the button on the intercom. Higgins opted not to leave yet, unless Worthley requested him to.

Roger's voice blared, "Herb, I didn't tell you! Our turpentine processing plant in Jessup, Georgia was damaged by fire. I received a call Friday from the plant manager. He told me a portion of the refinery was destroyed and must be rebuilt to resume operation. I checked some old files to see if we had insurance to cover the loss. Much to my surprise, we don't carry private insurance. I came across a memo of my dad's, dated Oct. 1937, canceling all insurance carriers, and designating Sunrise's general fund for emergency coverage. It was a cost-saving measure to eliminate premiums, since our general fund has been more than adequate for meeting such contingencies. I have dispatched a team from our engineering department to Jessup, to rebuild what's necessary and get the plant back in operation. You have my authorization to remit funds to them as needed. Mr. Coker is in charge. He will call you as invoices for building materials and labor accrue. The usual per diem, of course, will be included."

"A fire! That's too bad. I certainly will do as you say. I guess it's lucky the whole place didn't go up, with all the turpentine vats on location. I guess we are still ahead of the game after all these years of not paying premiums, especially on something as high risk as a turpentine plant."

Herb closed the connection and turned to Higgins. "You won't believe this, but at the last board meeting, Roland Powers advised the board that Durand dump the turpentine business, for a lot of reasons—one of them that the damn stuff is so highly flammable. Then our plant in Jessup, Georgia burns down. Durand must think Powers is psychic!"

Higgins merely shook his head and said, "Herb, if I wasn't here in your office, I probably would never have heard of that fire. Your office gets all the gossip. I wonder if Roger will switch to the good paint now? Oh well. Thanks a lot. When I need cash again I'll come begging." Higgins left, half a smile on his lips.

Lawrence Coker called Roger four days after arriving at the damaged turpentine plant. He said, "Mr. Durand, we have carefully assessed the damage here, and if we restore only the destroyed section, I estimate, and my colleagues agree, it will take about four months to bring the plant back into production. However, I must advise you, the whole facility is in rough shape. The part that's still standing is in such poor condition it should by all means be replaced and outfitted with new equipment. The grinding machines have been welded together numerous times. Broken gears have also been repaired. Our distilling vats are dangerously oxidized. Also, the housing for this equipment is absolutely ramshackle. The wooden storage building for the barrels of turpentine awaiting shipment leaks badly, and is dangerously close to the boiler room, which has two furnaces about to rust out. They are fueled by pinewood, which is stacked all over the place. I wouldn't be surprised if a burning twig from one of the boiler's smokestacks was what ignited the place. It's about time we replaced the boilers with the new oil-fired type. I suggest we tear this place down and build a modern refinery. Replacing the old part would be just plain foolish."

Roger interjected, "Coker, forget a new plant. By the time it's finished, our competitors would have the market sewn up, and we would be buying turpentine from them to supply our stores! We have a good five-month supply of inventory in those barrels you saw. Don't worry about the rusted boilers or the welded machinery. I was in Jessup eight years ago. They were in that condition then, and look how long they've served us. Get the job done in four months and get back here. I'll worry about everything else. That's my job. See you in four months."

It was Friday again—another weekend for Roger to enjoy away from the cares of his position. He decided to call his wife and ask if she would mind inviting George and Laurie for the weekend.

Sylvia responded, "Oh good. Laurie and I have a lot to talk about."

Roger said, "Fine. If you don't hear from me in the next hour, that means they can make it. I'll be driving home today. See you in a couple hours if I don't run into traffic. And tell Martha to cook something good. I'm mean when I'm hungry!"

His wife laughed. "What? Only when you're hungry? Drive carefully."

Laurie answered her brother-in-law's call and indicated she and George would be happy to sponge off the other Durands. She warned Roger that they had immense appetites and unquenchable thirst for the good stuff. Roger told her, "Good. Glad you can come and don't worry about food and drink, Laurie. We have three barrels of aged rainwater in our garden and a huge compost heap. You'll have a ball foraging in that good stuff. We would join you out there but Martha gets upset when we don't eat what she prepares. See you and my infant brother this evening."

Roger arrived at Golden Vista where he was warmly greeted by his wife, Laurie, and George, who was holding a glass of amber liquid in his hand.

"What's in the glass, kid brother?"

George replied, "My dear, ancient brother. This happens to be authentic aged aqua de rain barrel. And Laurie made these hors d'oeuvres de compost with her own lovely hands. Have some. May they soothe the frustrations of your recent labors."

Roger glared at his wife. "Did you show George where I hide my best liquor?"

Sylvia answered, "I got it from your hiding place. You can't hide anything from me."

Roger nibbled on an hors d'oeuvre as they headed for the family room. "This sandwich is delicious," he said. "Shall we hire Laurie for our party cook?"

"No, we can't hire Laurie. She is already working for George, like I work for you," replied Sylvia, poking her finger into his stomach.

Roger pulled up a chair. "Did you tell them about our fire in Jessup?" he asked.

"Yes," she answered. "Now let's all sit down and catch up on what's happened since the last time we got together. We're waiting dinner for Kimberly. No shoptalk, Roger. You can talk shop all day tomorrow."

"Amen to that," George spoke up. "We'll beat that horse to death tomorrow. It's never good to mix business with food or liquor, even when it's aged rain barrel water and fresh compost. By the way, Roger, would you like the fancy brown mustard, or imported soy sauce on your compost?"

"I prefer bordelaise sauce on my compost. You low lifers go for the mustard," Roger volleyed.

Kim arrived, and dinner was served. The family repeatedly derailed Roger's attempts to return the conversation to the fire in Jessup. George led the charge by injecting humor at every opportunity. Kim wondered out loud at the difference in temperament between the two brothers.

"Was Grandma Durand calm and easygoing like Uncle George, or more. . . uh . . . more like Dad?" she asked.

George replied, "She was almost always easygoing. I remember one time, a customer came into the store, hopping mad that the handle on a can of paint had let loose, spilling paint all over his walkway. Well, your grandmother didn't bat an eye at all his yelling. She smiled sweetly, handed him two gallons of paint, and said, 'I'm sorry about what happened. We didn't make the containers, but please take these—no charge.' That really knocked the wind out of him."

Roger disagreed with George's assessment. "She wasn't always easygoing," he said. "We moved from the store we'd been living in to a house on the outskirts of Hartford. It was like paradise after living in that cramped storeroom. The house had a large backyard with a small barn at one end. Next to the barn was a healthy crabapple tree. Your uncle and I used to climb up on the barn roof to pick the crabapples. Boy, were they sour. Anyway, the property next door had a wooden fence with wide spaces between the slats. On the other side of the fence was a big barn where they kept pigs. It had a chicken wire enclosure around each end, where the animals rooted around. George and I were on the barn roof one time when we got the idea that the pigs might like some crabapples. I think I threw the first apple and it hit a pig right on the nose. The pig squealed, grunted, and ate the apple. Hey, that was fun. So we both started winging apples at those pigs. Every time we hit one, we heard a squeal or grunt, but the pigs had a feast. We came down from the roof and were crawling through the fence to get a better look at the pigs when a man grabbed both of us by the suspenders, slapped our behinds, and threw us against the fence. We both screamed and cried so loud, you could hear us a mile away. Your Grandma came running out of the house, hollering, "Mr. Rand, what is going on?" He yelled back, 'Mrs. Durand, these two boys were on that roof throwing apples at my pigs.' So Ma said, 'Well, how do you normally feed your pigs—on a platter?'

"Just then, I cried, 'Mama, he threw us against the fence!'

"That did it. She lit into him. 'You big bully,' she screamed. 'Those pigs have more brains than you do. If my children come home with any bruises, I'll see to it that *you* end up in a pen!'

"I remember Mr. Rand looked really pale and shaken. He'd just seen a side of your grandmother she rarely showed."

Sylvia added, "But your grandfather—my dad, was the most serene person you could imagine. He never spanked me. If I was bad, he would say to me, 'You know what you did wasn't a very nice thing. When you do things like that it makes Mother and me very sad as we feel that we are not teaching you right from wrong. You don't want Mother to cry, do you?' And that would make me cry!

"One time he was driving my mother, brother, and me downtown for some shopping when he had to stop for a traffic light. We were sitting there, waiting for the green, when BANG—a car smashed into the back of our vehicle. When Dad got out to survey the damage, the other driver said, 'Mister, if you hadn't stopped so damn fast, I wouldn't have hit you. Didn't you know other cars were behind you? You probably wanted to get hit! I suppose you'll sue me now.' Dad answered in a voice perfectly soft and even, 'Sir, I was stopped here for over a minute. The light was red. You ran into me. You are right. I will sue you." He calmly filled out the police report and drove off as if nothing had happened. Maybe I inherited some of his temperament. It helps me put up with your father," she said with a wink.

Laurie countered, "You're lucky. My dad was just the opposite. Now, neither of my parents smoked, but dumb little me, fourteen years old, was palling around with my girlfriends in the park down the block. We met some young boys there, and of course that's when the trouble started. One of the boys— maybe 15 or 16 years old, had a pack of cigarettes. He offered some to us girls. Well, Margie took one, but Jenny and I said no. Margie started laughing at us, saying we were chicken, so I took a cigarette and started to smoke it. I choked and coughed, but foolishly kept smoking. After a bit, I felt a little woozy, and whispered to Jenny I had to go to the bathroom. When I got home, Dad opened the door and gave me a strange look. All I wanted to do was lie down, but as I hurried to my room, he was right behind me. 'Just a minute, young lady,' he said. 'Have you been smoking?' I almost lost it right there, but continued toward my room, Dad right at my heels. I said, 'I don't want to talk to you,' scooted into my room, and slammed the door right in his face. He banged the door open, slapped me hard across the face, and said, 'Don't you dare ever shut the door on me again. You do, and I'll smack your bottom so hard you won't sit down for a week.' I believed him. And, if that wasn't bad enough, he added, 'And you're not to go out or see your friends for two weeks!'"

Laurie's husband remarked, "Ha! So that's why you're only half spoiled. Your mother never punished you, but your dad made up for it!"

Laurie grinned. "Sure. Lord knows how I would have turned out if I'd had an easy-going father like you did," she said.

Kim leaned forward on her elbows. "Was Grandpa Durand really easygoing?" she asked. "All I ever hear is what a great businessman he was."

Roger launched into the conversation. "Oh, no!" he scoffed. "Dad sure had a temper and didn't try to hide it. Sometimes he'd fly off the handle for no apparent reason. When I was fourteen years old, living near Hartford, I got a part-time job as an errand boy, delivering orders for the Brook Street Market. I worked after school and all day Saturday. Well, one Friday my boss told me to be at work by six the next morning. He said he wanted to take me to the Wholesale Marketplace to pick up supplies for his store, that we had to leave early to get the best selection. I had Ma wake me bright and early, and headed in to work. I hopped into the truck with my boss, but instead of driving to the market, he went to an old warehouse building that was half burned down. A sign on the outside read 'Egg and Poultry Suppliers'. My boss went into the office in the unburned section. While he was talking to a man in there, another guy came out of the damaged part of the building carrying a crate of something. My boss put the crate in the back of our truck and we drove off. He stopped at an A&P store and sent me in to buy two dozen eggs. When I got back with the eggs, he led me to the back of the truck and opened the crate. He said, 'I get these for nothing,' and he began swapping the eggs I bought with eggs from the crate. One of them cracked, and, boy, did it stink! But he kept transferring them into the A&P cartons. Then he told me to return them to the store and get my money back. I must have looked confused, because he told me, 'It's all right. Those clerks don't give a damn. They will get credit from the company that sells them the eggs. Now go ahead. Tell them your old lady was mad as hell, if they ask you.' Well, he was the boss, so I did as he said. In fact, we did that all day long at a bunch of different stores. He got rid of 30 dozen bad eggs and got back 30 dozen good ones. He told me we'd get rid of the rest the next day. He also warned me to keep my mouth shut about it if I wanted to keep my job. I wasn't going to tell anyone, but Dad wanted to know all about what had happened at the Wholesale Marketplace that day, and I was having a hard time making things up. When I finally told him the truth, he was livid.

"He said, 'Why, that S.O.B. I read about that fire in the market district. Those eggs must have gone rotten because of the damaged refrigeration system. He made you do his dirty work, the louse. Monday you and I are going to see this scumbag.'

"Monday morning Dad and I went to the Brook Street Market and he confronted my boss. He said he should be jailed for theft and contributing to the delinquency of a minor. He created a scene in front of several customers and smacked the guy on the nose. The police came, and Dad was in trouble. They asked my boss if he wanted to press charges. He took Dad aside and said, 'Look, half a dozen people saw you hit me. If you keep your trap shut about the eggs, I won't press charges.'"

Kim sat on the edge of her seat as though watching a movie. "So what did he do?" she demanded.

Roger shrugged. "Dad agreed. But he said, 'I hope some day you get caught for such a rotten stunt. My son has to live with what he did for you, and what he saw here today will be with him for a long time.' We left the store, and Dad made me look for another job. I don't know what he was so miffed about, but that was Dad."

Kim's eyes widened. "Dad! You don't?" she screeched. "Your old boss would make a weasel look like an innocent pussycat!" She excused herself and bolted from the table. The guests withdrew to the library. The conversation shifted to lighter subject matter as they played bridge far into the night. Finally at 2:15 a.m. they enjoyed a nightcap and retired.

Kim left early the next morning to attend a basketball game with Carl at Windsor College. The others awoke later than usual to a satisfying brunch. Sylvia and Laurie decided to go shopping. They informed their spouses it would be a daylong spree, which pleased them, as Roger wanted to discuss the problems at Sunrise Industries, and George was eager to hear about them.

Sylvia alerted Gilbert that she wished to have the station wagon ready soon. The women dressed for the cool weather and set out for New Haven. Laurie mentioned that the station wagon seemed in good shape on the inside, but that the wood exterior appeared more worn than the upholstery.

Sylvia said, "I know. Rog tells me to buy a new car because this one looks shabby, but this car is my pet. I don't want a new one. I've decided to have the wooden surfaces refinished. Gilbert knows an expert at car refinishing."

The conversation turned to the latest fashions as the stylish but worn "woody" rolled along.

Back home, Roger suggested, "Let's have a few drinks. Then we can hash out some of the latest problems I need to resolve at work." The brothers raided his private liquor cabinet and consumed several shots of top shelf whiskey before Roger began, "I need to fire some personnel and get rid of a couple members on our board of directors, George. Maybe you can suggest how."

George put down his drink. "My God, what did they do?"

Roger sighed heavily. "One of the members humiliated me at the last board meeting. I asked for their suggestions on ways to increase our business. Beckhart suggested we stop production of turpentine and convert our plant in Jessup, Georgia to a paper producing plant. I said no. I don't want to decimate the trees on our holdings there. We need to produce turpentine for our Dura-best Paint stores. Well, this upstart, Roland Powers gets up without asking to talk and practically calls me a fool for not considering Beckhart's stupid idea."

"Did he actually call you a fool in front of the other board members?" asked George.

"No, but he accused me of having a fixation on turpentine. He implied that Dura-best stores were being supported by profits from our other companies. He assailed my judgment. And he swore in front of my secretary, Miss Saltmarsh."

"Really? What did he say in front of Saltmarsh?"

"He said hell, and then he said latex paints are giving Dura-best Paints a kick in the ass. I didn't like that one bit."

"Oh, you didn't like it. I doubt it bothered Miss Saltmarsh. She's heard a lot worse from you." George swirled the ice in his glass and took one more swallow. "You were mad because he told the truth about your paint," he said. "You have been trying to find out why Dura-best Paints aren't doing so well, but you won't listen to Roland Powers. I've read his articles in the trade magazines and newspapers. He is one smart cookie. You'd be making a mistake to kick him off the board. He probably gave you damn good advice, and so did Beckhart. You buy paper, whereas you could make enough of it for Sunrise's needs and sell tons of the surplus for profit! Who are the employees you want to fire, and why?"

Roger spouted, "Damn you. I waste my time telling you about the problems at work, and you're never on my side. I'm the boss of the place and I demand they do as I say."

His brother said, "Roger, let go of Dad's dream about Dura-best Paints. Things change, progress. Chemistry and other technology can't stand still. Now who are the ones you want to fire?"

Roger dragged his hand across his forehead. "I guess Sylvia told you—our turpentine plant in Georgia was partially damaged by fire a few days ago. Coker, our chief engineer, went to Jessup with a crew to survey the damage and make the necessary repairs to bring the plant back into operation. He phoned me a few days after he arrived and gave me a whole litany on why we should scrap the place and build a whole new factory. He was alarmed by the repaired machinery and the rusted boilers. Remember when we went there several years ago? We both noticed the condition those machines were in. Nobody thought they would hold up even another year, but they held on for several more, and they'll do it again. I told Coker to forget about building a new plant. Just get the repairs done and get back here."

George gazed off with his chin in his hands, then focused back on his brother.

"Yes, I remember how things were patched up at the Jessup plant," he said. "You can't fire him for suggesting we rebuild. Why, even back when we were there, I thought the place should be rebuilt."

Roger countered, "But that's not the main reason I want him out. It's because now if the plant blows up or burns, or some worker gets hurt or killed, Coker will be quick to tell everyone that he warned me it was a firetrap. I don't want him blabbing 'I told you so!'"

George said, "Wow! Fire a guy to cover your own ass? Roger, don't be so narrow-minded. The people who work for you aren't out to get you. The board members want to make money for Sunrise. They have to invest in the company. You can't be thin-skinned when they ruffle your feathers. Listen to them, even if you disagree. Give some thought to their suggestions. They may be right!"

Roger huffed. "Well, I can't do much about Roland Powers, but I'll keep an eye on Coker. If I ever hear he made a snide remark about my judgment, out he goes!"

George replied, "My dear brother, may the Lord give you the wisdom to retire soon. The rays of Sunrise blind your reasoning!"

Roger retorted, "Go jump in the lake. I'll run the place as I see fit! In a couple of weeks, those doubters will see Dura-best Paints yielding profits. Powers will eat crow when the board realizes he was wrong, and Beckhart will probably apologize for his suggestion. He's like that. George, no use talking shop with you. You're too much like Powers. Let's go have a game of billiards. You got me so mad I'm sure to win! Shall we play for ten dollars a game?"

George pulled a ten from his wallet and slapped it down. "Ten dollars it is."

Roger had Martha prepare a snack to go with the drinks. The brothers shot pool until George lost sixty dollars and Roger emerged in a good mood. He boasted, "The boss of the conference table is still the boss of the pool table!"

When the women returned from shopping, they entertained their husbands by trying on the new clothes they had purchased. They marched up and down the hallway, twirling and pausing like professional fashion models, much to the enjoyment of the two men. The remainder of the evening was spent in the living room watching "The Admiral Broadway Review" on television.

Chapter 15

Belated Thanks

Windsor's basketball team lost, but gave Yale some anxious moments. Yale had the advantage, as their best players had been selected from a much larger pool of athletes. The game was over by 3 p.m. On the way home, Carl told Kim, "Don't be peeved if I tell you I always root for Yale. I'm biased. Always liked Yale in all sports."

Kim said, "I can't be mad about that. As a matter of fact, when Windsor seemed to be winning, I wanted Yale to win, and when Yale was ahead, I was rooting for Windsor."

"Gee, Kim. You're fickle. That's news to me," teased Carl.

"No, Carl. Not at all. I'm an alumna of Yale and I teach at Windsor. Can you blame me for being ambivalent?"

"My gosh, you're right," said Carl. "How could I forget you attended Yale? Guess no matter who I rooted for, it would be OK by you. They can't call you a traitor, no matter which team you bet on."

She tossed her head and said, "Well, look at it from another aspect. I'm a traitor for the same reason!"

Carl reached over and tickled Kim's knee. "You're so clever . . ." Suddenly he whipped his head to the right. "Did you see that sign?"

Kim looked quizzically at Carl. "Yes. It said 'Saymour, 10 miles.' Why? Was that a test?"

Carl turned serious. "Kim, when I was in the Army Air Corps, I had the good luck of being commanded by an officer who came from Connecticut. His name was Colonel Walter Stone. He lived in Saymour. That's near Marlin's Dance Hall. If we get on the road that comes from Waterbury, we will pass right through Saymour. If he still lives there, I would really like to find him."

Kim said, "Then let's try. I might learn how you behaved yourself when I couldn't keep tabs on you!"

Carl said, "Oh, gosh! Now I'm a goner. He knows how many women I slept with in England. Oh well, we are engaged now, so you can't back out no matter how many women I slept with."

Kim said, "Yeah, you're right. I'm hooked. Let's see your colonel anyway."

When they crossed into Saymour, Carl stopped at a drugstore to find a pay phone. When he asked the druggist if he could use the phonebook, the man asked who he was looking for, as he knew most of the people in the small town.

"Sure, I know Walter Stone," said the pharmacist. "He lives at 35 Dunton Road, right off Sergeant Lane." He gave Carl directions.

Back at the car, Carl said brightly, "This colonel lives off a sergeant . . . Sergeant Lane. We should be there very soon."

Sergeant Lane led to a sparsely populated section of Saymour. They drove about two miles, and then came to the sign for Dunton Road. Three houses up, a blue mailbox with an airplane painted on it bore the number 35, with the name "Stone" printed below. Carl drove up the gravel driveway to a neat, two-story cape. He stepped out of the car, climbed the brick steps, sucked in a deep breath and rang the bell.

After several long seconds, Walter Stone opened the door. The features on his face convulsed, then froze in disbelief. Finally, he blinked hard and shouted, "Carl. Carl Emerson! My God! I thought you were dead!"

Carl thrust his hand out, overcome with emotion. He said, "Colonel Stone! I'm not dead. Feel my hand." They clasped hands for more than a minute before Col. Stone noticed Kim sitting out in the car.

"For God sake, call your girlfriend in," he said. As Kim ascended the steps, he remarked, "She's beautiful. Must be the angel that brought you back to Earth!"

Carl said, "Kim, this is Col. Stone, my commander when I had that cushy job in England."

The colonel shook Kim's hand and ushered the couple into his comfortable home. Carl quipped, "Yes, she does bring me down to earth on occasion. Don't tell her how badly I behaved and what a chaser of women I was."

The colonel said, "Yes, Kim. He went out with some real bombshells, but you know he really came down to earth on that last bombing run!"

After several more light exchanges, the former commander grew serious and asked Carl to explain what had happened after his plane was shot down.

Carl took a long breath and began, "Well, colonel, we were very happy on our way back from that bombing raid, having done so much damage to the Germans. But as luck would have it, an armed merchant ship hit our plane. We were almost over the Channel when it happened. Nothing could save the burning plane, and we crashed on the coastline of Holland. Only four of us were fortunate enough to survive and we were captured by the Germans. I was the only officer. Where they took the three enlisted men, I never knew, but they hauled me in a truck to a P.O.W. camp called Stalagluft Five. Boy, the ride in the back of that truck was almost as bad as the plane crash. You know, Colonel, having you as my commanding officer, from the same neck of the woods that I came from, was a coincidence no one could believe. Then, when I was interned at the P.O.W. camp, I was astounded to run into a buddy of mine and Kim's, Douglas Graf. We all went to the same high school. I still can't believe it. He was forced down in an air raid too, and became imprisoned at Stalagluft Five long before I was. Doug and I escaped, but, Colonel, if it weren't for you, we probably wouldn't have!"

"What?" exclaimed the colonel, scratching his ear. "I don't understand. How is that possible?"

"Colonel, you remember you gave me instructions on how to fly 'Snow White', that German aircraft? Well, some foolish German officer always left his plane warming up, unattended before he and his aide left camp. He was some kind of a prison inspector, I think, and went there three or four times a month to check the place. The plane was identical to the one you showed me how to handle. Well, a group of prisoners conceived a way to escape from under the prison, and Douglas and I were lucky enough to carry it out successfully. We stole the plane and flew to England. Colonel, you were a big help in our escape!"

"Damn, Carl. You were reported killed in an escape attempt. I wonder if you wouldn't mind writing down the details of the whole escape, what you and this Douglas had to do, and mail it to me. I write articles for an Air Force magazine. Your story would be great. They are always looking for interesting true stories about the war."

"Colonel, I sure will. I would love a copy of the article if they publish it."

Col. Stone assured Carl that he would send the copy. As Carl jotted down his address, the colonel gazed at Kim and remarked, "You sure know how to pick beautiful girls, Carl."

Carl said, "Thank you. Kim is the prettiest girl that ever graduated from Yale!"

Stone said, "By gosh, Kim, I went to Yale. Graduated in '35. When did you graduate?"

"In '48," she replied. "I majored in Economics. What course did you pursue, Colonel?"

"Aeronautical engineering. Always loved planes, and when I left college, I joined the Air National Guard. Trained others to fly. They decided to make me a Lieutenant Colonel after six years with the Guard. When we went to war, I was lucky. The Army made me a colonel and sent me to England. That's where I met your boyfriend, Carl."

Kim and Walter Stone discussed various instructors they'd shared at Yale, and swapped stories of their college experiences. The colonel threw his head back to dredge up his favorite account of dorm life:

"We had a classmate in my third year who always had a newspaper with him. Never saw him with any books. At lectures, he didn't carry a notebook—only his newspaper. On campus, if the weather was good, he would find a bench or seat and read the newspaper. He subscribed to at least three different papers. What drove us crazy was the fact that he always had the highest marks in class. One evening a student noticed that 'News', as we came to call him, had the door to his room open. The student looked in and saw News studying about eight engineering books at his desk. This same student came back from a date at 3:30 a.m. and News was still studying! Other students noticed that his lights were on at outlandish hours. No doubt, he was studying. No wonder he had such good grades.

"Often in winter after classes on Friday my student friends would congregate in one of our rooms for a bull session or beer bash. The student next door to News reported that his neighbor never locked the door when he took off for weekends. I thought News must be a trusting soul to leave his room unlocked, but it turned out—the only reason News never locked his room was that when he went away, he piled his books, clothing, towels, and who knows what else into a big suitcase and left an empty room, with nothing to steal. When we learned of this weird habit, one of us suggested we gather a bunch of newspapers. We told the dormitory janitor we were gathering bundled newspapers to sell as a fundraiser for a student who needed cash for tuition. The janitor was glad to get rid of the newspapers. One weekend when News left campus, we balled up the papers and filled his room with them. We went to work until the place was about five feet high with the stuff. We even filled the closet. From the hallway, we opened the transom over the door and threw the crumpled paper into the space immediately in front of the door. We did a great job. When our friend came back that Monday morning we ducked behind the doors of our rooms and watched. News opened his door, and an avalanche of papers cascaded into the hallway. He moved back and watched it spill, with his hand on his chin, as if he was thinking. Then he lugged the suitcase back down the stairs. We thought he went to get the campus police, but were surprised to see our victim return with the suitcase and a snow shovel. He shoveled our handiwork into the hall, picked up his suitcase, and strolled into his room as if nothing were amiss. The police arrived about thirty minutes later. Someone had reported the mess. As the pile of papers seemed to emanate from News's area, they knocked on his door and asked what he knew about it. He said he knew nothing. Nobody knew the truth but the janitor of our building, but since he gave us the papers, he didn't say a word, even though he had to clean up the mess."

The colonel held his stomach and roared with laughter. "Kim, we were crazy kids then, but when I see some of the guys who were in on it, we have a good laugh. News was really a good sport. He posted a note on the bulletin board that read, 'Dear Fellow Students, Next time please use the New York Times or the Washington Post. The rest aren't worth the paper they're printed on.'"

Kim and Carl laughed. Kim added, "Some student pulled a stunt that really broke us up. We don't know if a male or female did it. Anyway, while class was in session, someone went into the ladies' room and shoved a helium-filled balloon into each of about eight toilet bowls and put the lids down. Well, the lecture ended just before lunch break and we ladies went to freshen up. You should have heard the screams as each girl went in and lifted the lid. Some even got splashed by the released balloon. I speak from experience. Yuk!"

Carl remarked, "Never went to college myself." He turned to Kim. "Did you go to learn or have fun? No wonder you never talk about it. And you complain that I never talk about my military life!"

Kim looked at the colonel and said, "I think we should punish him for insubordination for that remark!"

Stone replied, "Hmmm. Let's see . . . What punishment is befitting a Lieutenant? The higher the rank, the more severe the penalty."

Kim interrupted, "Sir, then Carl Emerson must be punished more severely than a lieutenant. He's now a captain!"

Stone replied, "Really! I should have known that. I'm sorry, Kim. Capt. Emerson, you are hereby allowed only one kiss a day to your girlfriend until the end of this month!"

Kim gasped, "But you're punishing me. Always the woman who pays!"

Carl said, "Colonel, you were never so severe in wartime, but I will respect your orders, and kiss other women instead."

It was getting late. Carl told his former commander he was glad he and Kim were able to locate him and they should stay in touch. Kim thanked the colonel for the refreshments and for the fun of reminiscing about college days. As the couple was leaving, Stone reminded Carl to write about the escape from Stalagluft Five. He added, "My wife, Marla, is on jury duty in Waterbury—a murder trial. The jury has been sequestered a week now. I hope you can meet her sometime. I don't like being a bachelor."

On the way home, Kim and Carl talked about how difficult it had been throughout the evening not to divulge the secret of their engagement. They decided it was time to tell their parents and friends. Kim suggested the first Monday in April. Carl agreed, but suggested they make certain it did not fall on April Fool's Day. Kim agreed that was worth considering. They settled on the second Monday in April for the announcement and a June wedding, after classes at Windsor ended for the semester.

Chapter 16

Announcements

Carl entered the kitchen where his mother was busy putting away the dishes. He made several awkward attempts at small talk, and then sheepishly apologized for not having told her sooner. "Mother, I . . . I mean we—Kim and I—are engaged to be married in June," he stammered. Mrs. Emerson jumped down off the step stool and stumbled into her son's arms.

"Carl, my goodness! Tom, come here! Such wonderful news," she gushed. "Darling, I'm so happy for you! But why did you wait so long to tell us?"

Carl explained that he'd wanted to be on solid ground financially. He reminded his parents that Kim was from a well-to-do family, and he was sensitive to the fact that others might conclude he married for money. "When people learn I am branch manager of several stores, they'll be less apt to think that money was my motive for marrying Kimberly Durand, daughter of the Durands of Sunrise Industries," he said.

Mr. Emerson agreed and warned him, "Your marriage will be written up in the newspapers. Some may imply things, or even come out with headlines like, 'Poor boy, Rich Girl Tie Knot', or 'Kim Durand, Daughter of Industry Tycoon, Marries Son of Railroad Worker'. A little derision may creep into their account of your marriage. Of course, if you love one another, you shouldn't give a damn," he said.

"Yeah, Dad. Thoughts like that have bugged me," Carl agreed. "But Lord knows, we love each other."

Spring came none too soon to New England, as the winter had been a severe one. Roger harbored no regrets about the snow-covered hills losing their mantel of white, as beautiful as they had been. He kept close tabs on the earnings of the Dura-best Paint stores and outlets, in hope of detecting the first sign of an upsurge in sales. As in the past, the rural private stores showed a slight increase in sales. Farmers were restoring weather-beaten barns and farm buildings long overdue for a new coat of paint. But painting contractors and builders of suburban homes were simply not buying the Dura-best brand. The trivial increase of sales from the rural outlets fell short of meeting payrolls and expenses. The general fund continued to shrink as funds were tapped to cover the deficits.

Roger decided to reduce the manager's pay at each store by ten dollars a week, and fire two out of three clerks in each store. The managers would have to assume more of the workload. This cost reduction resulted in a savings of $4,400 a month, or $52,800 annually.

When the managers received notices of the reduction in help and their own pay, they knew lack of sales had driven the main office to take the unpleasant action. The bad news prompted the ten managers to call each other and plan a strategy to persuade the CEO to drop the Dura-best line of paints. Every manager agreed that the majority of customers preferred "that new paint that's so easy to clean up after." Potential volume buyers asked specifically for latex paint. Six managers from different areas decided to call Mr. Durand personally to plead for the new products on behalf of their customers.

The first caller said, "Mr. Durand, this is Victor Ward. I manage your Dura-best Paint store in Nashua, New Hampshire. I am calling about this notice you sent—two weeks' termination notice to two employees, and a pay cut for me. I would like to suggest you change from lead-based oil to latex paint. I am positive we can sell five times as much latex paint as the kind we carry now. Just yesterday, a building contractor wanted 500 gallons of latex for an 85-unit development in Amherst, and he is on the verge of starting another development. If you can meet the demand for this newer product and hold off on letting these people go, you will get a heck of a lot more business. They are building up here like mad!"

"Well, Victor, that's interesting," replied Roger, "but my order stands. These people that buy latex paint will be sorry in a year or two when the new homeowners bitch about fading colors and rotting clapboards, from the lack of protection that lead-based oil paint would have afforded. That's the word from this office, Victor. Have a good afternoon."

A few days later, the manager from a Dura-best store in Quincy, Mass. called Roger and made the same pitch. He told about hundreds of homes being built to the north and south of Boston. "Too bad we don't carry latex paint," he said.

Roger told him he was too busy to discuss the matter with him, and terminated the call. So it went for all six store managers.

One employee who received his discharge notice called Roger and said, "Hey, Mr. Durand, lead paint is poisonous. I won't promote that stuff anymore. I was quitting anyway!"

The entreaties glanced off Roger like raindrops off oilcloth. He dismissed the complainers as disgruntled employees over-reacting to a temporary setback.

Roger's brother subscribed to the New York Times and avidly read all business news—in particular, articles relating to construction. Every edition reported the phenomenal building boom in New York, New England, and other areas. He read help wanted ads and was surprised at the great number offering excellent pay with health benefits to workers required in the building trades. George decided to visit various sites where homes were being built. He could not find one new house, under construction or complete, that had been painted with lead-based oil paint. He questioned painters and their bosses about whether lead paint would provide better protection or ease of application.

The answers ranged from, "Hell, no!" to "What? And spend our time cleaning brushes with turpentine when we could wash them easily with water?" One said, "I used to use it but latex is much better all around."

When George returned home, he told his wife about his findings. "I've got to straighten Roger out. I'm going there tonight. Would you like to visit with Sylvia?"

Laurie nodded. "Sure I'll come," she said. Then, rolling her eyes, she warned, "But don't get your hopes up. You know your brother!"

George shook his head. "Yes. If only he would listen."

Laurie stood with her hands on her hips. "George, the rationale for dropping lead-based oil paints goes way beyond economics and convenience. A visit with Sylvia is all well and fine, but if I could corner Roger and share some facts I learned about lead-based paint in chemistry lab at NYU, it might scare him into dumping every can of that stuff Dura-best owns.

"The history of lead has many dark chapters. Wine consumed by the ancient Romans was often stored in lead bottles and served in lead goblets. Those who imbibed of it often went insane. Lead was the culprit."

George nodded resolutely. "Let's go visit my obstinate brother and bombard him with all this. Maybe between the two of us, we can pull him out of the dark ages."

When they arrived at Golden Vista, Roger was standing on the front porch. He called out, "Go away, George, but that beautiful lady is welcome." He turned to Laurie, "Ma'am, are you being harassed by this person?"

George said, "Actually, Roger, we're both here to harass you."

Sylvia arrived at the entryway, and George declared, "By gosh, you do have an eye for beautiful women. That's not one of your failings!"

"Me? Failings? I don't have any!" Roger shot back.

Sylvia said, "Thank you, George, for the compliment. I'm afraid Roger's failings are too numerous to be counted. Now please come in!"

George sidled up to Sylvia as they entered the foyer. "We really didn't come to socialize," he said. "We came on sort of a rescue mission concerning your husband's 'failings'. Maybe we can socialize after the rescue."

Roger overheard the last sentence and growled, "What the hell rescue are you talking about?"

George suggested everyone meet in the library. When they were settled in their seats, Roger said, "Every good rescue mission begins with a strong drink!"

George crossed his hands at the wrists and pushed them toward his brother. "No. Let's talk first," he said. "Business before pleasure."

Roger cleared his throat. "By God, I must be in a pickle."

George told about his survey of new homes, ending with, "And now my wife, the chemist, has some interesting information with which to enlighten you about lead paint."

Roger burst out laughing. "What the hell? Why bother me with all this drivel? The only reason those developers used that other paint is that they probably got it cheap. Some slick salesman gave the contractor a snow job about how good that crappy latex is supposed to be."

He saw Laurie gearing up for an argument. "OK, OK, Laurie. I'm ready for more laughs. Let's get it over with so we can pour the drinks and get down to some serious card playing or pool. Then maybe we can even talk sensibly."

Laurie bristled for a second, then drew a breath and said, "Roger, when I was in college studying chemistry, we were required to use breathing masks and rubber gloves in any lab work involving the element lead. Lead compounds are very interesting, but also extremely toxic. Did you know the lead acetate in your varnishes is poisonous?"

Roger replied, "So?"

Laurie ignored his response and continued, "And so is the lead carbonate used as pigment in your white paint."

Roger repeated, "So?"

Laurie maintained her composure. "Lead chromate, the pigment for yellow, is extremely hazardous."

Roger uttered a final "So?"

Laurie leaned in toward her brother-in-law, exasperation throbbing in her skull. "So, so, so, Roger! So people who use your product contract a slew of illnesses, from painter's colic to chronic intestinal pain, constipation, anemia, convulsions, and partial paralysis. And young children who ingest dried lead paint chips from windowsills and other painted surfaces can suffer brain damage. So—how can you keep selling that poison?"

Roger's face stared back, lips clamped tightly in a straight line. Finally he said, "So, if you're finished now, we'll have some wine."

Laurie pushed her face to within six inches of Roger's. "So, now that you mention wine, let me give you a little history lesson involving the ancient Romans, lead, and wine. . . .

When Laurie finished her speech, Roger shook his head and said, "You know, the radio and newspapers are all coming out with this same kind of garbage! My God, who in hell is going to eat or sniff paint like a dog? My parents painted miles of walls with lead paint and never got sick. I'm not going to abandon the most durable paint ever made just because a few stupid people got sick!"

George broke in and said, "You're wrong there too! Latex is better cover. It's like applying a rubber coating over clapboards or whatever. Truly waterproof gloves and galoshes are rubber coated. Try water-proofing a pair with lead paint."

Roger scoffed, "Forget this nonsense. Lead paint will be around long after the latex fad is over. When homeowners start complaining about fading paint and rotting wood from that watercolor stuff, these developers will be facing more lawsuits than you can shake a stick at. And mark my words, that will be the end of latex. Then watch Dura-best Paints take off! Where's Martha? Tell her to bring on the wine goblets!"

Sylvia threw her hands in the air. "Come on, Laurie, let's have cocktails in the den. You tried your best."

Five minutes later, George followed suit. "We failed. I can't believe it," he said to his wife.

Roger marched in, announcing, "Laurie, your husband puzzles and amuses me!"

Laurie looked up at Roger, her hands folded primly in her lap. "Oh? Please tell me why, so I may be puzzled and amused too."

Roger helped himself to a drink and said, "Last fall, he insisted we spend a couple of weeks at your place on Sebago Lake so I could forget my job. This evening, all he wants to do is talk about work. That's funny. I guess location dictates what we can talk about."

Laurie replied, "Of course. A time and place for everything. If you were planning to rob a bank, would you discuss it inside the bank in front of the tellers?"

The tension dissolved into laughter. Finally George said, "Roger, that vacation was intended to clear your brain so you could think more clearly. Now it's time to start doing that. Dad's world has passed. Sunrise Industries can't progress using the past as a mold. Go forward with new improved products. Now that's it! No more talk from me."

Roger sighed and uttered, "Amen."

The group played bridge for three hours. As George and Laurie were saying their good-byes, Kim entered the hallway. She halted her aunt and uncle. "Please don't leave yet. While you're here, I can kill two birds, or rather, four birds, with one stone."

George gasped, "Don't kill us. We're leaving now!"

Sylvia added, "Please spare your tired mother and father. Now hurry up and tell us your news, or you're a dead pigeon!"

Kim stood with her hands clasped behind her back, rocking back and forth on the balls of her feet. "Ma, Dad, Uncle George and Aunt Laurie, Carl Emerson and I are engaged!" She thrust out her left hand. "Look at the ring he gave me right before Christmas!"

They congratulated, hugged, kissed, and questioned Kim about her marriage plans. Like Carl's mother, Sylvia wondered why Kim hadn't informed them about the engagement earlier, when she'd received the ring. She explained that they both believed they should be employed and free of any money problems that might jeopardize a happy marriage. She and Carl now had good jobs. They could be self-sufficient.

The explanation vexed her dad. He remarked, "Well, my dear daughter, neither of you need worry about money. Your mother and I could give the two of you enough money to buy anything you might need or want, and cash enough to support you for the rest of your lives. You know that!"

"That's just what we don't want," said his daughter. "If you really knew Carl, you'd realize that he wouldn't marry me if you showered money on us. And I don't want you to either. I want to be able to say we earned the home we live in and all that we have, ourselves!" .

Sylvia, Laurie, and George applauded. Roger shook his head and said, "It's your choice." He wagged a finger in her face. "But we will have a big wedding for you."

Kim said, "OK on that. It may be late June or early July. We haven't decided yet."

Sylvia asked, "Kim, why didn't Carl come in with you tonight?"

"He has an early appointment in New York to meet his boss at a retail store convention. Something about building suppliers."

"Then we must toast without him!" exclaimed Sylvia, and they raised their glasses high.

On the way home, Laurie mentioned that Carl and Kim seemed equally endowed with good character. "That augurs well for their married life, don't you think?"

George agreed, adding, "Kim takes after Sylvia a lot more than she does Roger. As for that brother of mine, the way he is running things worries me. He keeps shoveling the corporation's money into Dura-best Paints, which is up the creek without a paddle, as far as making money is concerned. It's losing the profits made by the other branches of Sunrise. If the board of directors decides to push Roger out, I want to be on board to protect our interests. Maybe get the right man to take his place. I plan to buy a lot of preferred stock in Sunrise. Rog is so stubborn, he'd stick with a losing situation forever."

Laurie replied, "Amen."

Miss Saltmarsh perused the Wall Street Journal at the office as usual before starting work. She followed the stock market trends, and read various business articles that caught her eye, including news of company mergers and other industry-related items. This morning, her attention was riveted on a piece about Sunrise Industries, Inc., written by economics professor Damon Remick of Yale. The article, titled, "A Nightmare for Sunrise?" was reprinted in the Journal by permission of the trade magazine, "The Industrial Monitor." Amazed by the headline, she read on:

One of this country's best known corporations, which only six years ago yielded the third highest dividends of all major corporations, is expected to rank lowest of the 12 blue chip organizations this quarter. A recent study of Sunrise Industries, Inc. shows all of its subsidiaries yielding respectable profits for the past several years, with the exception of the well-known parent company, Dura-best Paints.

It is interesting to note that losses in the sale of Dura-best Paints have kept pace with the building industry's growing preference for latex paints. And it seems the burden of keeping Dura-best afloat has been imposed upon Sunrise's other affiliates. A conservative estimate of losses accrued over the past five years exceeds the five million dollar mark. From our perspective, it appears that Sunrise's top management displays an ineptitude amounting to a breach of the public trust. This bodes badly for stockholders or prospective buyers of Sunrise stocks.

Miss Saltmarsh, glued to the story, failed to notice that her boss had entered the office and was reading over her shoulder. As his eyes caught the headline, he said, "Good morning. I'd like to read that paper. Bring it to me when you're done reading it."

The secretary's stomach did a somersault. She thought, *Today is Friday. The monthly board meeting is at 10 o'clock. Better brace for some fancy cussing and yelling. Every month these damn meetings become more nerve-racking. First he tells me to write what is said, then if he doesn't like it, he orders me to delete it. What will it be today?*

It was past 10 a.m., and the board of directors was still awaiting its chairman. Finally at 10:15, Roger stomped into the room, making no attempt to hide his anger. He called out, "Who the hell gave inside information to Mr. Remick about our corporation?"

Herbert Worthley rose and said, "You mean Professor Remick? I didn't give him inside information, as you call it. The information was public, as required by law of any open corporation that offers shares to the public. He also retrieved information from our auditors, which, again, is public information. Withholding fiscal information is unlawful, as I'm sure you know."

"Either the professor exaggerated those figures he published in that damn story or you and the auditors are wrong. Five million? That's a bunch of crap!" Roger said, fuming.

"Well, sir," Herbert countered, "the lost revenue, the expense of maintaining payrolls, taxes, and advertising, mounted up after all those years. The figures are accurate, sir."

Summoning patience, Roland Powers raised his hand to speak. Roger said, "All right, Powers, what is it?"

In a calm, controlled voice, Powers replied, "Mr. Durand, Mr. Worthley had no recourse to what he told that author. Neither did the financial people. Why in heaven's name don't you yield to the facts of the situation about the paint business that exists now? Our other affiliates are doing well, but when the CEO champions the losing partner of the whole organization, to be frank, it makes him look like a horse's ass!" He glanced at Miss Saltmarsh, who had trouble concealing her grin.

Roger said, "Enough, Roland. Let's proceed to other matters." He asked for comments and suggestions about a new beverage machine for the cafeteria.

When the meeting ended, Roger returned to his office, trying to appear nonchalant. In truth, he was seething about Powers's likening him to the rear end of a horse. He did not, however, have his secretary delete the offending words from the minutes. He drove home early and planned to relax for the weekend. He would swim in the pool with his wonderful wife and enjoy a few cocktails. He would forget all those who tried to change his mind about Dura-best Paints.

The trip home was idyllic. It was warm for early May, and the lilacs were in bloom. There was little traffic for a Friday. When Roger arrived home, he greeted Sylvia with, "Darling, take off your clothes!"

She said, "My, did Miss Saltmarsh excite you today?"

He responded, "Oh, I mean take off your clothes and put on your bathing suit. Let's go for a swim. And, yes—she did excite me, but not in the way you meant."

Sylvia squeezed Roger's face between her palms and kissed him on the nose. "How, then?"

"I'll tell you after our swim." When Sylvia returned in her smart new two-piece swimsuit, Roger let out a sharp whistle. He eased himself into the water and said, "By the way, why wasn't your station wagon in the garage?"

Sylvia told him that she was having the wooden panels refinished. "Gilbert said the man doing the job is an expert at refinishing and painting cars. He picked it up a little while ago. It should be done in a few days," she said, poised for a swan dive at the end of the diving board.

After an hour of diving, swimming, and splashing around, the couple settled on poolside lounge chairs to take advantage of the fading sunlight.

"So, Miss Saltmarsh didn't excite you with some exotic perfume. Did she sit on your lap?" said Sylvia.

"I should be so lucky," responded Roger while Sylvia huffed. He continued, "No. This morning before work I caught her intently reading an article supposedly about Sunrise." Roger gave his wife a synopsis of the article, and told her about the trying board meeting.

They remained silent for several minutes. Finally, Sylvia said, "You know, dear, your own brother has been trying to convince you to change over to that modern paint. I wish you would listen to him and so many others who tell the same story. Even the president of the United States listens to his advisors. Anyway, if I had to paint, I would not use Dura-best. I heard that lead, besides doing all those other bad things, can cause blindness."

Roger said, "Oh, sure. If you drink it!"

Sylvia cast a doubting look at her husband. "You better think about it. I don't think Professor Remick is mistaken," she said quietly.

The sun's oblique rays no longer yielded comfort, so they retreated to the house to dry off and dress. Sylvia heard the front door close and checked the entry hall. It was Kim, arriving home later than usual. Sylvia asked what had delayed her.

Kim replied, "Let me get washed up and I'll tell you at dinner." Her mother caught a glimpse of Kim's fingernails, chewed down for the first time since Carl had returned from the war. At dinner, she prodded Kim for the story.

Kim explained, "For the past three weeks, I've been working on making up an Economics exam for my students' final this month. The exams were printed up last week. I had them under lock and key in my desk, ready to hand out in three weeks. After class was dismissed at 3 p.m., the students all left. I was closing the door to my classroom to prepare for a lecture session when a young man asked, 'Was that the Economics class that just let out?' I said yes. He looked around and said, 'OK. I have a couple copies of the final exam left. You can have one for twenty bucks. If you know anyone else who wants one, I can get more copies from a friend in the print shop. I'll be on the bench outside by the library main entrance, reading a book. Tell them $20 bucks apiece.'

"He thought I was a student! I paid him $20 and got the shock of my life when he handed me a copy of the exact same exam I had made for my students! I hurried to the Dean's office and told him what happened.

"Dean Cronin said, 'We'll get that rotten cheat,' and he called security to his office and asked his secretary to help. His secretary, an attractive redhead about 22 years old, was given twenty dollars to approach the man selling the exam papers and buy a copy. The security man watched the transaction from the library window, and when the money and exam changed hands, they nabbed the seller and brought him to the dean's office. When he saw me, he said, 'I didn't think a pretty co-ed like you would rat on me.'

"Dean Cronin told the fellow he was in serious trouble and he had better tell who he got the exams from in the printing shop. It was nearly time for my lecture hall, so I asked the dean to excuse me and told him I would return after class. I thought, now I have to make out another exam. Damn that printer and his buddy! Cronin later informed me they'd arrested the 'two idiots', and thanked me for unraveling a problem they had suspected was going on.

"I groaned about having to make up a new examination paper, but he said, 'No, you don't. I will have my secretary retype the exam and scramble the order of your True or False questions. Then our printers will make new copies. They should be ready by Monday.'

"I said, 'Mr. Cronin, how will that do any good? They still have the correct answers from the original they bought.'

"He answered, 'Miss Durand, I am also a psychology teacher. The ones who got those copies won't even try to read the questions. I am sure with 30 questions, they will just memorize the proper numbers to mark true or false, or perhaps jot them down on a small sheet of paper. I know all their little tricks. I will scramble the questions so none will coincide with the correct answer on the original sheet.'"

Sylvia was amazed at her daughter's story and remarked, "No wonder some teachers shun having children. They have their fill of sneaky kids that can't be trusted. How did you react to all that?"

"Ma, I must have had a dozen reactions. I was horrified at first. I was frightened for a while. When they brought the crook to the dean's office, I was flattered that he referred to me as a pretty student. Then I became damn angry at the thought that I would have to redo the exams. And silly me, when Dean Cronin thanked me for unraveling the problem, I felt like a hero. Now all I feel is cheated of my 20 bucks!" Kim laughed.

Roger remarked, "That dean is a fool! The kids who bought the exams have all the right answers by now. They'll pass the test, hands down. What the hell was Cronin thinking?"

"Dad," his daughter tried to explain. "If a student writes the correct true or false answers from the original on the new exam, then he or she gets them all wrong. But if the student bothers to read the questions on the new exam, then the dean's psychology succeeds. They either don't know the material and fail, or they know it and waste twenty dollars!"

Roger was not convinced.

The semester ended on the third week of May. Eight out of 29 students failed the final in precisely the same manner. Each was re-tested and consequently charged with possession of stolen property and cheating.

Kim enjoyed a break from teaching until the start of summer session in mid-June. Those sessions would be far less demanding, granting her more free time. Her workweek would vary from two to four days. She could have any three weeks in July for vacation. She thought, *we could get married on the last week in June and have our honeymoon in July. A June bride! That is, if Carl can get his vacation in July. We must talk.*

On the third Friday of May, Kimberly Durand and Carl Emerson announced that the big day would be the last Saturday in June. Their three-week honeymoon would begin on the first of July. Carl was quite sure he could get two weeks off, and since his marriage coincided with his vacation, he was positive he could take the third week as well.

Roger's return to the office the following Monday began a week of frustration. Professor Remick's article proved most troublesome. The editor of the New York Times column,

"Advice for Investors," called about the derogatory editorial. He asked, "How is it that Sunrise has fallen to the bottom of the blue chip companies?"

Roger answered, "Remick is exaggerating."

The editor said, "I checked Remick's facts. He's not lying. Mr. Durand, my job is to advise people interested in investing in stocks and bonds. Unless I'm missing something, I must counsel that buying stock in Sunrise is not a good investment at this time. I don't write a critique of a company's operations. If you can give me any reason for optimism, please do and I'll pass it along. Otherwise, I must support Remick's conclusions."

Roger glanced at the calendar. He could no longer claim that profits would rebound in the spring. "I'm sorry. I can't discuss it right now. I'm in a meeting," he said, and threw the receiver down.

Other reporters and editors requesting comments added to Roger's discomfort. Calls from stockbrokers poured in from all across the country. The most annoying calls came from managers of the affiliates of Sunrise Industries, Inc., asking their CEO for guidance in responding to queries about the company's financial status. It seemed that everyone was conspiring to ruin him, just because Dura-best Paints was in an extended slump. *Well, time will prove they are wrong as hell— exactly the amount of time it takes for that cheap latex paint to begin chipping and peeling!*

Gilbert called Sylvia on the intercom. "Mrs. Durand, can you come to see your new old station wagon? The gentleman just arrived with it."

Sylvia hurried to the garage, anxious to see her beloved car. Her reaction assured John, the expert refinisher, that she was well pleased. She asked what the job cost. John replied, "I was going to ask $130, but my wife was not available to follow me here with our car, so if someone can drive me home, I'll knock off $15."

Sylvia paid John $150 and asked Gilbert to drive the man home in "our new limousine." Her station wagon looked showroom new, and she was delighted with his work.

Occupants of Golden Vista were bustling about with an odd mixture of joy and anger. Sylvia, all the servants, and of course Kimberly were excitedly planning the wedding. However, Roger remained aloof and detached from the process. He concealed his anger toward the columnist and his readers by appearing simply busy with the day-to-day operations of the corporation, while Sylvia conferred with Martha and Gilbert about elegant wedding foods, decorations, and beverages. She and Kim selected the bride's and bridesmaids' gowns, drew up the guest list, and handled invitations. They hired a 10-piece band for the reception and attended to the thousands of details necessary for hosting a wedding consistent with the Durand status. Kim placed great importance on having Carl's parents attend a get-acquainted dinner at Golden Vista before the big day. Her mother agreed and called Mrs. Emerson. They set the date for the second Saturday in June.

Meanwhile, the paint business slumped into deeper trouble. Herb Worthley reminded Roger week after week that maintaining the Dura-best stores was bleeding the corporation's profits at an unsustainable rate. It had to stop, or the consequences would devastate Sunrise. One noon, following one of Herb's reminders, Roger told Miss Saltmarsh he had to leave the office for some important business. Then he headed straight home, hoping to escape the office and calm his nerves. When he drove into the garage at Golden Vista, he spotted the station wagon at the back of the guests' parking area, gleaming in the early June sun. He approached his wife's pet car and examined it closely. He ran his hand over the smooth wooden panels, surprised at the perfection of the refinished woodwork. Gilbert came to greet Roger and noticed his boss's interest in the vehicle. He said, "How do you like Mrs. Durand's new wagon?"

Roger replied, "Fantastic. It looks like it just came from the showroom! Wonder where the paint came from?"

Gilbert answered, "The man who did the job works at a paint store in New Haven. He gets a discount on all his supplies. Nice store. I've been there several times."

Roger said, "I want you to drive me there now. I must see who my competitor is. Let me call Mrs. Durand on your intercom. We should be back within the hour, shouldn't we?"

Gilbert said, "Yes sir, just about an hour, this time of day."

Roger informed his wife of the plan. She said, "I'm surprised you're home so early. It's a shame you have to run right back out again."

Gilbert drove into the parking lot of a brilliant yellow building with lavender trim. He stepped out and opened the door for his boss. "Well, Mr. Durand, this is the place— Everbright Paints. I'll wait here, sir."

Roger entered the store and browsed through the aisles brimming with a wide selection of paints. When he concluded that none of the gallon size cans contained lead-based oil paint, he told the clerk he couldn't find what he was looking for and left. His only comment on the drive home, was, "So that's where the paint for her new wagon came from."

"Your station wagon looks dandy," he said to Sylvia upon his return. "I've got to find who owns or runs that paint store. It's our competitor." He kissed his wife and said, "When I'm finished with the call, I'd like a cocktail. Is Kim home? She might want one too."

He rushed to his study and phoned Herb Worthley.

Miss Chadwick recognized Roger's voice and said, "Mr. Durand, Mr. Worthley is on another line. Can he call you back?"

Roger replied, "No, Miss Chadwick. Just tell him to come to my office first thing tomorrow. It's important."

Roger fetched his much-needed drink, and went to talk to his wife and daughter, who had seemed difficult to communicate with of late, due to the high priority of wedding plans. Upon entering the den he said, "Ah! My two favorite ladies, the young Mrs. Durand and the younger Miss Durand!"

Sylvia raised her eyebrows. "Well, that's an abrupt change of mood. Welcome back to Earth! What brought on the improved spirits and why are you home so early?"

Kim added, "Yeah, Dad, was Sunrise brighter today? — Pun intended."

Roger grimaced at his daughter's humor. "You're right. A plan is brewing in my mind that I believe will turn a gloomy situation bright. But, as my little brother, George, would say, 'Let's forget shop talk now.'"

Sylvia laughed, as she always did when Roger referred to George that way. He was easily six inches taller than his older brother. For the first time since Prof. Remick's annoying article, Roger engaged in conversation with his wife and daughter about wedding plans. After a fine stuffed fillet of sole dinner, amiable conversation filled the Durand household for the remainder of the day.

Sylvia welcomed bedtime, exhausted by the travails of planning the elaborate wedding. Roger encouraged her to get some rest, saying he wished to stay up and write plans for the next day's work. The plan was actually simple. It was to have

Worthley locate and contact the owner or owners of Everbright Paints, and determine the value of the company through the bank. Then he was to make attractive offers to entice them to sell.

The next day, Mr. Worthley waited in Roger's outer office as requested. He asked Miss Saltmarsh why the boss wished to see him. She speculated it was about the article in the Wall Street Journal, but didn't really know. Before he could interrogate her further, Durand entered and bade them both good morning. Coffee awaited them in Roger's office, courtesy of Miss Saltmarsh. Both chatted over the brew prior to any business talk. Then Roger said, "Herb, I'm aware that banks have access to lists naming the owners of major businesses. I want you to find out who owns Everbright Paint Company. I think we must acquire that outfit. We have enough capital for the purchase, if we make it attractive enough to the owner or owners."

Mr. Worthley's jaw dropped in shock. "What? You don't really mean. . Oh my gosh!"

Roger glared across his desk. "What the hell's the matter with you? Have you gone nuts?"

Worthley said, "Mr. Durand, you gave an order long ago not to, or rather you didn't want . . . "

Roger tapped his pen impatiently.

"Oh, what the hell," blurted Worthley. "You own Everbright Paint Company! They are a Sunrise affiliate!"

Roger eyed the bank president suspiciously. "What in hell are you saying, Herb?"

"Roger, for the love of Mike, do you think I am making this up? I have a copy of the minutes of the board meeting just before the war, when you and Higgins had that tiff about creating new business to take advantage of the demand for war goods. When Higgins said, 'Are you afraid to make money?'

210

you got teed off and told him to start a company with Sunrise funds. You didn't want to know a thing about it. On your say-so, he established Everbright Paints with the firm's money. Merchants Trust owns Everbright Paint, and Sunrise owns Merchants Trust! You never once inquired about Higgins or what he did for Sunrise, but it's been substantial."

Roger eased his chair back from his desk. He dropped his head back and pinched the bridge of his nose, trying to recall that meeting so long ago. Worthley was right.

Roger's anger dissipated for the moment. In a conciliatory tone, he stated, "By gosh, you're right! I remember now." The clock ticked noisily for several seconds. Then Roger exploded. "Why that bastard! He had the gall to start a paint business! He has been competing with Dura-best Paints all these years! No wonder my paint business has been slowing down. He really hurt us!" Worthley watched silently as Roger's expression transformed from one of shock to sheer malevolence. "That makes it easy," the CEO mused. "Herb, I'm ordering you to shut down Everbright Paints. The termination order I made back in 1942 to close down any enterprise not useful to Sunrise still stands. I declare Everbright no longer useful to this corporation. You have a copy of that directive. Implement it tomorrow morning!"

Herb was horrified. "Roger, we have twelve Everbright stores. You can't shut them down. They make money for Sunrise. They made up for your losses and then some!"

"Like hell I can't," Roger barked. "You do as I say or your ass is out too!" In a more moderate tone, he added, "You may go now. This meeting is over. I want to see a copy of the vacating order on my desk by tomorrow afternoon."

Worthley was shaken. He found the task more distasteful than anything he'd undertaken throughout his entire career. He marched out of Roger's office, his mind in turmoil.

That afternoon, the order was forwarded to Mr. Andrew Higgins. Two days later, Higgins picked up the notice and read:

> Att: Andrew Higgins.
>   Termination notice to Everbright Paint Company, pursuant to directive dated 12 March 1942, from Sunrise Industries, Inc. and Merchants Trust Bank. Everbright Paint Company, beholden in its entirety to Merchants Trust Bank, shall cease all operations within 30 days of receipt of this notice of June 2, 1949.

Higgins read all the fine print regarding money due employees, creditors, and insurance. When he finished, twice he exclaimed out loud in the empty office, "The guy is crazy!"

Higgins immediately called Worthley for his thoughts on the directive. "Is this a joke?" he demanded.

Herb said, "Andrew, I am still on the board of directors. If it's any consolation, I'll fight this stupidity tooth and nail. I know a number of board members who feel the same way I do about Roger Durand. He will ruin Sunrise if he doesn't step down. It is in all the stockholders' best interest to fight this and get rid of him!"

"Damn right," Higgins said. "I'm with you. We have 30 days to fight the closing. Call me at home and we'll arrange to get together."

The bad news spread fast. Higgins was obliged to inform his employees. He could have given them two weeks notice, but opted for 30 days, which he felt they were due for their loyalty to the company. The notices stated:

Due to a situation beyond my control, the Merchants Trust Bank, our holding company, will terminate Everbright Paint Company 30 days from this day, 3 June 1949. All funds accrued by employees, including vacation pay plus two weeks' severance pay, shall be paid two days prior to closing.

Chapter 17

In Deep Water

Everbright's employees were astounded, as all were certain that business had been flourishing. Some anticipated that the company would be sold to another corporation, and new owners would hire them. Carl did not see that possibility. Devastated, he watched his hopes of marrying the woman he loved wash down the drain with Everbright Paints.

Carl lay awake that night, anguishing over how to break the dismal news to Kim. He decided to tell her on the weekend, when they'd planned to attend an exhibition at the Boston Museum of Fine Arts. The show was to open at 9 a.m. Leaving Milford at 8 would put them in Boston by 11, with ample time to view the exhibition after lunch. However, the trip never took place.

Carl arrived at Golden Vista shortly before 8 a.m. He spotted Kim sitting in the gazebo, enjoying the fresh June morning. He left his car in the guest parking lot and approached her. She looked absolutely dazzling, sunlight filtering through wisps of golden hair whipped into disarray by a persistent breeze. It only served to compound his distress about what he had to tell her. He stepped tentatively, Kim's joy at his arrival turning to concern as she watched him draw closer.

She asked, "Carl, what's wrong? Are you hurt or just tired?"

He kissed his beloved and eased himself next to her on the bench. He clasped her hand in his and wrapped his other arm around her waist.

"Kimberly, I have some news that makes me sick to think what it will mean to us and our folks." He felt her fingers tighten around his.

"In a few weeks I'll be without a job," he continued over a sharp gasp from Kim. "I'm not sure, but I heard the Merchants Trust Bank—I guess they own Everbright—sold our company to some big corporation. Anyway, all Everbright stores will be closed. About 40 people will be out of work soon. Kim, we have to postpone our wedding. I know this is terrible for you and your mom and dad, after all the plans you've made." His voice cracked. "Kim, I'm so sorry."

Kim willed the tears brimming in her eyelids from spilling over. In a tiny voice she said, "But we can still get married. I am working, and my folks will give us anything we need. Money is not a problem."

"Kim, you know how I feel about marriage. We discussed this a long time ago. Look, we can wait. I should get a good recommendation from my boss that may help me get another job with decent pay. When I do, maybe we could just have a quiet wedding—you know—just our families and a few close friends. Not the big one we were planning. Kim, I haven't told my folks yet. I wanted you to know first, but I dreaded telling you."

George Durand pulled into the space beside Carl's car. He stepped out of his car and spotted his niece and Carl in the gazebo. As he neared them, he noted they did not appear as cheerful as he'd expected the prospective bride and groom to be. He remarked, "Hey, you two aren't married yet! No arguments now. Maybe next year!"

Carl solemnly shook his head and motioned for George to come and sit down. Then he broke the bleak news.

George said, "Damn! Kim, is your dad home? I noticed the car isn't in the garage."

Kim answered, "No, Uncle George. Dad went to the office today, even though it's Saturday. He told Mother some urgent thing had to be taken care of. He expects to be there the rest of the day."

George told the couple, "You two cheer up! Things can change. Kim, tell your mother I said hello, but right now I need to see my brother. I'll see you later on." He dashed back to his car muttering, "Hmmm. Must be pretty urgent," as he slammed the car door.

Recognizing the CEO's brother, the building custodian admitted George to Roger's outer office. George knocked on the door and Roger called out, "Come on in, Herb."

When George appeared, Roger did a double take. "Hey? What are you doing here? I was expecting Herbert Worthley."

George answered, "I was told you had some urgent business to attend to. It must be, for you to come here on a Saturday."

"Yes, that's right. My wife told you I was here?"

"No. It was Kim. What's going on, Rog?"

Roger rubbed his hands together, as if relishing what he was about to say. He told his brother, "George, just before the war, I got some sass from Higgins about my not wanting to try other business ventures opening up due to the coming war. I wanted him off my back, so I told him to start a business with our bank funds, using our bank as the holding company. I told him I didn't want to know a damn thing about whatever business he went into. He did as I suggested. But the bastard went and started a paint business. He had the gall to compete with his benefactors. I found out the other day, he's president of Everbright Paint Company!"

Roger flung his hands out as if checking for rain. Then he clasped them together and said, "But, by God, I got even with him! I had our bank shut his company down. All twelve of his stores! Worthley's to arrive momentarily with a record of the yearly earnings of Everbright since its inception."

Just then, Herb Worthley entered the office. He shook hands with George and said, "Good to see you again, George. Are you here to watch the slaughter? You know, of the goose that laid the golden egg?"

Roger said, "That's enough, Herb. Higgins competed against his own corporation. He caused all the grief for Dura-best Paint Company."

George commented, "So you shut down a branch of the corporation making a good profit! That's the dumbest thing I've ever heard! No wonder Sunrise has been getting bad reviews in the financial pages, and derogatory articles by economists!"

His brother raised his hand and said, "Cut the crap! If you came here to criticize me, go home! I want to look over this financial report."

Worthley shifted uncomfortably as the brothers argued. He said, "There you have Everbright's earnings report. I have to get back to the bank to complete the paperwork and closure statement you ordered."

Roger dismissed Worthley and ordered George to go with him. On their way out of the building, George suggested, "Herb, let's talk in your office. We have to put a stop to my brother's craziness." Worthley agreed. They met in the bank president's office and George began, "Herb, this bothers me. He is my brother, but I am afraid he is no longer fit to run Sunrise. Only appointing another chief executive can halt his adherence to the outdated, unpopular, and even harmful product Dura-best sells at the expense of the rest of the firm. Lord knows, I've tried for a long time to point out how wrong he is in his thinking."

Worthley's face relaxed for the first time since he'd walked into Roger's office. The bank president agreed and assured George that other members shared his concerns. He said, "I will convene as many board members as I can and set up a meeting in the board room adjacent to his office, for the purpose of appointing a new CEO. We'll invite Roger as a professional courtesy. If a two-thirds majority of the stockholders supports our resolution, he's out."

George agreed, but warned Worthley that Roger would fire him from his position as Merchants Trust president.

Herb replied, "I'm aware of that, but I am also a board member and can only be removed by concurrence of the board. Anyway, let him fire me. Who knows what will happen after the vote."

"OK, Herb. I'm with you on this. Let me know what develops."

George shook Worthley's hand and drove back to Golden Vista as fast as traffic would permit. He wanted to tell Sylvia all that had transpired and explain the reasons behind his plan to oust her husband from Sunrise Industries, Inc. He knew that his brother's ineptness of late, and his constant complaints about the board members worried her. Perhaps she would understand, or even welcome the course of action. He hoped so.

As George wove through the Saturday traffic, Kim told her mother about Carl's decision to postpone the wedding. She added, "I told him we could still get married, even if he is out of work, because I'm still working and you and Dad would help, but you know how he feels about that!"

Sylvia replied, "Oh dear. What a thing to happen now. I feel just terrible. Let's hope something changes for the better before the company folds."

After a period of silence Kim said, "My mother, ever the optimist." She blew her nose and said, "I'm mentally exhausted. I'm going to see if I can get some rest." Sobbing, she hugged her mother and plodded to her room.

Several minutes later, Martha opened the door for George. He joined Sylvia in the den and told her the whole story of why Carl was losing his job, and Roger's involvement in the whole mess. Finally, he squared his shoulders and divulged the plan to remove Roger as head of Sunrise. He watched his sister-in-law's expression cautiously, as if she might be holding a trump.

Sylvia's face brightened. She sat up straight in her chair, slapped her hands on her thighs, and said, "Well, I'm glad! I hope they succeed. Roger really must retire." She cupped her chin and stared at George for several minutes, then said, "He didn't know Everbright was a branch of Sunrise, his own firm? Why, that means Carl was working for my husband—something he said he would never do!"

George said, "That's right. But let's see what happens. I think Rog is in for a shock! He has lost too much for the firm and his credibility as CEO is shot." He said he would keep her posted and left. Sylvia did not mention the plan to Kim. Neither did she say anything about Carl's position in the family business. The poor girl's nerves were frayed enough already.

That afternoon, Worthley was able to contact all members of the board of directors. He informed them that an urgent meeting was scheduled for 9:00 a.m. that coming Thursday to consider the ouster of Mr. Roger Durand and the possible appointment of a new CEO of Sunrise. As an act of fairness, Roger was invited.

Stockholders were also invited by phone or mail to attend a meeting at 10:15 that same morning to vote their approval or disapproval of the board's decision.

Roger was incensed when he received a telegram of the notice. He called Worthley and screamed, "You ungrateful back stabber! When the board votes and I am still in charge, you are out the door. Fired! Just remember that!"

Worthley said, "I realize that, but let's see what the board does with you."

Roger was torn by conflicting thoughts as he drove home. One part of him felt it ludicrous to think that the board would even consider ousting Roger Durand, their longtime and capable CEO. Another part was still smarting from George's charge that he had been "dumb" to close down a company that was earning such high profits for Sunrise. Roger fought with his own mind not to accept his brother's assessment. He finally consoled himself by equating Dura-best Paint's losses with Everbright's success. He decided to carry on as though nothing had happened. He would not tell his family that he was responsible for Everbright's closing. He never wanted to know about the damn company in the first place.

Meanwhile, his wife, inwardly seething with the knowledge that her own husband was at the root of Kim and Carl's problems, decided not to divulge what she knew of the situation.

When Roger arrived home, he dutifully kissed his wife and casually inquired about Kim.

Sylvia answered, "She's in her room, very upset. I'd rather she be the one to tell you why."

Roger shuffled his feet and mumbled, "OK. I guess I can wait." Then, brightening, he added, "What say we have a cocktail before dinner?"

Sylvia replied flatly, "I guess I don't care for one."

Later at the dinner table, Roger watched his daughter pick at her food, her face downcast and sullen. He cleared his throat and asked, "Kim, what's wrong? You look like you've lost your best friend."

Kim looked dolefully up at her father and in a voice choked with emotion said, "That's pretty close, Dad. My wedding's been called off. Carl's about to lose his job at Everbright Paints."

Roger's mouth went instantly dry. He had trouble swallowing his last piece of filet mignon. Sylvia eyed Roger accusingly and discreetly nodded her head.

Roger wiped his mouth and folded his napkin. Then he focused across the table at Kim. "Why, I can give Carl a wonderful job at Sunrise. Call him here this evening so we can discuss the matter."

Kim and Sylvia responded in unison, "He won't work for you!"

Roger boiled over. "Then to hell with him! Let him scrounge around for work and money. This discussion is closed." He stood abruptly, knocking his chair over, and abandoned the table.

For the next four days, the atmosphere in the Durand household hung heavy like oily rags. Few words passed between father and daughter, husband and wife. Kim and her mother kept busy with projects around the house while Roger commuted to the office as usual.

That Thursday, all members of the board of directors, with the exception of one abstention, voted to terminate the current CEO of Sunrise Industries, Inc.

Mr. Robert Beckhart was appointed to succeed Roger Durand. Beckhart was considered well qualified, with a Masters degree in business administration. The board's vote shocked Roger to the depth of his being. But the vote could still be reversed by a two-thirds majority vote of the stockholders.

A half hour later, Douglas Graf and his father entered the meeting room. Kim had had an hour-long conversation with

Hazel about the marriage postponement, and Hazel had told Douglas, who wondered if the stockholders' meeting was somehow related to Carl's employment situation. Doug spoke to his dad and they both decided to attend.

The stockholders meeting convened at 10:30 a.m. as scheduled, Herb Worthley presiding. He waived reading the explanation for the meeting, as all in attendance had received letters. He then invited members of the board to explain why Roger Durand was voted out of office, and Mr. Beckhart elected to succeed him.

The first speaker was Mr. Roland Powers. Powers addressed the group, "Ladies and gentlemen, I take no pleasure in the ousting of Mr. Roger Durand. But for the good of Sunrise and its stockholders, I must ask you to agree with the board's determination. I give only one reason among many, why I voted against him. Recently a member of the board suggested we convert our turpentine plant in Georgia to a paper producing plant. Many of us agreed this would be a wise business move. Sunrise owns vast pine forests there that are wasted in manufacturing turpentine, which is in very low demand today, due to the construction industry's recent shift to latex house paint. Sunrise purchases paper from another company to manufacture its paper products such as napkins, picnic plates, cups, cardboard boxes, you name it. Supplying our own paper pulp would increase profits by about a million dollars annually. Mr. Durand's rejection of the board's suggestion is the only thing that stands between Sunrise and that increase. Please keep in mind—your dividends are dependent upon our performance!"

Andrew Higgins spoke next. "Stockholders, I am, or perhaps was, president of Everbright Paint Company, a branch of Sunrise Industries. We've had tremendous success in the sale of our paint products, as we have taken advantage of the latest technological advances in chemistry. Over the past seven or eight years, we have been producing state-of-the-art lacquers and paints for the extremely favorable home building boom. We have expanded to twelve stores in that time. Before the war, Mr. Durand and I had a disagreement at a board meeting, the details of which I shan't go into right now. But he angrily told me to go and start my own business with our bank's money. He stated he didn't want to know a damn thing about the venture. I think he wanted me to disappear. He said my firm must pump up a certain percentage of the profits to the bank, which in reality owned Everbright. Funny thing, the profits from my venture ended up offsetting the losses from his pet, the Dura-best Paint Company. Over the years, he lost sight of "Hig", as he often referred to me, and the fact that Everbright was a part of Sunrise Industries. A few weeks ago, Mr. Durand shut down the company that he had not known existed and was his benefactor. I had no choice but to vote against his retention."

The third speaker was not on the board, but the members felt his input was important. He was Sunrise's head industrial engineer, Lawrence Coker.

Coker stated to the shareholders, "I can give you some insight into why the board voted against Mr. Durand. You heard Mr. Powers speak about a turpentine plant in Jessup, Georgia. A portion of the plant was recently destroyed by fire. A crew and myself were sent there to assess and repair the damage. I could see the section of the plant not touched by fire was a mess—a real hazard to life and limb of our personnel. I suggested tearing down the dangerous remainder of the building and reconstructing the whole plant. Mr. Durand would not listen to reason. He told me in no uncertain terms to do what he ordered and get back here as soon as the damaged part was rebuilt. The old part of the plant is a fire hazard. I feel sorry for those who work there. It is not safe, with all that flammable turpentine stored on site. As stockholders, you bear the burden of that liability. Enough said."

The next speaker was Mr. Stephen Zedonick. Herb jokingly introduced him as "the youngest of our board members—eighty-two years young! He wishes to explain his reasons for abstaining from the vote to replace Durand."

Mr. Zedonick said, "Thank you, Herb, for the compliment. Maybe he has those numbers in reverse. Let me tell you nice people, I do agree with the board's decision. However, Roger is not a bad person. You know, I have been with this firm since his dad was the big wheel. He was a tough egg and demanded absolute adherence to his orders. He wanted this outfit to succeed at all cost. He lost his parents at age twelve, I think, and his life was an uphill struggle, from what he told me. His son, Roger, was put in charge here with a stern lecture that he must keep Dura-best Paints paramount to anything that might threaten its high standing. Roger tried too hard to emulate his dad and follow his orders. I believe it blinded him to progress and change. He hurt the firm, but not intentionally. I wish him a happy retirement. Thank you for listening to the junior board member."

The last person to address the stockholders was George Durand. Mr. Worthley said, "Let us now recognize Mr. George Durand, Roger Durand's brother. He is not a board member but wishes to address the stockholders."

George told the audience, "I came here to praise Caesar, and to retire him also, because I have an interest in Sunrise Industries, and I love my brother. Mr. Zedonick is right. My dad, rest his soul, was bitter due to the loss of his mother and father so early in life, and his struggle to build the corporation we have here today. My brother loved his dad as I did, but he unrealistically aspired to be the exact person he believed my dad had in mind. I am sure Dad did not require him to become the highest earner in the country.

"During the war, my brother nearly succumbed to participating in a scheme of collusion involving government contracts. His wife and I dissuaded him from going through with the plan. Thank God, Roger realized he was playing a dangerous game and backed out before the damage was done. This close call and numerous others made me realize that my brother must step down. He is too easily tempted by the pitfalls of easy money—enormous sums he believes our dad meant for him to acquire. I'm convinced the time has come for Roger Durand to stop and smell the roses before we all become impaled on the thorns. Thank you."

Before marking their ballots, the stockholders were asked for their comments. One painting contractor said, "I often wondered why Dura-best didn't sell latex paint. I use hundreds of gallons of it in my business. I don't like oil paint, and I especially dislike lead-based oil paint. It's a hazard to my workers."

Douglas Graf's father said, "I hope he retires. He is a member of our country club but I hardly ever see him there. I miss playing golf with him."

A low rumble of laughter spread through the room. Then Douglas jumped up and said, "I hope he retires too. My friend wants to marry his daughter."

Mr. Worthley and several others in the room looked around blankly while a few voices chuckled. Worthley said, "I don't understand that last statement, but if there are no more I suggest you mark your voting cards and leave them in the box by the door. Mr. Roger Durand has declined to comment."

Roger exited the room several minutes before the meeting adjourned. The attendees chatted quietly and partook of refreshments at two tables along the side wall, while George lingered at the back of the room talking to Mr. Zedonick. Roger reentered the room to seek his brother, and eyeing Zedonick, sheepishly approached the two men. He said, "Mr. Zedonick, I never knew my dad told you those things. Anyway, thanks for the kind words. George, I guess I'll leave my car here. Can I bum a ride home with you?"

George noted Roger's trembling hands. He put an arm around his brother's shoulders and said softly, "Of course. Of course you can." Zedonick turned his face away and excused himself.

On the way home, Roger confessed, "You know, George, maybe I was acting a little swell headed. I screwed up by believing everybody would buy our paint just because it was the Durand's brand. 'They've been in business for years and they know paint.' Damn, I was wrong. This new latex stuff beat the crap out of us! Dad told me and you to undersell the competition but goddamn, we can't do that with an inferior product. I hope Beckhart will do the right thing, and I'm sure he will. Keep Everbright going with 'Hig' at the helm. Poor Kim and my wife. What a problem I made for them and Carl. It's the second time I goofed up with him!"

George stopped his brother. "Forget it now. It's over. I had it easy while you had to do what dad wanted, just because you happen to be older than I am. In this life you have to play with the cards fate deals you. Rog, don't tell anyone, but at one time I was planning to take over your job at Sunrise. Boy, am I glad I didn't go through with it. The hand fate dealt me was a straight flush!"

Roger sat motionless, absently watching the road ahead. "You know, being the boss of a big firm made me feel important," he mused. "I liked it. I was proud. I guess it's true—Pride cometh before a fall, and goddamn it, I fell hard!"

He turned to face his brother. "But George, I'm a free man now!"

Sylvia ran to the door and greeted Roger with a heartfelt kiss. She said, "I was afraid you two might wind up on bad terms with one another. I was wrong, wasn't I?"

"Hell, why should I be mad at him? He's my little brother. I can still boss him around," said Roger.

George laughed. "Between you and Laurie, I'm a doomed man!" he said.

"So what happened at the big meeting, Roger?" his wife inquired.

"Sylvia, you are going to have a man around the house day in and day out, and night time too. They sacked me. Even the stockholders agreed with the board of directors. But we won't starve. They voted a good pension for me—$150,000 a year plus other goodies.

"My goodness! That was a generous gesture," exclaimed Sylvia.

Roger nodded. "Is Kim home?"

"Yes, she's in her room—Same place she's been for the past five days. She's not too happy—calling off the wedding at the last minute, everything ordered, 120 invitations or more ready to be mailed, all for nothing! No June wedding for Kim."

George broke in, "Hey, you two, not so glum. How about a July 4th wedding?"

Sylvia said, "Carl won't get married with the prospect of losing his job in a few weeks."

George responded, "Stop. Listen to me. Today, just before the meeting adjourned, the board of directors advised Mr. Worthley to retract the order to dissolve Everbright, and make every effort to inform the employees they still had their jobs and the company was not going to be closing. Mr. Zedonick told me

Mr. Higgins will remain president. He further stated that Dura-best stores would be converted to Everbright Paint stores. The old codger remarked, 'Now your name won't be tarnished.' Rog, he said that right before you came over to speak to us."

Roger was taken aback. "Why in hell didn't you tell me that? We drove all the way home from the plant and you didn't say a word about it!"

"Well, my dear brother, you were admitting your mistakes, and talking about what felt good about running Sunrise. I decided to let you get all that off your chest. Now we can share the good news with the family."

Sylvia clapped her hands together and said, "Oh, my lord, now Kim can get married! I must go tell her the good news."

Roger said, "Let's go to the den. I'll serve enough of my finest liquor to cheer everyone, myself included."

Sylvia entered the den with a depressed Kim, who pointed to the five glasses filled with amber liquid and said, "Why five glasses?"

George answered, "When you hear the news, you'll be happy enough to drink the extra glass. Maybe your unemployed father would like to tell you."

"What's this all about?" Kim asked. "Dad, unemployed? Is this a joke? My fiancé Carl will be the unemployed one. I hope you don't think it's funny."

Roger feigned ignorance. "Oh, my God, don't tell me your Carl works for the Everbright company! I remember something about him working at some paint place. Guess I didn't pay much attention. Was it Everbright?"

George interrupted. "Your dad shut down Carl's firm."

Kim, on the verge of tears, demanded, "What is Uncle George saying? Damn it, Dad, did you manage to buy out Everbright and boot every employee out? What a lowdown thing to do! I thought you liked Carl! My own father, undermining me!"

"Wait, Kim. I did not know we, Sunrise, owned Everbright, so help me God! Let me explain . . ."

Kim screamed, "I don't believe you! How is that possible?"

"Kim, Kim, please calm down," Sylvia pleaded. "Dad is telling the truth. And he is no longer the head of Sunrise. He is through there. Unemployed. He was, well—how else can I say it? —kicked out by the board of directors. Another man was appointed CEO. The new boss was advised to reinstate the Everbright establishment and all its employees, so Carl will still have his job and you two can get married!"

Kim's hands flew to her mouth. Her pupils widened as if she were wearing magnifying glasses. "That's incredible," she said. "Carl swore he would never work for Sunrise, and he never knew that he was! I'll have that drink now, and another one pretty quick!"

She placed her hand on her father's arm and laughed. "Dad, when my class starts next fall, why don't you enroll? I'll teach you a thing or two about economics and business! Now I'm going to call my future husband and tell him to come over for some good news and booze. He was so down in the dumps, this'll send him to the moon!" Kim ran to a secluded phone in the sitting room and began dialing.

Carl arrived at Golden Vista about 20 minutes later. He suspected Kim would try convincing him to marry her in spite of the loss of his job. She greeted him with a huge smile and a kiss, led him to the sitting room, retrieved his favorite cocktail, and said, "Carl, I'll trade you this drink for a smile! Then follow me. I want you to meet another unemployed person."

Carl smiled weakly, took the drink, and followed her to the den. Her parents rose from their seats, raised their glasses, and said, "Here's to a happy Fourth of July wedding!"

Carl exclaimed, "No, no! Kim, didn't you tell your parents the reason the wedding is off?"

Her Dad interjected sternly, "What? You don't want to marry our daughter, after all the planning and preparation we went through?"

"Mr. Durand," Carl said angrily, "I'm unemployed, or will be soon. She works. You're rich. Sure looks like a case of poor boy marries rich girl! I can't do this . . ."

Roger interrupted, "I'm the unemployed person here."

Carl responded, "I don't understand. What are you talking about?"

Roger responded, "Since you won't be working for me any longer, there will be no preferential treatment for you to worry about. And if your boss treats you unfairly, I don't have a damn thing to do with it!"

Carl scratched his head. "All right. Who's going to tell me what's going on?"

Sylvia took a deep breath and said, "Here's the story. You are not, and will not be unemployed. Everbright will not close. It is co-owned by Sunrise, but my husband is no longer the CEO. His board of directors fired him, thank goodness. The new CEO rescinded his order to shut down Everbright. Carl, believe this. You worked for Roger and didn't know it. Roger didn't even know. And about your not being rich. What the hell do we care about that? When my mom and dad settled in Boston, they were poor Irish immigrants. Work was very difficult to find. There was a lot of prejudice against the poor Irish. My mother told me there were help wanted signs in store windows that said, "Irish need not apply!" I was poor. George here knows about being poor and so does my husband, but I think your future father-in-law here became a little swellheaded being the CEO of the firm his dad founded. Now he is a poor, unemployed rich man! And you are free to marry our daughter.

We are going to send out invitations to our friends and relations inviting them to our daughter's wedding to you on July 4th this year. We all love you, Carl."

Carl said, "Well, I'll be damned." He gulped down his drink, pulled Kim close to him, and said, "Kim, let's get married on Independence Day. I'll mail those invitations today. Just change the dates on them." He kissed her openly in front of her parents, and kissed Sylvia also. After shaking hands with George, he reached for Roger's hand.

Durand grasped Carl's hand and said, "Son, the fourth of July won't be your independence day. You'll be tied up with my daughter. It will be my independence day. No more work, no more commuting, no more responsibility!"

Sylvia said, "That's right. I'll make all the decisions." She placed a finger on her cheek and thought for a moment. "I think we will commute all over Europe. And Rog, our gardener needs help, so there is still work for you."

George remarked, "You better not argue with her, or the fireworks will be starting early!"

A few days later, the Durands invited Carl's parents for a get-acquainted dinner. Tom Emerson sat on the plush dining room chair and said, "You know, Mr. Durand, the railroad is getting newer, more comfortable cars to ride in. I've seen you on our run several times. Too bad you won't be commuting anymore."

Sylvia corrected Tom. "We intend to commute all over North America, and Europe too. I'm sure Roger and I will appreciate the new cars."

Roger said, "Another unilateral decision."

Carl's parents exchanged puzzled glances while the others laughed.

The Fourth of July was perfect for the wedding ceremony, performed poolside at Golden Vista before a throng of Kim and Carl's relatives and friends, including Capt. Campbell. Douglas was best man, and Hazel, matron of honor. Kim looked radiant in a flowing silk organza wedding gown with a pearl-studded, floor-length mantilla. She carried a bouquet of rare mixed orchids, trailing antique ribbons edged with hand-tatted lace.

After a banquet unsurpassed by anything any of the guests had experienced, Carl called Douglas over to the pool area and said, "I'd like to present Capt. Campbell with a gift. Would you please call him over? Bring Hazel too, and our immediate families."

The designated group moved to the pool area, chattering excitedly in anticipation of the presentation. Carl called out, "Ladies and gentlemen, I'm so pleased to present this meager gift to a fellow who had a dream that became reality for me and Douglas—our means of escape from the devil's own home. I won't tell you the details of his dream. Some of us here know them already. But it worked, and we are happy that it did. Captain Campbell, Douglas and I would like you to have this."

Campbell accepted the package and shook it curiously. Then he tore off the wrapper and showed its contents to the gathering. "A nice white scarf," he said, waving it in the gentle breeze. "I'll need it this winter in Canada."

Carl explained, "The silk scarf is courtesy of the fat German whose plane we stole."

Campbell burst into laughter as the guests cheered. Then he reached into the box and unwrapped a bulky object. He stared at it for a moment, threw his head back and howled with laughter. "Oh, my silver flask!"

Half the spectators laughed too, while the rest whispered back and forth to each other, puzzled looks on their faces. Carl said Campbell would have to explain later.

The groom then turned to Douglas.

"Doug, a long time ago, you beat me at tennis. After the game you pushed me into this swimming pool because I claimed to be the best man. Another time you let the air out of my tire. For a long time, I owed you two. But since you helped in our escape from prison, I now owe you just one."

Doug looked at the people crowded closely around him, then down at his spit-shined shoes, suddenly aware he was standing inches from the edge of the pool. In a panicky voice he bellowed, "Oh no, you don't!" and jumped into the pool with a huge splash, scattering the guests in all directions. When he surfaced, he tossed his wet hair and said, "Remember, Carl. Today I *am* best man."

Martha stopped serving refreshments and frowned at Douglas as he climbed out of the pool, water streaming down his clothing. "There they go again," she muttered. "Damn, I hate drying and pressing tuxedos!"

About the Author

Harold L. Prevett is a WWII veteran and retired aerospace engineer who worked with NASA designing early technology for the Mars and Jupiter probe landings. Not one to shrink from new endeavors, he took up water color painting as a hobby upon retirement. Later, he designed drawbridges for miniature railroads. At age 80, he built a cello, using only a child's violin as a model. At age 85, he enlarged the concept to construct a bass fiddle. In 2003, at 88, he completed this, his first novel, incorporating many vignettes from his own life. It places him among the last WWII survivors to reflect upon the social and corporate climate of that time.

It was a great honor and privilege to work with him on this project.

His editor and daughter,

Jeanne Prevett Sable